THIS BOOK BELONGS TO

Kal

Library of Congress Cataloging-in-Publication data is on file with the publisher.

Text by Alison Sage
Text copyright © 2015 by HarperCollins Publishers Ltd.
Illustrations © 2015 by Sarah Gibb
First published in Great Britain in 2015 by HarperCollins Children's Books
Published in 2015 by Albert Whitman & Company
ISBN 978-0-8075-7351-8
Printed in China
10 9 8 7 6 5 4 3 2 1 SCP 20 19 18 17 16 15

For more information about Albert Whitman & Company,
visit our web site at www.albertwhitman.com.

SLEEPING BEAUTY

Sarah Gibb

Albert Whitman & Company
Chicago, Illinois

O nce upon a time, there lived a king and queen who had almost everything they could possibly wish for. But neither was content for there was one thing missing…they both wanted a child.

One day the queen saw a rosebud floating in the fountain and it smelled so sweet, she put her hand in to pull it out.

Just then, a bright green frog leaped out of the water and spoke to her. "Don't be afraid," he said. "I have good news for you. Before long you will have a baby girl." And he jumped back into the water with a tiny splash.

The queen was overjoyed and ran straight inside to tell the king what had happened.

The following spring, just as the frog had promised, a beautiful little girl was born, and the palace bustled with joy. The king and queen were so delighted that they decided to celebrate with a magnificent party.

"Everyone in the kingdom will be invited," said the king, beaming with pride.

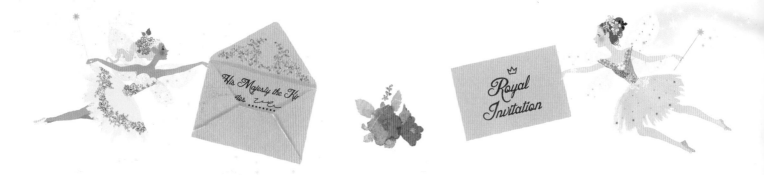

In those days it was the custom when a royal baby was born to send out invitations to all the fairies in the realm, from the tiniest to the most powerful. Messengers were sent out all over the land.

But one fairy, who had not been seen for more than fifty years, was forgotten. And she was the oldest and most powerful of all. Her name was Malevola.

"So, they don't want *me* at the party?" she snarled. "Well, let's see if they like my gift!"

On the day of the party, the king and queen welcomed the fairies as they arrived and led them all into a beautiful hall full of flowers.

"The princess's name is Rosebud," announced the king as the fairies came forward to give their magical gifts.

"Then she will be as beautiful as a rose," said the first fairy.

"Everyone will love her," said another.

"She will be very clever," promised a third.

"…kind…"

"…graceful…"

"…lucky in love…"

As they went on, the queen began to lose count of the wonderful gifts being showered upon little Rosebud, sleeping sweetly in her arms.

All of a sudden the air grew freezing cold, and at the entrance to the hall was Malevola hidden in shadow.

"You didn't ask me to the party, but I've come anyway!" she cried. "And here is my gift…Beautiful and clever she may be, but when she is sixteen, the princess will prick her finger on a spindle and die!"

The other fairies shrieked with horror, and the queen held her precious baby close. But Malevola had already disappeared into the night.

Just then a tiny fairy with a wand that shone like pink fire flew out of the shadows and hovered above the little princess. "I haven't given my gift," she said.

The queen lifted her baby up to the fairy.

"When you prick your finger, you shall not die, Rosebud," said the fairy. "You will fall into a deep sleep until a hundred years have passed, when a prince will wake you."

The king and queen wept as the fairies said good-bye. What a terrible future for their little princess.

The king was determined to beat the evil spell. The next day
he ordered that every spindle in his kingdom be burned on a
huge fire.

The little fairy, who had stayed behind to keep watch over the
princess, shook her head and whispered, "What's done cannot
so easily be undone!"

Years passed and the king and queen began to believe that they had outwitted Malevola.

Rosebud grew as beautiful, clever, and kind as the fairies had promised. She was as graceful as a deer and so loving that no one ever wished her a moment's harm.

But the little fairy waited and watched over her with an anxious heart.

On the morning of her sixteenth birthday, Rosebud woke up feeling strangely restless. She wandered from room to room and soon found herself in a part of the palace she had never seen before. Excitedly, she climbed faster and faster up the steps of an old tower until she reached a door at the top. It opened at the lightest touch, and there in front of her was a little old woman working at a spinning wheel.

Rosebud had never seen a spindle before and it seemed like magic. "What are you doing?" she asked. "Can I try?"

"If you like," smiled the old woman, taking Rosebud's hand.

But as soon as Rosebud touched the spindle, the sharp needle pricked her finger and she fell at once to the ground in a deep sleep.

"See! You can't escape from my spell!" hissed the old lady, for she was Malevola in disguise. And then, triumphantly, she slipped away.

Luckily the little fairy was already searching for the princess. She warned the king and queen, and they hurried to the tower. There they found Rosebud fast asleep by the spinning wheel.

All day they wept and called her name, gently touching her face and rubbing her hands, but it was no use. Rosebud remained asleep, smiling prettily as though she was dreaming.

At last with a heavy heart the king carried Rosebud to her
room and laid her on her bed.

Then it was time for the little fairy to carry out what she had been planning ever since Malevola cast her evil spell. Gently, she touched the king and queen, who yawned and soon sank quietly into a deep sleep.

One by one, the fairy touched the cooks and the courtiers, the pages and the maids, until the whole palace was quiet except for the sound of gentle breathing. Even the cats and dogs slept, the mice in the corn, and the doves in the hayloft.

Outside in the gardens the wild roses quickly began to grow and huge briars covered the walls of the palace. Days passed, weeks, months, and then years. Still the palace slept deep in enchantment, encircled by a forest of wild roses.

In the outside world, a legend grew of a princess cursed by a wicked fairy. Everyone agreed that there were great treasures to be found in her palace but that it was unlucky to go anywhere near it. Some, braver than the rest, tried to hack through the briars. But at every stroke of their swords, the thorns grew back thicker, and they gave up, scratched and bleeding, and slunk back home.

Almost a hundred years had passed when a young prince went out riding in the forest. Prince Florizel soon found himself separated from his friends with no idea where he was.

With growing excitement, he saw that he must be near the enchanted palace of the legend. Through the trees was a vast wall of wild roses and their scent flowed around him like honey, drawing him closer.

He jumped from his horse and raised his sword, ready to fight his way through.

But to Florizel's amazement, the thorns melted away and the roses parted in front of him.

Soon, the huge stone walls of the palace loomed above him, overgrown with brambles and moss. Florizel saw a watchman on guard and held his breath until he heard snoring. The man was fast asleep.

Florizel crept forward, past guards in the guard chambers and

horses asleep as they stood. Cooks slept in the middle of stirring their pans and children lay curled up, their toys still clutched in their hands.

As if in a dream, Florizel climbed the cobwebby stairs until he came to a door and pushed it open…

The most beautiful princess he had ever seen lay on the bed asleep. Florizel leaned forward and kissed her hand, and her eyes fluttered and opened.

"My prince!" she said sweetly. "I have been dreaming about you. I knew you would come!"

And before they knew it, the prince and Rosebud were talking and laughing as if they had known each other all their lives.

Meanwhile, the palace had also woken up and everyone was getting back to whatever they had been doing when they went to sleep. The dogs were chasing the cats, the sparrows were pecking at crumbs, the stable boy was leading out the horses, and the cooks were getting the kitchens ready for supper.

The king and queen soon discovered that the spell on their daughter had been broken and they wept tears of joy.

Not long after, it was announced that Prince Florizel and Princess Rosebud were to be married.

Everyone in the kingdom was invited to their magnificent wedding in the palace rose garden.

Rosebud wore an exquisite silk wedding dress, and as she walked by, fairies showered her with fragrant petals.

Never had she looked more beautiful than when she looked into the eyes of her handsome prince, and, smiling, each said, "I do."

It was the happiest day of their lives and the celebrations lasted well into the night.

The princess, who became known as Sleeping Beauty, and prince lived happily ever after, forever grateful for the magic of the little fairy.

DECORATING

DECORATING
A Realistic Guide by Mary Gilliatt

Book design by Janet Odgis and Photos by Michael Dunne

with Michael Nicholson and others

Pantheon Books, New York

First American Edition

Copyright © 1977 by Mary Gilliatt

All rights reserved under International and Pan-American Copyright Conventions. Published in the United States by Pantheon Books, a division of Random House, Inc., New York. Originally published in Canada by Random House of Canada Limited, Toronto.

Acknowledgments for the photographs are to be found on page 271.

Library of Congress Cataloging in Publication Data
Gilliatt, Mary, 1935–
Decorating: A Realistic Guide.
    Includes index.
    1.   Interior Decoration—Handbooks,
        manuals, etc.
I.   Title.
NK2115.G425   747'.8'83   77-4769
ISBN 0-394-40700-8

**Printed and bound in Italy by A. Mondadori
Editore - Verona.**

For Barbara Plumb, whose idea this was, with love

Acknowledgments

A heavily illustrated book on decoration must be dependent on many people for ideas and suggestions as well as on those willing and kind enough to allow their houses to be photographed as examples. I am grateful for the time given to me by Joe D'Urso, Mark Hampton, and Chuck Winslow, whose work I much admire, and for all the cooperation I received in both the United States and Europe. The Caxton Publishing Company, Ltd., London, England, kindly gave permission to reproduce the wallpaper and paint calculation tables in the chapter on planning, and Luciano Zucchi and Janet Turner of Concord Lighting (Great Britain), gave me much knowledgeable and efficient help with the lighting chapter.

On a personal level, I would also particularly like to thank my editor, Barbara Plumb, for her invaluable help and unstinting generosity; Janet Odgis, who designed the book with such verve and enthusiasm; Jeanne Morton, for her great patience; Connie Mellon; and everybody else at Pantheon who made working on this project such a pleasure. On the home front, I want to thank my patient friend and colleague Virginia Bredin, who always gave me encouragement when it was most needed; Harry Weblin of Liberty's for his kindness and example, and Charles Baxter and all my other colleagues at Liberty's for their steady cooperation; Drusilla Beyfus of *Brides* Magazine for her unerring clarity of mind and for the opportunity to include bits of articles I wrote for her within my chapters; Michael Dunne, who took most of the photographs in this book, for his energy and perception; Jerry and Mary Cookson, for letting me write a good part of this book in their house; Esom and Millicent Alintah and Henry and Myra Shaw for being such helpful clients; Nancy Oranie for her loyalty and help, which make my life so much easier to encompass; and finally my husband, Roger Gilliatt, and my children, Sophia, Anne-Louise, and Tom Gilliatt, for their constant support and understanding.

Introduction

A curiously large number of people do not realize that decorating a home is just about the most creative and revealing enterprise that they could embark on, money or no money. In fact, not having much money to play around with helps the creative process. A home should be an accretion or an adaptation of ideas picked up over the years; a definite statement of pleasure in color and light and objects; a statement, in fact, of all one's preferences which, put together with confidence, amount to individual style. But a sense of style is a precarious thing that needs to be cultivated most carefully.

One of the first pieces of information I picked up as a design consultant was that there are many more choices to make, many more details to consider, and many more facts to become acquainted with in home decorating than newcomers to the process can begin to realize. Many people fancy that they have definite tastes until they begin and find the choice bewildering, or as it happens sometimes, inadequate. Many others start off thinking they have no ideas and end up, via a long process of elimination, knowing exactly what they want. Some people can envisage the finished result from the start (which is of enormous help). Others, again, have absolutely no idea what is going to happen.

In my role as design writer turned design consultant, I have at times felt guilty about actually designing, as if I were trespassing on a territory that I have no real right to, although I have—as I need to remind myself—been designing houses for a good fifteen years.

As it happens, I know I am wrong. It is illogical to feel guilty about helping other people to design their own houses, if through my writing, and through all the inevitable seeing and noticing and studying of what is best in domestic design, I have been fortunate enough to learn the basic premises which remove the mystique from decorating. I have now been on both sides of the domestic design business long enough to know it

inside out. As a customer and a representative of customers, I know most of the pitfalls. As a design consultant, I try to provide the solutions. And to be both informed consumer and purveyor is, in a way, a unique position. It is just because I have, as a former amateur, experienced all the difficulties and finally learned to employ the methods and shortcuts with comparative ease that I feel I can usefully pass on the information.

By passing on this information, I am no more doing decorators out of a job than having basic general knowledge about the insides of an automobile would obviate the necessity for motor mechanics. Even if one could employ a decorator—and most people decidedly cannot—it is as useful to have a good working knowledge of the intricacies related to the whole business of doing up a house as it is to know about the basic workings of an engine. How else would you know what to get repaired, or if the repair was satisfactory?

What I particularly wanted to achieve, though, was not only a book that would implant some good working knowledge of decoration (for after all, there are several good reference books on that subject) but a book that dealt with the actual "cosmetics of design" and showed how to decorate memorably and idiosyncratically, with style and warmth and humor. Moreover, I wanted to show that effect really need not depend upon money—or not much; that the conventional is not necessarily right or even desirable; and that the most important things to strive for in a home are comfort, individuality, and flexibility.

To this end, I have tried to take people through the whole process of planning a home—or a room—in simple and logical order. I have taken up the difficult basics of how to use space and light, color and texture; gone into all the elements of a room, the furnishings and accessories; and illustrated more or less every point with photographs showing just how much can be achieved with ingenuity, imagination, and clever compromise.

Some of the houses and apartments I chose to have photographed were pro-

fessionally designed; some belong to professional designers. They are designers whose work I admire, who have a lot to teach by example, and whose ideas can well be adapted to different circumstances and different possessions. Just as the home dressmaker adapts ideas from the great couturiers, so the layman decorator can try out ideas from the interior designers' work.

Most of the rooms, however, were achieved by nondecorators: by painters, illustrators, writers, architects, landscape designers, manufacturers, academics, teachers, dress designers, and just generally creative people with an eye for color and detail. Some rooms had a lot of money spent on them, some the minimum possible, but all of them are in some way constructive.

The text has had to be repetitive in parts so that people could dip into it at any point to search for something they were interested in, as well as to read it all the way through. Each section had to be able to stand on its own; but to make the book as helpful as possible, I have cross-referenced other useful sections whenever it seemed apt. I hope very much that it serves its purpose.

1. Planning

Probably the most comforting homily to remember with regard to any sort of domestic design is that most successful decoration is the result of successful elimination. If that sounds depressingly practical rather than comforting, write down all the things that could possibly be needed, quite apart from being wanted, for an ideal renovating or redecorating scheme and count up the costs. Most people will find the sum involved disastrous and will promptly decide on an alternative master plan, dealing with essentials first and with other details as and when they can afford them. This is just as well. Few people have the infallible taste or knowledge to get things right the first time—why should they, with little or no experience? And going slowly, working within some kind of framework, gives them more time to think and learn.

Planning

The Essentials

Important questions to ask at the initial stage of doing up a house or an apartment are: How do you eliminate successfully? and, What are the real priorities in any decorating job? As is often the case, the essentials are rather boring, but nevertheless, the first step (in any owned property, at least) should be to attend to the most pressing structural alterations, like repairing a leaky roof, ripping down or putting up partition walls, strengthening the structure where important, mending plasterwork, repairing floorboards, renewing decrepit plumbing and electrical wiring, or putting in a burglar alarm. However obvious this all sounds, it is worth stressing here, for any decoration done when the structure is in a bad state and the basic services unattended to is bound to end in disaster. Even so, it is remarkable how many people do embark on the more creative painting and papering before tackling the heavy work.

So that details are not missed which will later prove essential to remedy, however expensive, it helps to make a checklist under the two main headings of Services and Structure. These can be subheaded as follows:

Services	Structure
Electricity	Roof
Gas	External walls
Heating	Internal walls
Air conditioning	Floors
Ventilation	Insulation
Water	Cracks
Plumbing	Damp
Drainage	Leaks

Making out a list like this might serve as a reminder of other details or faults. Make a note by each heading of the current state of affairs: whether the service exists or not; what condition it is in; and what improvements or repairs are needed.

Rentals, of course, are another matter, for it is to be hoped that the landlord will have taken care of the structural needs in the first place. But even if there is no necessity for heavy structural work of the kinds listed, think long and hard about the needs of each member of the family—if there is one, or might be—bearing in mind that during a long-term stay these needs will change, so that the place must be capable of flexibility. Although it is not easy to plan for an unknown future, it is useful to make certain assumptions and to ask certain questions:

What is the maximum number of rooms needed, and for what uses?

How much space can be made multi-functional?

Can the sort and number of rooms needed be provided from existing space, perhaps by putting up a partition across one large room or by changing levels with platforms? Or can a hitherto neglected roof or attic or basement space be remodeled?

Should there be plans for an eventual extension—or another move?

Once any necessity for structural work is either established or eliminated, the decoration and furnishings can be decided upon. Again, rooms should be approached in order of priority: most usually, kitchen, bathroom(s), principal bedroom, living room, followed by other rooms in due course. Even then, stick to basics, like getting the framework of walls, floor, ceiling, and windows right before furnishing. This is what distinguishes a well-thought-out plan from the all-too-usual patchwork process. Like most frameworks, the plan can be deviated from if it is understood that this could increase costs. In any case, it is useful to have something cohesive from which to deviate.

If the thought of discomfort ahead is a melancholy one, remember that if the place has to be lived in while all this is going on—and most do—it will help to keep spirits up if at least one and preferably two rooms can be made comfortable right away, if by no means in their final form.

In a kitchen-living room, this can be achieved with surprising ease, and without benefit of paint or paper if need be—though these certainly help— by adding a cheerful tablecloth, plants, prints or posters, good-looking pillows, a rug or two, and any decent pieces of furniture that are already in existence.

In a bedroom, it helps to have a comfortable bed, a rug, a good, well-lit mirror, a reasonable amount of storage space, and a chair. Or you may have the bed in the living room and cover it with pillows or cushions so that it can be used as a general lounging area. Bed manufacturers would disapprove, but never mind. Some friends of mine in Paris got so used to having their bed in the so-called *salon* that they never did get around to having a proper bedroom, and turned the space into a library instead.

But to go back to the master plan: When the most important points have been decided—or mostly decided, because fresh ones will always be occurring—make another list for every room and include every single thing that you think you will need, in principle, in each. I say in principle, because there will be a great many things that can be filled in only as the job progresses. The list supplied here might be useful as a guide, and it can be added to or subtracted from as necessary. When it seems as complete as possible, figure out the maximum sum that you can afford, remembering that it is wise to keep a sum in reserve against the emergencies and extras that invariably turn up to spoil the best-laid plans. It is no good thinking that with luck it will somehow all get done without mishap: it almost certainly won't, or at least not cheaply. And if by some rare chance it does, there will be the agreeable bonus of extra money to spend.

A Checklist

This checklist indicates probable necessities that will have to be bought. However elementary they may seem, they are all too easily overlooked in the grand scheme of things and have a bad habit of adding up to a nonelementary sum. Reading the list may bring to mind other particular or personal needs. Note them all. Clarity in the beginning will prevent much confusion and regret later on.

Probable needs

Apart from the costs of moving, some or all of the following items will need to be either arranged for or bought.

For all rooms

Any repairs or alterations

Painting or wall covering

Floor covering, whether carpets and padding rugs, or hard flooring like tiles

Curtains with appropriate hardware— poles or traverse rods, etc.—or window shades

Checking of electrical wiring and its possible renewal

Lighting fixtures and their installation

Insulation

Heating and air conditioning

Attention to plumbing where necessary

Living and dining rooms

Seating

Dining table, chairs, serving table

Bookshelves and storage units

Desk or writing tables

Coffee table

Television set and aerial

Stereo equipment

Telephone installation

Accessories: cushions or pillows, paint- ings and prints, plants, clocks, wastepaper baskets, ornaments

Kitchen

Stove (and its installation)

Grill

Refrigerator and freezer

Washing machine (and plumbing and installation costs)

Dryer, ironing board, and iron

Dishwasher (and plumbing and installa- tion costs)

Kitchen cabinets (and their installation)

Sinks and drainers

Ventilator

Pots and pans, utensils, knives, wooden spoons, basins, storage jars

China, glass, cutlery

Toaster, rotisserie, mixer, coffee grinder, juice extractor

Table linen, dishtowels

14

Vacuum cleaner, floor polisher, brooms, mops, brushes, cleaning cloths

Stepladder

Bathrooms

New sanitary equipment: bath, basin, vanity unit, shower, bidet (and their installation)

Tiling

Towel racks

Mirror

Electric-razor outlets

Medicine cabinets

Clothes hamper

Stool or chair

Towels, washclothes, bathmats

Bedrooms

Beds, mattresses, sheets, blankets, bedspreads, pillows

Storage units

Dressing tables

Bedside tables

Chests of drawers

Chairs

Garden

Mower, roller, gardening tools

Garden furniture

Barbeque equipment

Plants

Cutting Down Costs

Apart from drastic pruning of ideas, there are various other ways of paring down costs without losing too much in impact and comfort. In fact, most of them turn out to be more idiosyncratic and therefore more interesting than more conventional and expensive solutions.

Shop around for contractors if they are needed. Try to find out about handy- men working on their own. Or possibly, the work can be done without outside help. After all, almost everything structural *can* be done quite successfully by the amateur determined to apply himself or herself, and the things that are deemed too difficult can be subcon- tracted out. Bear in mind that surpris- ingly good furniture can be homemade: see Clement Meadmore's book *How to*

Make Furniture Without Tools (New York: Pantheon Books, 1975; $4.95)— not, alas, available in England.

If the job requires renovation or remodeling, hunt around in demolition yards and junkyards for materials. It is possible to find doors, fireplaces, porches, staircases, balustrades, floor- ing, paving stones, tiles, and old bricks, as well as baths, basins, and toilets which can be restored to a near- immaculate finish.

There are almost always bargains and shortcuts for the furnishings. Look in the yellow pages for remnant stores that buy up remnants of carpet, mill ends of fabrics, and offcuts or leftovers from large contract jobs such as hotels and stores. I once carpeted an entire vacation house with offcuts, and very good it looked, too, at a fraction of the normal cost. But watch out for fire or flood-damaged goods: they have a tendency to rot.

Another possibility is to dispense with floor coverings altogether and strip and polish, strip and stain, or strip and paint the floorboards. Old floors can be stained or painted in bright colors or black or white. Use floor-weight felt for bedrooms with the occasional rug.

Shop around for discounts off major electrical goods, or for "seconds" from reliable brand names or manufacturers. Buy up fabric remnants and mill ends for curtains, bedcovers, tablecloths, pillows, and window shades. The last are comparatively easy to make at home (see instructions on pp. 182-88), since rollers to mount them on are widely available, and they use only a fraction of the material needed for curtains.

Buy linens, towels, china, glass, cutlery, furniture, kitchen utensils, and household equipment on sale. It might seem unnecessary to say that almost all household goods and furnishings can be bought on sale, given patience and determination, but people do forget. And when money is short, the assiduous inspection of stores for bargains, and of newspapers for advertisements of sales, can save a lot of money.

The great thing to remember about bargain hunting is to make sure that the purchases are indeed bargains. Striking

a bad bargain is the simplest way to waste money, and can result in longtime discomfort—the wrong mattress, for example, or a cheap carpet on a hard-wear area that dissolves into threads in no time.

Secondhand stores and thrift shops can be searched for cheap furniture to be stripped and painted or lacquered or re-covered. Cheap tin trunks make reasonably good side tables as well as providing extra storage. Big, plump pillows can substitute for chairs. Boxes can be built in along sides of rooms, topped with fabric-covered foam, and used for both storage and seating. Indian cotton bedspreads at either $5.00 or £3 apiece make a cheap and original form of wall covering and can be stapled onto walls quite easily.

These shortcuts might sound hackneyed, but they all help. Learning to pare costs, to substitute, and to eliminate builds up an attitude that can only improve with practice.

Saving versus Spending

Without experience it is difficult to know exactly when to save and when to spend. As a general rule, the most money should be spent on items that will have to last the longest, will get the most wear and tear, and will make life more comfortable. The corollary is that savings can be made on nonessentials and less-used furniture and furnishings where substitutes will do as well.

In the first, "spending," category come all structural repairs, any re-wiring, and efficient heating, air conditioning, and insulation where needed, followed by necessary appliances and furnishings: kitchen and washing equipment (stove, refrigerator and freezer, washer, dryer, and dishwasher); beds; at least two good, comfortable chairs; first-class lighting; generous cupboards and storage units; first-quality stair and hall carpet; rugs for floor areas that are not to be carpeted; and stalwart, good-looking, comfortable kitchen flooring.

In the second, "saving," category comes a good deal of furniture,

Ideas from public places: a tile in St. Mark's, Venice. Proportion and detail dictate their own design (right).

especially dining tables (which can be more flexible, more practical, and a better size when made from wood fixed to a steady base and covered by a floor-length cloth); conventional window treatment, which normally presupposes yards of expensive fabric; first-quality carpet in areas where traffic is not heavy; and expensive glass, cutlery, china, linen, and other such luxuries.

Obviously, both lists could be longer, but they are given here more as a guideline than as a set of definite rules.

Once a decision has been reached on the sort of budget that can be afforded for a home and on the necessities that will have to be provided, the master plan can be worked out in detail. But again it is important to be realistic about ideas, to make sure that what looks good actually works, and most of all, to be clear about one's tastes, wants, and ideas of comfort. This last might seem to go without saying, but many couples, determinedly different from their elders in every other way, automatically take over their parents' criteria for decoration without giving much thought—at least until it is too late or too expensive—to what would be most practical for themselves.

A Clear Head

Even if one can afford to hand the job over to a decorator and thus avoid the onus of all the organizational details, it is still important to know what one wants (or mostly), to explain it clearly, to be prepared to listen to ideas, and to spend time on discussions, decisions, and shopping. That is, if a home is wanted that is in any way personal, interesting, and comfortable. Otherwise, it is unfair to the decorator, who is left to do what he or she thinks best from only the sketchiest of indications; and the results will almost certainly be disappointing for the client. It is to be hoped that both will at least have learned something from the experience.

If there is no question of affording or even wanting a decorator, and one's taste is still uncertain and untried, a good way to firm it up is by analyzing one's choice of clothes, the colors one normally likes, and the line: is it spare? is it tailored? is it soft? This should give some guide to a familiar, easy style. Think what is particularly attractive about other people's rooms. Or make a list of all the things you do not like. As I have said before, most style is developed from elimination and constant pruning. And once given a start on the right lines, the majority of homes just evolve in their own good time.

To a certain extent, too, plans should be dictated by the proportions and period of a house or apartment, its situation, condition, and natural light. I am not suggesting that all buildings should be decorated according to their period, but rather that they should be treated with sympathy, and that their natural ingredients should be used to the best advantage. By natural ingredients I mean windows, views, doors, staircases, the differing proportions of various rooms, interesting floorings or moldings if they exist, and all the integral details of a house.

Normally, this sort of empathy with a building can only be achieved after several relaxed visits while it is empty. After a time it should be possible to

absorb its shapes, surroundings, details, and potential to the extent that certain types and colors of furniture can be imagined in their appropriate settings. And there should be a good idea of what features to emphasize and what to diminish.

Once a building has become properly familiar, planning can begin in final detail. If possible, take time to find a starting point. Ruffle through books and magazines for sympathetic arrangements. Scour the shops, stores, and showrooms for wallpapers, wall coverings, carpets, hard flooring, and fabrics, and collect samples of anything that suits your impression of what the place should be. A good idea is to stick these samples up on a corkboard. Put together like that, they should start to give some firm ideas, if only on what to discard.

Adapting Ideas

Room settings in stores (like the legendary Bloomingdale's operations), model apartments or houses, permanent exhibitions, restaurants, museums, hotels, and public foyers can all help with ideas, or the beginnings of them. Never underestimate the private ideas that can be culled from public places.

A ceiling treatment here, a floor there, an arrangement on a table, a particular way of covering a wall, or a certain juxtaposition of coloring can all start off a train of thought, or be stored to click into place at some later date. Learn to carry a notebook around for jotting down descriptions or making quick sketches of anything that is appealing. Never rely on memory alone; these impressions hardly ever last without a reminder.

If a good idea cannot be used right away, or soon, it might come in useful later, or help to put other ideas into context. In any case, it will all help to build up a sense of style, a sureness of what is best suited to one's circumstances and tastes.

Being Flexible

When it is analyzed, the chief asset in people who decorate successfully and

idiosyncratically is the ability to be flexible. No flexibility almost inevitably means frustration. Furniture and fabrics that have been decided on are much too expensive or suddenly unavailable. Ideas about furnishing set by years of planning in theory, if not in fact, prove to be impractical both spacewise and financially. Having lived in a city for years, someone has to move to the country or another state or continent, so that tried and tested belongings suddenly become unsuitable. All these, and many more difficulties which at the time might seem insuperable, can be overcome by an open mind.

Never be bound by intransigent rules. Never think that it is imperative to have a particular item, a particular color. Decoration is supposed to be a background, an expression of personality. Therefore, it is important to do what is most comfortable. If a compromise becomes inevitable, remember that compromise is—or can be—an art in itself. I never believe that it is impossible to substitute, but I do think that it is important not to make an uncaring substitution. It is much better to go off on another tack than to give in on something which is not to one's taste and with which one will always feel uncomfortable.

Almost all the best interiors, when you go into it, have been the result of some sort of compromise or accident. And remember that perfect, or would-be perfect, rooms have an uncomfortable habit of turning out to be boring. People aren't perfect. Why should rooms be?

Planning to Scale

Unless one has had a good deal of experience in furnishing or has an exceptionally accurate eye, it is easy to overbuy or to make mistakes in size so that pieces of furniture turn out to be too numerous, too big, or too small for the room. A sensible way to avoid this is to draw the room or rooms to scale on graph paper and to work out from there the number and approximate sizes of the pieces that are needed. Such scale plans are also useful for builders, contractors, and furniture movers, since

a good plan includes positions of electrical outlets, radiators, breaks in the walls, and so on.

Start by making a sketch of the shape of the room. After that, measure the lengths of walls, the widths of doors and openings, the sizes of windows and fixtures, the thickness of partitions, and the distance of fittings from one another, as well as the position of electrical outlets, telephone attachments, and radiators or other permanent heating appliances. Mark all of these clearly on the sketch. This will be the preliminary survey.

To draw up the plan proper, you must decide on the scale. A quarter of an inch to the foot (1 in 50 centimeters) is reasonable for general areas, but half an inch to the foot (1 in 25 centimeters) might be better for kitchens, bathrooms, and laundry rooms, which have to take a lot of fixtures and where every inch counts. If working in inches, use graph paper with the inch squares divided into eighths and then take two (a quarter-inch) for a foot. See the illustration on page 19 for an example.

With a sharp pencil draw the perimeter of the room to the chosen scale. It is important to do this accurately. Mark in door openings, windows, radiators, electrical outlets, and any other fixtures, again making sure that everything is completely accurate. I know it is tedious to keep stressing accuracy, but from bitter experience I know how the slightest inaccuracy can ruin the brightest idea. Correct measurement of doors and windows is particularly important as far as the moving of furniture is concerned. Many a double bed, piano, sofa, or large armchair has had to be sent back unused because although the room was big enough to accommodate it, the doors and windows simply weren't.

When the room plan is finished, concentrate on the furnishings. Draw to scale, on a piece of colored or plain card, any bits of furniture you possess, and cut them out. Do the same for any pieces of furniture that you would like to buy. Or work out the approximate size of pieces that will go best in the space as well as fitting the budget, and

These illustrations show the sort of floor plans that can be drawn up in order to avoid mistakes in scale when buying or rearranging furniture. Above on the left is a "before" version of a room. On the right, a newly planned version shows a possible rearrangement of the existing furniture with some subtractions and additions. Below is a drawing, or visual, showing the actual pieces of furniture in their new positions. In this way, it is possible to juggle around possessions—or possible possessions—with the minimum of aggravation, quite apart from physical effort.

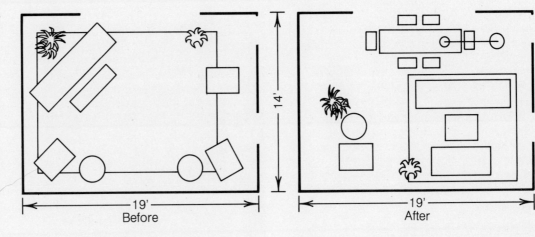

Before

After

look out for them, not trusting to luck when you find what seem to be the right things, but making sure of the measurements first. Don't forget to identify each piece by labeling it "armchair," or whatever; otherwise it will get confusing.

Bearing in mind traffic routes, focal points, electrical outlets, and lighting positions, juggle the pieces of card around on the plan to form different arrangements. This is the best way to make the most practical use of the space that is available.

Work Schedules

Whether or not a contractor or builder is being used, the kind of work schedule that is prepared will be the keystone of a successful remodeling, renovating, or straightforward decorating job. Of course, it is quite possible to explain to a contractor what is wanted and hope that he takes it all down, has understood, can fill in any outstanding gaps, and will estimate accordingly. But there is no doubt that a concise, comprehensive, and decisive list of works that has been drawn up with care and thought will avoid a great many extra explanations and misunderstandings about cost. It might be taxing at the time, but the amount of money—and man-hours—it will save in the long run is immense. It is so easy for the amateur to forget the most obvious and necessary items, which will then have to be done piecemeal, so that the cost mounts up over and above the original estimate, ending in a hefty shock when the final bill is received.

If a contractor is to be used, it is sensible to get estimates from two or three companies, unless one firm is known from experience to be particularly reliable. It is equally sensible to give them all the same work schedule from which to make their estimates—an obvious point, but not one to which people automatically adhere. However, if it looks as though the job is going to be really costly or complicated, it might be well to employ an architect, at least on a part-time basis, to prepare a professional specification that takes into account the

White, down to the palm trees, in a Californian room.

homemade one. This is wise, for there will almost certainly be methods for tackling particular problems that the nonprofessional will not know. Even if a contractor is not going to be used, it is still useful to prepare a work schedule and to adapt the points that I made about contractors for personal use.

The master plan and checklist described on pages 10–14 should be helpful as a nucleus for the work schedule. If lists have not been made already for budgeting purposes, go through the house or apartment room by room, noting everything that needs to be done from repairing baseboards or skirtings to replacing door hardware. State where old paint needs to be stripped off and the number of coats of paint needed for a good job (this is always open to discussion with the contractor); what pipes, if any, will need to be concealed; where new electrical outlets should be positioned and how many will be needed; where radiators, air conditioners, and other appliances should be placed if any are to be installed.

When every item has been written down, divide up the work into what needs to be done on the exterior and what should be done on the interior, room by room, and floor by floor if it is a house. Put plumbing, electrical work,

carpentry, or plastering under separate headings so that there can be no possible confusion as to what is needed in these fields. Then make separate lists for the various rooms, noting all the background work and repairs that must be done before the decorating and finishing touches can be added.

It is important to prepare a carefully detailed decorating schedule to be included with the general schedule of works (it may be, of course, that the decorating schedule is all that is needed). If there is no such schedule, contractors will allow provisional sums in their estimates for the actual painting and wallpapering or covering of rooms, which can be very misleading. Their ideal wall coverings, after all, may well not be the same as their customers'.

In any event, it is necessary to give the contractor a clearly written list of instructions to avoid expensive and sometimes irreparable mistakes. Have an original and three carbon copies made of each schedule: one for the contractor, with samples of paper and colors attached; one so that the appropriate sheets can be pinned up in each room to be decorated; and two to keep—one spare, which should be kept in a separate place in case the first is lost. Then, if the contractor makes any mistakes, you need only point out the relevant instructions on the carbon copy, and he will be forced to make it good at his expense, not yours. Moreover, if the relevant schedule is fixed to the walls of each room, painters or wallpaper hangers can refer to them if the foreman or client is not around to ask. This way, it should be possible to avoid trouble even if the place to be decorated is miles from your present address.

I have found that the most foolproof way to prepare a decoration schedule is to write down each room at the top of a separate sheet of paper, with headings underneath something like the example given on page 21. Where one would otherwise specify a particular manufacturer's name and the number of the product to be used, I have simply put "Manufacturer's" and "no. — ."

SAMPLE DECORATING SCHEDULE

Hall/Staircase/Landing Area

Floor	Hall:	*Manufacturer's apricot/white striped tile no.—, as sample*
	Stairs:	*Apricot carpet by manufacturer, as sample*
	Landings:	*Apricot carpet by manufacturer, as sample*
Walls		*Manufacturer's wall covering no.—, name, color, width*
Ceiling		*Manufacturer's white flat paint*
Woodwork		*Manufacturer's white satin finish*
Radiator		*Manufacturer's paint no.—, to match wall covering*

Kitchen

Floor	*Manufacturer's apricot/white striped tile no.—, as in hall*
Walls	*Manufacturer's white satin finish*
Ceiling	*Manufacturer's white flat paint*
Tiled wall area	*Manufacturer's apricot/white border no.—and manufacturer's white tile no.—*
Woodwork	*Manufacturer's white satin finish*
Radiator	*Manufacturer's white satin finish*

Powder room

Floor	*Manufacturer's apricot/white tile no.—, as in kitchen and hall*
Walls	*Manufacturer's wall covering no.—, name, color, width*
Ceiling	*Manufacturer's white flat paint*
Tiles	*Manufacturer's white plain tile no.—,*
Woodwork	*Manufacturer's white satin finish*
Radiator	*Manufacturer's white satin finish*

Living room

Floor	*Manufacturer's apricot carpet, as sample for stairs*
Walls	*Manufacturer's wall covering no.—, name, color, width*
Ceiling	*Manufacturer's white satin finish (n.b.: not flat paint as usual)*
Woodwork	*Manufacturer's white satin finish*
Radiators	*Manufacturer's paint no.—, color*

Bedroom 1

Floor	*Manufacturer's apricot carpet, as sample for stairs*
Walls	*Manufacturer's paper no.—, name, size of roll*
Ceiling	*Manufacturer's white flat finish*
Woodwork	*Manufacturer's white satin finish*
Radiators	*Manufacturer's white satin finish*

Bedroom 2

Floor	*Manufacturer's apricot carpet, as sample for stairs*
Walls	*Manufacturer's wall covering no.—, name, color, width*
Ceiling	*Manufacturer's white flat finish*
Woodwork	*Manufacturer's white satin finish*
Radiator	*Manufacturer's paint no.—, color*

Bathroom 1

Floor	*Manufacturer's cream carpet no.—, as sample*
Walls	*(Above tiling) Manufacturer's wall covering no.—, name, color, and size of roll wallpaper*
Ceiling	*Manufacturer's white flat paint*
Woodwork	*Manufacturer's satin finish no.—, color*
Radiator	*Manufacturer's satin finish no.—, color*

Bathroom 2

Floor	*Manufacturer's cream carpet no.—, as sample*
Walls	*Manufacturer's satin finish no.—, color*
Ceilings	*As walls*
Woodwork	*Manufacturer's cream satin finish no.—*
Radiator	*Manufacturer's cream satin finish no.—*

Paper and Paint

If painting or wallpapering is to be done without professional help, it is important to know how to calculate the amount of whatever materials are needed.

Most rolls of American wallpaper are 8 yards long and, when trimmed, 18 inches wide, or 36 square feet. French and European rolls are 9 yards long and, when trimmed, 18 inches wide, or 40½ square feet. English rolls are generally 12 yards long and, when trimmed, 21 inches wide, or approximately 7 square yards. Bearing in mind these differences, always make sure to find out the roll sizes and the origin of the paper before you order.

One would think that having ascertained the roll size, it would be easy enough to calculate the quantity by measuring around the four walls of the room and multiplying this by the height from the top of the baseboard to the top of the wall, deducting spaces for windows, doors, and fireplace opening. In practice, however, this is not so accurate, because in large-patterned papers there is a great deal of waste in matching, and this is unavoidable. So look at the tables on pages 21-23. Ceiling measurements—if the ceiling is to be papered—are taken by measuring around the four walls of the room, including doors, windows, and so forth, and following the appropriate table.

When walls are to be painted, the number of feet around the room multiplied by the height from baseboard to ceiling will give the area, and calculations will be reasonably accurate on the basis of a gallon of paint (4.5 liters) to 60 square yards (50.2 square meters). This should be adequate for most walls, but new plaster is more absorbent and might take a gallon for 40 square yards (33.4 meters).

If the contractor or builder is to obtain all the merchandise, it might also save time to include the supplier's telephone number for quicker ordering. This should be followed up in writing as a guarantee in case of disagreement—and remember to keep a carbon copy of the letter. It is equally important to remember to give roll sizes of papers with information about repeats, and in

AMERICAN WALLPAPERS

A table to calculate the number of pieces of paper required for any room

Calculated for paper 20 inches wide (18 inches when trimmed) and 8 yards long. Over doors and under windows not calculated for in this table.

N.B. If calculating in Europe, remember that 1 inch equals 2.5 centimeters; 1 foot equals 30.5 centimeters.

Explanation: Look for height of ceiling at top of column; number of feet of wall around the room in the lefthand column; in the table will be found the number of pieces required.

Example: Number of feet of wall around room, 36; height of wall to ceiling, 11 feet; in the table will be found 12 pieces.

Ft. Around Room	Height of Wall to Ceiling (Skirting to Cornice)						
	8 ft.	9 ft.	10 ft.	11 ft.	12 ft.	13 ft.	14 ft.
28	7	8	9	10	11	11	12
32	8	9	10	11	12	13	14
36	9	10	11	12	13	14	16
40	10	11	12	14	15	16	17
44	11	12	14	15	16	18	19
48	12	13	15	16	18	19	21
52	13	15	16	18	19	21	22
56	14	16	17	19	21	22	24
60	15	17	19	20	22	24	26
64	16	18	20	22	24	26	28
68	17	19	21	23	25	27	29
72	18	20	22	24	27	29	31
80	20	22	25	27	30	32	34
84	21	23	26	28	31	33	36
88	22	24	27	30	32	35	38
92	23	26	28	31	34	37	39
96	24	27	30	32	35	38	41
100	25	28	31	34	37	40	43
104	26	29	32	35	38	41	44
108	27	30	33	36	40	43	46
112	28	31	34	38	42	44	48
116	29	32	36	39	43	46	50
120	30	33	37	40	45	48	51

FRENCH WALLPAPERS

Table for calculating number of pieces required

Height of Wall   Measurement Around the Walls in Feet, Including Doors, Windows, Fireplace Openings, etc.

Height of Wall	28	32	36	40	44	48	52	56	60	64	68	72	76	80	84	88	92	96	100
7 to 7½	6	6	7	8	9	9	10	11	12	12	13	14	15	15	16	17	18	18	19
7½ " 8	6	7	8	8	9	10	11	12	12	13	14	15	16	16	17	18	19	19	20
8 " 8½	6	7	8	9	10	11	11	12	13	14	15	16	16	17	18	19	20	21	21
8½ " 9	7	8	8	9	10	11	12	13	14	15	16	16	17	18	19	20	21	22	23
9 " 9½	7	8	9	10	11	12	13	14	15	16	16	17	18	19	20	21	22	23	24
9½ " 10	7	8	9	10	11	12	13	14	15	16	17	18	19	20	21	22	23	24	25

the case of wall coverings, to give the widths of the pieces, for this again will help the contractor with an accurate estimate of quantities.

If fixtures or semifixtures such as kitchen units, appliances, and sanitary fittings are to be installed, they must be chosen at this stage. Find out what is currently available, collect every possible brochure, and make a choice. It is important to allow plenty of time for the ordering of this sort of equipment, so check on delivery dates before placing an order. If the promised date is too far away, a substitute will have to be found.

Once the final choice has been made, even if many of the items will have to wait for financing, a master checklist can be drawn up for each room. These lists, which will combine all previous lists, should act as a progress guide to the job as well. Draw them up as in the example on page 23, and keep them together with a large envelope or a file full of samples and any relevant literature that has been collected.

Contractors

Scary stories about the misdemeanors of contractors, their carelessness, incompetence, and gross overcharging, are so commonplace that it is worth putting on record that skilled, conscientious contractors who take a pride in their work really do exist. The only trouble is finding them. It is comparatively easy when there is an architect as guide and mediator. But when there is not, what is the best way of going about it?

One good way is through a confident recommendation by a friend or neighbor whose judgment can be trusted in such matters and whose home can be taken as an example. A helpful architect in the vicinity may be prepared to suggest contractors he knows to be reliable even if he is not being employed professionally himself. And a local hardware store or builder's merchant, who doubtless supplies most of the contractors in the neighborhood, might be induced to part with his opinion on the subject.

After a suitable list of contractors has been worked out and their financial stability checked as far as possible, ask

ENGLISH WALLPAPERS

Table for calculating number of pieces required

Height of Wall   Measurement Around the Walls in Feet, Including Doors, Windows, Fireplace Openings, etc.

	28	32	36	40	44	48	52	56	60	64	68	72	76	80	84	88	92	96	100
7 to 7½	4	4	5	5	6	6	7	7	8	8	9	9	9	10	10	11	11	12	12
7½ " 8	4	4	5	5	6	6	7	8	8	9	9	10	10	11	11	12	12	12	12
8½ " 9	4	5	5	6	7	7	8	8	9	9	10	11	11	12	12	13	13	14	14
9 " 9½	4	5	6	6	7	7	8	9	9	10	10	11	12	12	13	13	14	15	15
9½ " 10	5	6	6	7	7	8	9	9	10	10	11	12	12	13	14	14	15	15	16
10 " 10½	5	6	6	7	8	8	9	10	10	11	12	12	13	14	14	15	16	16	17
10½ " 11	5	6	7	7	8	9	9	10	11	11	12	13	13	14	15	16	16	17	18
11 " 11½	5	6	7	8	8	9	10	10	11	12	13	13	14	15	16	16	17	18	18

Stripes go off in all directions in this English hall. Cut-out walls (left) make an interesting space.

at least three of the firms to come and inspect the house or apartment, and give them each a copy of the general work schedule and the decorating schedule in order to get a competitive bid or estimate. This might seem a lot of fuss and trouble, but it could save a corresponding amount of money, since contractors' bids often vary wildly.

Once all the estimates have been received, damp down the spontaneous inclination to chose the cheapest, unless you have heard particularly good things about that firm, or unless all the bids are close together in price. The very lowness of the price, or comparative lowness, might reveal a contractor more concerned to land the contract than to carry out a good job. Do not forget that bad workmanship that has to be redone in a matter of months will clearly be much more expensive in the long run. Instead, look carefully and in detail at all the bids.

Do they all specify a similar quantity and quality of paint and the same number of coats? (If the specification was prepared properly, they certainly should.) And do they all estimate for exactly the same amount of work and materials? Pay attention to the provi-

SAMPLE MASTER CHECKLIST: LIVING ROOM

	Product, Make Color, Etc.,	Size, Amount, and Number	Date of Order	Date of Delivery	Price
Walls					
Ceiling					
Woodwork					
Flooring					
Windows Curtain rods					
Doors Hardware					
Fittings					
New fixtures					
Furniture (sofa, chairs, coffee tables, tables, wall units, etc.,)					
Heating					
Lighting					
Hi-fi					
Television					
Mirrors					
Accessories					

sional costs in the bid, that is to say, the imponderables, and the materials the contractor cannot estimate for exactly because they have yet to be chosen. These are the uncertainties that contractors can make most of their profit on if they are lucky, or if their client is careless, so beware.

Are there any conditions in small print on the back of the bid that should be read over and thoroughly understood? Denials of obligation, for example, if the contractor's employees cause damage or breakage or fire, or if materials disappear from the site? Are there loopholes that will enable the contractor to wriggle out of the results of any complications and delays he is likely to encounter?

If the bids vary only slightly, then the final decision should be made in favor of the contractor who gives the earliest firm finishing date (to which you can usually add at least an extra month or two in your head); the contractor who is the largest (bigger contractors have less need to subcontract); or the contractor who is willing to let you meet the foreman assigned to oversee the job—a very important man and a personality that might well make all the difference in the final choice.

Keeping a Check

In the section on budgeting (pp. 10-16), I strongly advised keeping a sum in reserve for emergencies because extras have a regrettable habit of cropping up, however carefully prepared the complete list of works. In an old house, the very act of disturbing the structure by, say, installing a heating system might bring to light all sorts of hitherto unsuspected faults, and removing unsightly plaster or outside finish could reveal deep cracks in brickwork, the cause of which must be investigated with all possible haste.

In order to keep bills to the minimum, it is important to ensure that all extras are quoted for in writing and that they are attached to the main bid; otherwise, it is a glorious opportunity for the contractor to double his bill in no time at all.

Another good plan, if the job is of any size, is to arrange a meeting at the site

24

once a week. Take the checklist and go over the house or apartment, room by room and floor by floor, with the contractor, his foreman, the electrician, the plumber, the carpenter, or whoever is relevant and whoever can be mustered. Take down in writing—even if the contractor appears to be doing this already—anything and everything that is said and arranged, and file these notes too, making sure that each one is dated, and that each person has a copy which has been approved and initialed by the contractor. Most trusting clients would not imagine that such extreme precaution could be necessary, but all too often, however good the relations, contractors will deny that alterations have been asked for or specifics ordered.

If the job is smaller or is near to your present home, it will probably be as well to visit it every day. In any event, try to visit the site as often as possible, just to check that work is progressing and to iron out any problems. One sprightly, courageous, and curious female friend of mine actually took the trouble to climb the scaffolding to the roof of a three-story nineteenth-century house to see how work on replacing an old chimney was progressing. The men were amazed. She thought the work seemed shoddy and asked the contractor if it was necessary to leave such jagged cement. He inspected the roof himself and found that the work was indeed bad. It only goes to show that even in the safe hands (as you like to imagine) of a professional, nothing should be taken on trust.

Most likely, arrangements for paying will have been included in the contract. That is to say, the contract will state whether a sum should be paid every month as the work progresses, or in thirds, or by whatever method seems mutually convenient. But whatever has been arranged, it is wise to leave the settlement of the final account until all work has been completed absolutely satisfactorily and has proved to be durable over a period of several months. When all is said and done, this is probably the only real safeguard against bad workmanship.

It is very easy to get upset with contractors, however agreeable and willing

they are. Renovating or decorating a home is an understandably emotional process to the owner. But one cannot expect everyone else to be as emotionally involved in the project, however physically embroiled they may be. If things go wrong—and some things will undoubtedly go wrong—it may well upset all sorts of schedules and arrangements and be financially inconvenient if not disastrous, but to the contractor and the labor he employs, it is just another delay to which they are well used, and for this reason they may appear infuriatingly phlegmatic and unsympathetic.

Provided notice is taken of the safeguards I have suggested, the job should be completed as satisfactorily as possible. But do not expect any but the most dedicated of men to stay on after hours to finish a job, however tantalizingly near to completion it is. I have known the extreme case of a young plumber leaving an essential drainage pipe unfixed on the optimistic grounds that it would be quite all right as long as it did not rain. It did, and in the middle of our first night in our first home we awoke to the ominous sound of water pouring down from floor to floor, destroying the decoration of every single one of the rooms it gushed through in the process. To be fair, that was an extreme example, and the contractor was just as shocked as we were—as well he might be, since it was clearly his liability and he had to pay.

Do not expect contractors to make any design decisions for you unless you have implicit faith in their judgment, or no ideas at all of your own. On the whole, their taste is not going to be your taste. By the same token, try not to be offended, cast down, or worse, swayed in your own judgment by a contractor's obvious denigration of your choice of colors and finishes. You can be illogically cut to the quick by the derogatory remarks passed by workmen. I still am, and I have been designing rooms for years. But take heart from the fact that you are going to live in the place, not they. Besides, you might just be more unconventional than other clients they have had, and they might end up by liking your choices after all.

2. Space

Space is almost always the bugbear of decoration.
There is normally never enough of it. Occasionally there
is too much of it. It is interesting how rarely it seems
right. Yet many of us just accept or adapt to the given
space in a house or apartment without ever thinking
how it could be changed around, expanded, or rethought
for the better. This chapter shows how to create space
visually, how to exaggerate it, and how to tame it. It
shows how to expand space by furniture arrangement,
by decoration, by mirrors, by creating perspectives, and
by the use of light. And it gives advice on cultivating
a sense of scale, as well as on effecting minor changes.

Preceding page: *Different spatial images are revealed at every turn of this spectacular soaring staircase.*

Above: *Just about every trick in the trade has been brought into play to exaggerate the space in this small bathroom. Cleverly used mirror visually doubles the existing area; long windows with vertical louvers and inset lighting strips give new perspective.*

Right: *The problem in this vaulted Spanish room was how to minimize the space. Shelves at one end curtail it, as do the massed paintings.*

Since the means for radically changing the basic structure of a home are limited, if not impossible, for many people—and people living in rentals are just as hamstrung as people who are short of cash—one of the first considerations must be how to make the space *seem* more expansive. Careful exploration of all the possibilities within an existing building can make a useful difference to its feeling of spaciousness, if not to its square footage.

Sensible apportioning of space usually depends upon lifestyle. Open-plan living has much to recommend it for the single, or for childless couples. But a family has to balance the need for as much elbow room as possible with the equally pressing need for occasional privacy and quiet and different spaces for work and play, for adults and children. This presupposes a proportion of general areas for everyone's use with private spaces for individuals; a ration of formal space and a ration of informal. When space is tight, living areas should be as large as possible, and bedrooms can be as small as is compatible with basic sleeping and dressing needs. It may help, for example, to organize so-called reception-room space into one large kitchen-living-working room with bedrooms and bathrooms off it to which people can retire to sit and read, or talk or work, whenever they want to be alone.

Far left, above and below: *Toilet, washbasin, shower, dressing table, and closets are neatly slivered off from the main dressing room–study area in painter Hélène Fesenmaier's London house, making maximum use of available space without destroying proportions.*

Center: *New York painter Jack Ceglic has an all-white, entirely open-plan loft in Soho which is brilliantly designed. The only closed area is the bathroom, where services are run down through a simple chrome tube to keep the effect as uncluttered as is compatible with efficient plumbing.*

Above: *The kitchen area in the same Soho loft consists of one fixed and two maneuverable wood-topped blocks holding appliances and accessories. The castored blocks can also be used for serving since they can be wheeled anywhere. Again, services are concealed in slim chrome tubes.*

At a very simple level, a home that is owned, as opposed to being rented, might well be improved by the elementary expedient of changing the functions of the various rooms, or by changing the layout. It is taken for granted, in many houses, that bedrooms are upstairs and living rooms downstairs, but if the view and light are better higher up, why not live up there and sleep below? Why keep a kitchen inconveniently at the end of a long corridor, just because it was always there, when that space would make a better laundry room, and an area could be sliced off the living or dining room to make an efficient galley kitchen? I did that in our present house, and I cannot say I really miss a large kitchen—not too much, anyway. And I could not do without the laundry room. Another good idea I noted in a large dressing room was a whole wall of louvered doors, neatly concealing separate compartments for toilet, washbasin, dressing table, and shower.

32

Above: *A series of platforms covered in carpet and shaggy fur rugs have been built into Philip Guadaynino's Manhattan apartment by New York architects Louis Muller and William Murphy. They were designed to cram maximum seating-lounging space into a long narrow area with the minimum of clutter. Extra storage and hi-fi equipment are tucked away under another platform (not shown), and the only movable furnishings are the glass and steel occasional tables.*

Center left: *Attic space is well used for a child's room in this London house. A fresh pink, white, and apricot wallpaper is extended up and over the sloping ceiling to make the room seem more spacious.*

Proceeding up the scale:

Old doors can be blocked up to make new wall space, and new ones can be cut into more convenient bits of wall.

Walls can be cut halfway down, or at either side so they form a dividing slab rather than a solid mass; or shapes such as long slits or ovals can be cut through them from top to bottom, so that the adjoining space shows through.

A gallery or a platform can be built into a room with a particularly high ceiling.

Take advantage of an attic or a basement, and generally use the space available as the flexible entity it can be. Landings and hallways should be used to their maximum advantage; it is surprising how often they will take the odd piano, desk, or table for extramural eating.

More ambitiously, it is possible to be as ingenious with space as money, basic structure, foundations, and any legal requirements for the district or building allow. A new basement can be excavated, a roof raised, and any internal walls that are nonsupporting can be knocked down.

Obviously the structure of a building, its position, whether it is a rental or not, and the state of its heating, plumbing, and wiring will all have a bearing on any decisions. But there are very few hard and fast rules to be followed, except those dictated by finance, practicality, and common sense, once the decision has been made to use the space at hand as freely and imaginatively as possible. All the same, it is just as well not to make any momentous decision to hack down all partition walls —or put a whole lot up—before finding out whether there might not be some simple cosmetic solutions, some visual trickery that could be played, with equally gratifying results.

Center right: *This rather Eastern-looking room merges with the courtyard outside to give a greater sense of space, which is in turn exaggerated by the low stools and cushions piled on the right.*

Above: *A wall cut away at either side in painter Jack Ceglic's New York apartment becomes a screen dividing off the dining space.*

Below left: *The same sort of cut-away wall device is used behind the bed in the Dykers' apartment, designed by Mark Hampton. It looks very clean-cut.*

Below right: *A new staircase goes up from the new extension in architect Bernard Hunt's conversion of a Victorian terrace house. The brick structure in the background holds a laundry and powder room squeezed into minimal space.*

Expanding Space by Furniture Arrangement

The cheapest and most obvious way to gain apparent extra space is to be rigorous about the amount of furniture that is used and the way it is arranged. Pare down as much as possible, though don't pare down to the extent that all individuality is lost in the process.

As a guide:

Two small sofas look neater than four chairs.

Two small seating units pushed together take up less room than two individual chairs spaced apart.

Storage all down one wall is better than separate desks, liquor cabinets or trays, shelves, tables for television and hi-fi units, and the various other appurtenances of living rooms.

Corners can be used more: for beds, cupboards, desks.

Built-in cupboards or seats with storage under them can be tucked in wherever possible to obviate clutter.

Big pieces of furniture should be kept against a wall.

Fold-up and thus get-riddable-of furniture should be used whenever possible.

Tables, occasional tables, and desks made of plexiglass, Perspex, or glass or surfaced in mirror look much lighter and more insubstantial than the same pieces made in wood or chrome, plastic or marble.

In a one-room apartment, a double bed looks both obvious and bulky. Have a couple of good daybeds piled with cushions or pillows instead. By day they will take care of seating needs and at night they can be pushed together.

A room that might seem too small with a double bed plus sufficient wardrobe space will work better if the wardrobes are built around the bed.

If you decide to have the minimum of furniture in order to make more room, make sure that the pieces require the minimum of maintenance; being fewer, they will get twice the amount of wear.

Above left: *Clean-cut furniture grouping, a carpeted seating platform, and spare Plia chairs hung on the wall help to exaggerate the given space in Kate Curry's small London apartment.*

Above right: *A pair of Italian Cassina canvas chairs set into an angle make maximum use of rather awkward space.*

Below: *Transparent pieces set in front of white storage, white walls, and an off-white carpet add to the sense of space in this small apartment.*

Far right: *Two chairs pushed together and two small sofas facing across a glass table make compact seating for six in the Dyker's apartment.*

Expanding Space with Mirror

Mirror will always give depth and added length and width to a room, even if it is expensive depth, length, and width. If it can possibly be afforded, use it on one whole wall, or in a dark corner, and use it generously from floor to ceiling and right up to a corner if the space could do with doubling. Extending from floor to top of window height in the space between two tall windows, mirror will make an enormous difference to light and brightness. In an alcove or on a recessed wall, it will give a feeling of depth.

If unadorned mirror seems unsubtle, one compromise is to carefully insert metal supports between lengths of mirror to hold glass shelves for books and objects. Lit from underneath, the whole will take on an interesting brilliance as well as adding perspective to a room. Etched, sandblasted, or patterned mirror put up on a wall can be decorative in its own right apart from its reflective value. Find out from an art school or college about craftsmen who work with glass. Many students or ex-students will be glad of the opportunity to design a single job in this way.

Expanding Space with Perspective

An alternative to making space with sheets of expensive mirror is to create perspective whenever and wherever you can. Think consciously of creating a foreground, middle ground, and background, a definite three-dimensional effect. A mirror on a table or mantelpiece with a plant or small objects in front of it will give depth, as will a hinged screen with, say, a small table and lamp in the foreground. Similarly, the eye can be drawn out and along by diagonal or zigzag lines painted on doors or walls, or by similar geometric or directional patterns on the floor.

Far left: *Mirrored mosaic tiles with a border, patterned foil paper, more mirror on the ceiling, black-and-white-striped tiles, and a white floor make for a mesmeric effect in Anthony Redmile's small bathroom. The varying reflective surfaces seem to break up boundaries and push the room on forever.*

Center: *Mirror extends across the corner made by an angled seating platform in Alan Schlussel's New York apartment designed by Louis Muller and William Murphy.*

Above: *Waist-high angled mirror divides a bed from storage units in Philip Guadaynino's bedroom designed by architects Muller and Murphy, who seem to have a gift all their own for ingenious space-pushing.*

Expanding Space by Decoration

Thoughtful decoration is important when space is limited. There are various simple rules for exaggerating or diminishing a given area:

The same floor covering running through a whole apartment maximizes floor space. If walls and ceilings are kept the same color as well, the space will flow uninterruptedly. Variations on the same color scheme from room to room give an illusion of space because of the continuity.

The lighter the wall and floor color, the bigger a room will look. Pale colors recede; strong, intense, or dark colors come towards you. If a ceiling is too high in proportion to a room, a strong color will bring it down. If it is too low, a light shade will appear to heighten it.

A continuous band or stripe of color or a contrasting picture molding around a room will make it seem more compact. Likewise, the removal of a picture molding will make it seem more spacious.

Shine and reflection will increase a sense of space, while a soft, matte surface will blur and diminish it.

Patterns with a strong directional or geometric feel can appear to push out and extend floors and walls. Patterned carpets or wall coverings with a light ground give a feeling of depth. Patterns on a dark ground enclose. If you want to have an all-over motif on walls, try the same motif on a smaller scale for curtains or shades, covers, and so on. This will push the walls out.

Take advantage of any good long view to be had from a window, or even any greenery. Furniture and curtains should not be allowed to impede the view in any way, so that the eye is drawn into the distance.

Use window shades instead of curtains.

Pictures hung on either side of a narrow corridor or room will push walls out in a quite surprising manner.

Far left, above: *The view from the Avray Wilsons' sitting room behind the Côte d'Azur stretches over the garden to slopes tangled with vines and flowers, joining room to landscape.*

Far left, below: *Cool white walls and ceiling blend with white tiled floor in a gently revamped chateau in the South of France belonging to the Bernard Sterns.*

Center: *Directional stripes of expanding widths on walls, tented ceiling, mattress, and floor exaggerate space which is already cleverly dispersed in British designer Nicholas Hill's London home.*

Above: *Pinky-apricot baseboards and stair rails delineate and pull together a high white studio.*

Above: *The space around this staircase seems enormous, which is entirely the result of the painted lines drawing the eye upward and along the area.*

Right: *Supergraphics by English designer Alan Grainger add to the marvelous space in the Washington house designed for Gerald and Jo Frey by architect Wendell H. Lovett. The graphics make the seating area seem more contained and the staircase appear to soar, as well as outlining the diamond-shaped window.*

Far right: *This exercise in perspective in a New York loft was arranged by British designer William Waldron. It makes a narrow corridor seem spacious. The alternating zigzag on the door adds interest to an otherwise bleak area.*

40

Expanding Space with Light

The lighter the colors in a room, the larger a room will look, but light itself, whether natural or artificial, can make a dramatic difference to space. The whole subject of lighting is treated in chapter 3, but its proper control, arrangement, and direction can change a room beyond recognition, and what is more, change it in several different ways.

Natural light can be filtered at the source by blinds or shades, or screens of one sort or another, to give it a softness and subtlety which in itself diffuses space. Floor-to-ceiling panels of glass let into interior dividing walls give extra light to halls and corridors, as well as doubling the sense of space and perspective by showing glimpses of rooms beyond. Uplights and downlights used instead of table lamps; pools of artificial light from judiciously placed spotlights; light trained onto particular things like paintings, plants, or objects; light controlled by dimmer switches: all these soften and blur the hard confines of a room so that its limits seem to expand.

A Sense of Scale

The importance of a sense of scale is often underestimated in furnishing and decorating. By a sense of scale, I mean things like knowing how to deploy height and width, when to use large patterns and when small, when to offset an angle with a curve and vice versa, all of which are just as crucial as a clear sense of style and color.

Some people are born with an accurate sense of scale just as others are born with perfect pitch or a useful color sense, but whereas perfect pitch is an absolute and is either there or not, a sense of color and a sense of scale can be learned with time and experience, which is at least encouraging.

Try to analyze the parts of any room, or photograph of a room, that looks good. Note how things are placed and in what proportion, what seems to enlarge a space and what to dwarf it. It will be noticeable, for example, that if furniture in a small space is deliberately kept on a small scale, the area will seem agreeably larger.

Normally, too, it is possible to get an enhanced sense of space by keeping most furniture at much the same low level, remembering, though, that the effect of the continuous low level is set off to advantage by at least one tall object like an old cupboard, a tall bookcase, a rangy plant, long windows, or a canopy. Try to balance solidity with delicacy, angles with curves, height with depth. Rooms that show this awareness of balance have much more ease about them.

Above: *Light streams in through the tall windows at such an angle that the fireplace wall stands out sharply and the recessed walls fall right back.*

Far left: *(Top) A sense of scale is shown in the deployment of heights with depths, angles with curves, and solidity with delicacy. (Second from top) Light filtered through screens makes this window wall seem less confining. (Second from bottom) The parameters of this space are given a deeper perspective by floodlighting the table and objects placed in front of the screen. (Bottom) There is a sure sense of scale here in the placement of painting and sculpture.*

Simple Structural Changes

If it is possible to make some minor structural changes in a home, it is worthwhile to bear in mind a list of potential alterations that involve comparatively little upheaval and expense.

Doors

It may well be that a door into a room is not strictly necessary and that its removal will give more space and flexibility. Either take it straight out from its frame—remembering to make good the places where the hinges and locks were—or remove frame and all and repair the surround. If the latter is done, a further step could be to round the top to form an arch.

Less drastically, circulation can sometimes be helped by rehanging a door so that it swings in the opposite direction. This is often a simple aid in the rearrangement of furniture, perhaps enabling an extra bedside table to be placed by a bed.

If space is minimal but a door seems necessary, consider changing the original door for one that folds in on itself rather than opening outward, or narrow double doors that just swing in when pushed. If there is space to the side, try a sliding door on a track. If a new partition wall is being built anyway, it might be possible to have the door slide into it. If all these solutions are impossible, consider a curtain, which may be in fabric, beads, bamboo, raffia, or rattan—anything that will hang well and take up no space.

Windows

The number, shape, and size of windows can make a radical change in the sense of spaciousness. Many people put in large areas or walls of glass to make a room merge as much as possible with the outside view, but this can raise problems of its own with heating and security, and not least, diminish wall space so that there is no room to hang paintings or prints or to set up bookshelves.

Windows do not have to be of conventional shape and size: this is only habit. A long, thin slit of a window, whether vertical or horizontal, is dramatic and throws interesting light from both extremes of its length as well as providing extra depth to a room. Small, narrow windows in a wall, set on either side of a fireplace, for example, will add new views, give slivers of extra light, and subtract very little valuable wall space. Nor should one forget the extra space for furnishings that can be made by raising sill levels if there seems to be too much window and filling in the space below.

Center: *The table in this house on Fire Island designed by Horace Gifford makes maximum use of the seating platform and obviates the need for conventional chairs, as does the platform below with its comfortable pillows. The varying levels and the unbroken areas of glass and wood enhance the space.*

Above: *Glass walls and an arched door make all the difference to the sense of space in this London conservatory extension to a cramped Victorian house. The new wood staircase branches off the old main stairs, giving a feeling of lightness and suspension which is underlined by the pale gold of the wood strip floors, the cane furniture, and the rangy plants in cane baskets. The house belongs to architect Bernard Hunt and his green-fingered wife.*

Fireplaces

A room can be made to look bigger by blocking up a fireplace (and so giving more room for furniture), and a great deal bigger by removing the walls on either side of the chimney breast if the fireplace happens to be set in a dividing non-load-bearing internal wall. This will give a feeling of being divided from the room next door as well as providing an increased sense of space and continuity.

Ceilings

It is much cheaper to build a flat ceiling, so naturally, conventional ceilings are flat. But different shapes in the upper level can make an enormous difference to the space, style, and interest of a room. One part can be lowered—say, over the table in a dining room—and the apparent size and shape of the room will be considerably altered. Or a ceiling can be lowered all around the perimeter of a room so that the middle appears to soar. Chimney breasts, too, can be made to jut out, giving an unexpected new angle of interest.

Above: *The fireplace in this California house has not been removed but so recessed in the surrounding chevron-patterned wall that it adds depth and perspective to an already large and clean-cut space. The wide polished floorboards in quiet contrast to the wall stripes increase the sense of space and continuity, and the indoor tree in its loosely woven cane basket gives added height.*

Right: *The chimney breast juts out at an unexpected angle in this basically one-room apartment designed for Suzanne Klevoric by Joe D'Urso. Three stepped platforms define eating, sleeping, and sitting areas, and the quiet black, white, and dark grey scheme is another contributing factor to the flow of space. A mass of pillows on the sofa bed adds pattern, as does the spiky foliage of the plants. In this basically neutral scheme every stroke of color stands out sharply.*

All these changes can be effected fairly simply with plaster or wallboard, with plywood for straight shapes, or with plaster on expanded metal for curves or undulations—although this last would be an ambitious undertaking for anyone but a skilled contractor.

An extra bonus of dropping a ceiling is that it creates more space for storage above and gives an ample recess for inset spotlights or downlights, which is, of course, one of the most satisfactory ways of lighting.

Corners

Just as most people think of ceilings as being flat, so too they think of corners as being angled. But there is really no reason —except the very salient one of cost—for not having rounded corners, which again make a difference to the feeling of space. The more angles and joins are made to seem blurred and indefinite, the bigger a room will feel.

Curving corners is a more complicated structural exercise than the previous changes I have mentioned, but the final effect is worth the effort. It involves using an expanded metal lath and wood frame, which is then plastered to fit in with the existing plaster. There may be a difference in level between the old plaster and the new, but this is easy enough to disguise by covering the wall with a thickish fabric or paper. If a plain painted finish seems preferable, cover the wall with a thick lining paper first and paint over the top. Alternatively, one can achieve much the same effect cosmetically with a tall hinged screen, although, of course, it will be gently angled rather than rounded.

Changing Levels

Introducing extra floor levels to make a multilevel room is a particularly effective way of altering and enhancing almost any sort of space.

If a space is very high, a balcony or gallery reached by a staircase can be built in, which can then act as an extra sleeping area, a music room, a study/work area, or extra display space for art. The staircase might well be a spiral, since they take up the least possible room. To digress a little here, Michael Dunne, who took most of the photographs in this book, managed to fit his wife, himself, and five children into one small London mews house with incisive planning, excellent storage, and a self-designed spiral staircase.

Left: *Two parallel walkways reached by a double-height spiral staircase create three separate levels in Bernard Stern's London studio converted from an old church. If too much space is a problem, this is one good way to bring it into scale for living.*

Above: *Max Clendinning designed this towerlike structure as living space within a working studio in London. The ground-floor level is for eating (top) and cooking (below, right). The dark-painted bedroom (below, left) with its stepped wardrobe and cupboard space looks like a domesticated version of battlements from the outside. This bedroom has its own bathroom at the far end. The whole structure works successfully as a separate entity.*

Even if a room is not particularly high, it is quite possible to build in a variety of platforms, depending on where the room is situated in a building and on the state of the building's structure. Given reasonable height and size, conversation pits of varying depths can be inserted in the middle of a room by building up the space around with plywood, and that change of level can be compounded by putting, say, a platform for dining on one side and having still another level for working on the other. Again, a platform can be run all around a room, leaving a well in the center; or one can be built across one end of a room with storage cupboards underneath and perhaps a balustrade above—or low bookshelves which will act as a balustrade.

Bedrooms often look a great deal bigger if the bed is either set upon or sunk into a platform. Alternatively, a covered mattress can be put onto a carpeted base, or a sunk-in mattress can be covered by day with yet another level of seating platform. Depending again on the height of the room, this platform could be quite high and reached by steps, which will give extra storage space underneath.

If the ceiling of the room below is sufficiently high, it might be possible to cut through a wood floor, dropping the floor in the room above and lowering the ceiling in the one beneath. If the room is on the ground floor, it is sometimes possible to excavate a seating well. But even the simplest platform is a way of gaining a seating area without the need for extra furniture, as long as one can forgo the flexibility. Covered blocks of foam can be placed on top of a raised level for yet another change of height.

Although the difference made to a room by a multilevels is often quite extraordinary, a good carpenter should be able to introduce the various levels that are wanted without too much difficulty. It is certainly interesting to be able to change the whole feeling of space through the floors as opposed to the walls.

A particularly imaginative spatial solution that I saw in London involved the building of a towerlike structure within a studio. The painter-owner wanted living space that did not interfere with and was quite separate from her working space, and yet was totally integrated and added to the look of the space. The ground floor of the tower held a tiny kitchen and dining area and the second floor a skillfully constructed bedroom and bathroom. But before embarking on any spatial experiments, one should be quite sure that the structure of the building will stand the alteration.

Far left, above: *Curved corners on this stairwell in a converted nineteenth-century terrace house in London greatly enhance the feeling of space.*

Left, above: *Michael Dunne designed this staircase, which takes up surprisingly little room in his small London mews house that nevertheless holds a family of seven plus rather large dogs. Mirrors, shades, and the same pale sisal carpet throughout also help.*

Far left, below: *A mirrored screen reaching to the ceiling gives added height and depth to this dining room in Mark Hampton's New York apartment. The geometric-patterned carpet, reflected in the screen, further encourages the important spatial illusion.*

Left, below: *A seating platform runs the length of this room, which is architects Louis Muller and William Murphy's office as well as living space. The mirror, which lines the entire side wall, doubles the arch and the small space in general.*

Above: *A mattress, now fur-covered, is sunk into a seating platform in Kate Curry's London flat.*

Room Dividers

So far, I have been mainly concerned with opening space up rather than dividing it more efficaciously, but most dividers do just as their name implies without blocking off natural light or being as solid as a built-in wall. Many of them can act as extra storage receptacles, as well as combining disparate pieces of furniture like shelves, cupboards, and working surfaces into one unit.

There are a number of commercial room dividers available, ranging from simple, free-standing shelves in different shapes and sizes to elaborate structures that incorporate shelves and cupboards, desk units, and stereo storage and are much like ordinary wall storage units except that they are free-standing.

Then there are the various types of screens and their off-shoots, whether free-standing, fixed, solid, or see-through, which are being developed all the time. Ordinary wooden garden lattice is cheap and can look effective, fixed at floor and ceiling for solidity. I have also seen handsome three-quarter-height curved white screens (they could also be covered in stretch fabric of any color) used to divide off an apparently semicircular room, like a dining area, from a larger space. A hinged screen can be effective in a bedroom, a kitchen-dining room, or a one-room apartment. Put a table and a lamp on one side, for example, and use the other as a headboard for a bed. More ambitiously, a series of sliding screens can be set on runners to divide up space at will. I have seen screen walls that pivot and walls that turn on small wheels.

A well-designed fabric, or even strong coarse net, can be stapled to battens (slim pieces of wood) attached to floor and ceiling and stretched between them, or hung like a banner or just plain curtains from the ceiling alone. A large unframed painting can be fixed to a vertical wood or metal post attached to floor and ceiling. Many people use vertical blinds as room dividers; these are especially effective when they are left half-open to give small vistas through into the next area.

A mirrored screen is effective, since it reflects and divides at the same time. In a bathroom, something as simple as a towel rail hung with towels divides up areas efficiently. Tall, broad-leaved plants like the arums with their particular sculptural quality act as good dividers, and virtual walls of plants can be made by setting several large plants of various sizes side by side in baskets or planters.

Left: *A curved screen made from shining strips (above) reflects and exaggerates the light as well as defines the dining area in architect Paul Rudolf's New York apartment. Lighting strips embedded in the carpet (below) make the room appear to float above ribbons of light at night. The curved seating unit, wrapping its way around the table and down the side of the room, is another space-saver, as are the muted, neutral colors.*

Right: *A screen wall in this Californian lobby is hung with a large mirror in a deep frame which reflects the cactus plant in front of it as well as the window and the view beyond. This extra dimension and the domino-striped cushions on the floor all help visually to enlarge the area.*

3. Light

"Architecture," said Le Corbusier, "is the knowing, correct, and magnificent play of masses brought together in light." To a great extent, so is the home, for light plays a key part in showing everything to its best advantage and in diminishing faults. But knowing the correct way to bathe a home in the right sort of light for the right room is not so easy. The choice of lights themselves is vast, but it is rare to get advice on how to use them, or even to see them as they should be seen, in the correct situation. Here, the various methods are all set out and illustrated, and the choice of lights explained and rationalized along with notes on their proper control.

Lighting

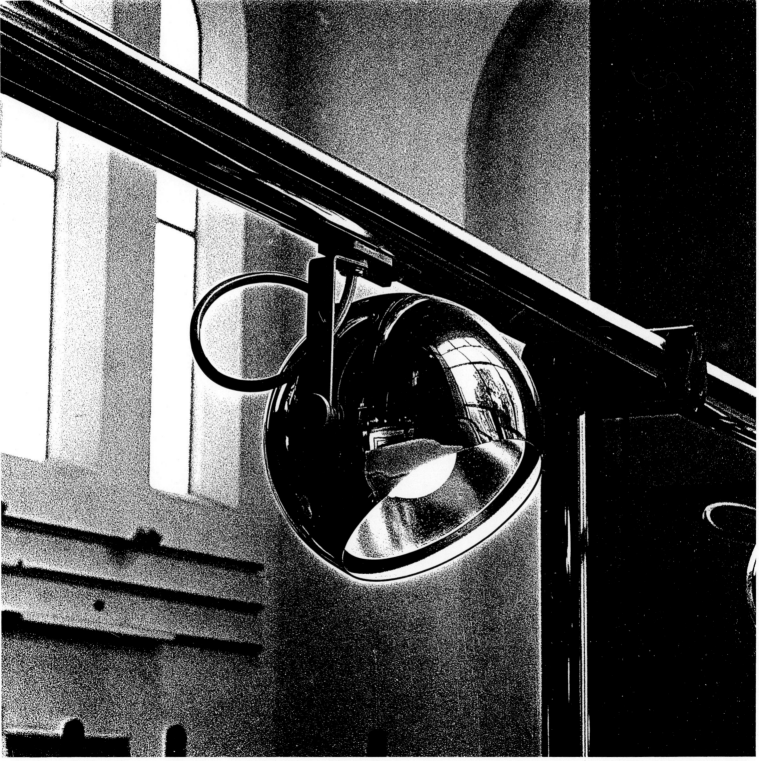

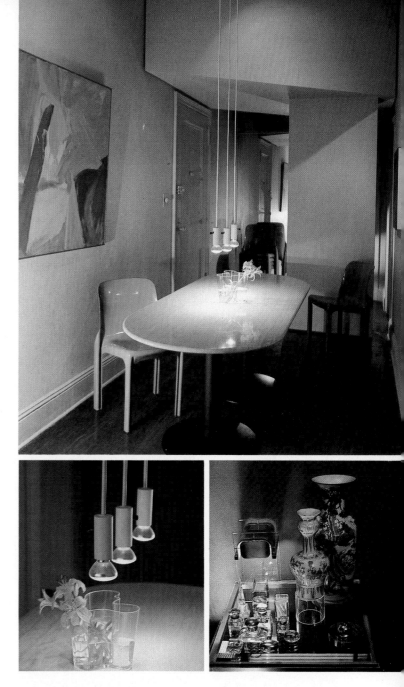

Good light and good lighting, the one natural and the other man-made, are as central to the success of any room as they are to sight, and yet, curiously, they are often the least planned, the least thought-about of all domestic ingredients—very much the afterthought, in fact. It is odd, for after all a mass of daylight is one of the few free assets anyone is likely to get with a home and should be made the most of—enhanced, filtered, or allowed to flow to the best of one's ability. Artificial lighting, on the other hand, is certainly the most flexible way to change mood, atmosphere, or feeling, and will exaggerate space or diminish faults at the flick of a switch or the turn of a dimmer. Unconsidered lighting can make an otherwise exemplary room look dreary, whereas imaginative lighting can imbue the simplest ingredients with a near-mystic excitement—almost as if they had never really been contemplated before.

Ideally, architects should give the same amount of thought to the planning and placing of lighting equipment as they give to the proportions of windows and their treatment. But then, everybody should have the same concern for artificial light as they do for daylight. More, perhaps, because it can be controlled and manipulated at will. That there is not the same concern—that there is often a failure to make the most of even the daylight that is given—seems such a waste.

The reason for this disregard—at least as far as artificial lighting is concerned—is mostly, I think, that many people tend to light their homes as their forebears did, though with electricity instead of oil, candles, or rushlights. They seem unaware that artificial lighting has developed from being a poor daylight substitute to the point where its potential has a fundamental influence on design. When they think of lighting, they think of lights, or lamps, the actual fixtures, rather than how to manipulate the stuff. When they buy fixtures, they buy them very often for their shapes and looks but neglect to find out about their effect. Even when they are searching out the more sophisticated lighting in a store or in a catalogue—the spots and wallwashers, the downlights and uplights—they mostly buy for looks rather than for what those looks will achieve.

And it *is* difficult to display the effects of lighting anywhere except in a showroom devoted to nothing else. How could it

Preceding page: *Multipurpose track supports spots, loudspeakers, and air conditioning.*

Far left: *Spots and reading lamps fixed on the uprights of the bookshelves, and more spots suspended from the ceiling track, cast warm pools of light on the bed and the pillow painting in painter Jack Ceglic's Soho, New York, apartment. By day the space is a blaze of light; by night it is splashed with a quite different kind of mellowness.*

Above, and below left: *Three spots suspended over the dining table in an apartment by architects Louis Muller and William Murphy. The light gives particular intensity to the vase of flowers.*

Below right: *A lucite and chrome table lamp exaggerates the transparency of glass on glass.*

Above: *These three photographs show several uses of a drainpipe-shaped Concord spotlight, which can be wall-mounted or used free-standing and is flexible enough to be twisted at any angle. In this way, it can be used for working, sewing, or reading, or just to highlight an object or a wall. It is typical of the many multipurpose lamps that are internationally available.*

be possible to show how the position, color, and intensity of light sources will give definition to various spaces in a house; to display light and shade, strength and subtlety, in a cramped area full of dozens of different fixtures crammed together for maximum choice?

Whenever possible, if only to get an enlightened view of current techniques, it is wise to visit proper lighting showrooms. If it is not possible, take careful note of pleasing lighting in other people's houses, restaurants, museums, and galleries—anywhere and anything that seems translatable into a domestic setting. For reference, here is a summary of the choice of lighting generally available.

Types of Lighting

There are basically four different types of domestic lighting equipment—six, if you count the most subtle but the least effective for seeing, candlelight and firelight. These are downlights, uplights, spotlights, and floodlights, which have all been adapted from theatrical and industrial lighting; conventional ceiling lights, wall lights, table lamps, floor lamps, and strip lights; fluorescent lighting; and the more ambitious lighting equipment that makes light a decoration or an architectural element in itself. This last will be dealt with separately later in the chapter.

Downlights

Downlights are just that: round or square metal canisters that can be recessed into a ceiling, semirecessed, or ceiling-mounted to cast pools of light on the ground or any surface below them. The kind of pool of light depends on whether the bulb inside is a spot, a floodlight, or an ordinary bulb. A spot will throw a concentrated circle of light, which is at its most effective bearing down on a plant, or a bowl of flowers, or a collection of glasses as on a dining table. A floodlight will give a wider, less intense, cone-shaped light, and an ordinary bulb will provide soft over-all lighting.

Most downlights are fitted with some sort of antiglare device, and some of them are half-silvered to give a directional light. Some types can be used for wallwashing and some for pinpointing. By wallwashing, I mean literally bathing a wall with light. Angled close to a wall of paintings, wallwashers will splash light onto the varying surfaces, leaving contrasting shadows in between. Or they will simply make a color more brilliant or a molding more effective.

Uplights

Uplights are downlights in reverse, round or square metal canisters in different diameters, which will hold varying intensities of bulbs. Put them on the floor, under glass shelves, behind sofas, behind plants, and in corners, and they will give a beautiful, dramatic accent light, bouncing reflected light off ceilings and into the room, creating shadows and moods that could never be imagined by day. A well-placed mixture of uplights and downlights, judiciously bolstered by pinpointing spots and light to read by, gives great atmosphere to a room, as well as the sort of reflected light that lighting designers consider the best since it gives the least glare.

Spotlights

Spots are used for accent lighting and to give strong, direct light. The simplest spotlight consists of a reflector fitting that will take an ordinary bulb. Others take specially designed spot bulbs, which are often internally silvered with built-in reflectors for special intensity. A third variety hold low-voltage transformers to cast especially narrow beams on small objects or narrowly defined areas. Although normally the hotter the wire or filament, the brighter the light, a low-voltage transformer will produce the same amount of light from a lower-wattage bulb, so that in this case the lower heat makes it possible to have brighter light. There are also eyeball or framing spots for the specific lighting of paintings or objects.

Most spotlights can be mounted straight into the ceiling, onto walls, or onto tracks and pointed at anything that would benefit from special illumination. Some small spots have a magnetic backplate so that they can be attached to any surface and pointed in any direction. These are useful for concealing on the sides of bookcases or in wall recesses or ceiling angles to give extra accent. Even smaller free-standing eyeball spots or miniature free-standing high-intensity, low-voltage spots can be pushed in among books or objects on shelves to give more pools of light and shade. These eyeball spots can also be recessed in the ceiling.

Tracks are an excellent way of getting a lot of light from one outlet without extra and expensive electrical work (as well as the making good afterwards that such work generally entails). Mount them on or recess them into a ceiling or down the side of a wall. Arrange them in lines or rectangles or squares or circles a few feet out from the edge of the room, or straight down the middle. On them go spotlights or floodlights, which-

Above: *Suspended from the top lighting track are, from left to right: a flood or wallwasher, two internally silvered bulbs with built-in reflectors, another wallwasher, and a reflector fitting with an ordinary bulb. Immediately below these are three bulbs of the type to go around shaving or make-up mirrors, a low-voltage transformer, and a variety of table, floor, swivel, and wall spots.*

ever seem best for the purpose, or a mixture of both that can be angled at will. Some of the more sophisticated varieties contain multicircuit systems to allow even greater flexibility of control. Plug-mold strip is another variation and comes in a variety of lengths. It can run around the edge of a room behind a concealing baffle or pelmet of some sort. It will take any variety of bulb with the use of a socket adapter, and bulbs can be plugged in at 6-inch intervals for varying effects, but it is particularly good for wallwashing. Plug-mold strips can also be mounted on shelves and covered with opal acrylic or frosted glass, or used as ribbons of light in much the same way at the base of a seating platform. LyteTrim, a miniature track with miniature spots, is also extremely useful for shelves, bed-heads, and so on.

It is particularly important for spots or floodlights to be used in conjunction with dimmers so that their intensity can be controlled at will; besides, dimmers both save energy and prolong the life of the bulbs. Most dimmers are combined with an on/off switch and can be installed quite easily. If it is impossible to rewire a room for one reason or another, a dimmer plug, which is a little like an adapter, can be used to control a couple of fixtures. Unlike a regular dimmer, however, a dimmer plug uses as much electricity as any ordinary fixture.

Conventional Lights

Conventional lights and lamps of this sort need little explanation, and there is an enormous choice of shapes, colors, and materials, depending on taste and space and pocket. But some are more suitable for certain purposes than others. And some, such as those Italian snaky coils of light, are like pieces of sculpture or art objects in their own right, quite apart from their light-throwing qualities.

Pendant fixtures are ubiquitous, but they tend to flatten shadows and do not give enough light by which to read or work comfortably. The amount of light they let out depends very much on the type of shade used and the height at which they are hung. Directional pendants, which are good over dining tables and sometimes over side tables, have opaque shades so that the light shines downward. The shade should be deep enough to prevent light shining into eyes, and the pendant is best mounted on a rise-and-fall fixture. Ceiling-mounted lights give good over-all general light, but it looks flat unless this general source is used in conjunction with other types of light.

If wall lights are used, or have to be used because that is the way a space has been wired, they are best if they are direc-

60

Above: *Ralph Bisdale is one of the most talented of American lighting designers. He uses light as the subtle, maneuverable force it should be, as here in this dramatic room with the trickling illumination down the sides of objects to be picked out. The flower stands out in this extraordinary illumination.*

tional and used to bounce light off a ceiling or off the wall itself, or to light an object, picture, or surface. Other wall fittings, such as bare bulbs placed at the side or the top of a mirror as in a theater dressing room, give an exceptionally good light for putting on makeup or shaving.

Table lamps are meant to provide concentrated areas of light. Again depending on the type of shade, they will bounce light up or down or spread it horizontally. Directional desk and table lamps for working by should be adjustable and let the light shine down on the paper or work in question.

Floor lamps give general or directional light depending on type and shade, and the variety fitted with spots can be a good substitute for spots or track. They make useful reading lights and can be moved around, set to shine on a book—preferably over the left shoulder—or directed onto a wall or ceiling. When choosing shades, remember that translucent silk shades are the best light diffusers, followed by linen and paper.

Strip lights of the incandescent variety, as opposed to fluorescent tubes, are useful for concealed lighting when they are put behind a baffle or pelmet to shine down on shelves in an alcove, or to light up curtains or a working surface.

Fluorescent Lighting

Fluorescent tubes, either straight or circular, give about three times as much light as a tungsten or filament bulb of the same wattage and have an average life of 5,000 hours. They are, therefore, a good deal more economical to use where high levels of light are needed for long periods at a time. In fact, for maximum efficiency these lights should be switched on and off as little as possible. The tubes are best masked by a baffle of some sort, or by a panel of milky plexiglass or Perspex.

Because fluorescent light can distort color, it is important to choose the right color tube for a particular area. If tungsten and fluorescent are to be used together, for example, "de luxe warm white" is the nearest in feeling to tungsten light and when diffused is useful for kitchens and bathrooms. "De luxe natural" gives reasonable color quality, is tolerably warm, and is quite good for kitchens, but because it dramatizes color, it is not so good in bathrooms. Used with discretion, a little can be mixed with candlelight for dining in a working kitchen. "Plain natural" simulates daylight and can be used as a booster when daylight lacks luster or penetration. But tubes sold with names like "warm white" (without the "de luxe"), "cool white," and "daylight" emphasize greens and yellows and kill pinks.

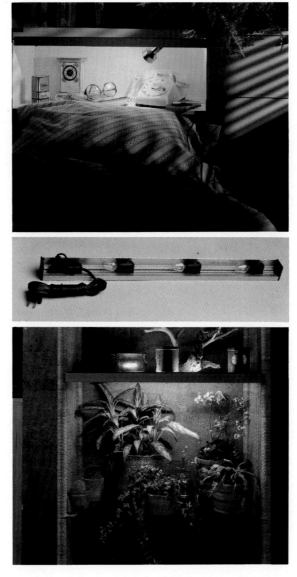

Above, top to bottom: *A superior new lighting product is Lyte Trim, a miniature track that can be fitted onto shelves, into cabinets, above headboards, or below furniture with the twist of a screwdriver. It takes very small bulbs to give a soft wash of light, fluorescent lights for a flood, and tiny swivel spots for sharp punches.*

Useful Principles

The most common lighting problem is how to improve the light in existing houses, especially when there is no lighting consultant on hand to give advice. Unless there is already a well-planned electrical layout that provides for all kinds of lighting, or an enormous number of electrical outlets—both of which are desirable but unlikely—the choice is either to add new outlets to existing circuits (which is best, but expensive) or to install lengths of lighting track, which can take a variety of extra fittings, to the odd ceiling outlets that are in place already. If there are no ceiling outlets, make do with the kind of floor lamps that carry adjustable spots. If major rewiring is proposed, it should be planned in detail before the electrician starts work and completed before any decorating is begun.

Left and above: *Architect Paul Rudolf's New York sitting room was shown in the space section, but in the early evening. At night, it assumes quite a different guise: melodramatic in the twilight, with light glancing off the ribboned screen, along the thin curves of the bookshelves, and on the backs of the sunken seats; razzle-dazzle at night, with strings of minute lights striping the carpet like a road to the Milky Way. And indeed, the city lights twinkling and winking and flashing through the great sweep of window at one end of the room do look like some sort of Mecca to be approached by a dramatic wide road of blazing light.*

In any event, whatever the circumstances and the problems, it is useful to know something about the principles behind modern lighting design. I have divided them into the practical considerations (making the most of daylight; what works best where; the comfort factor; the safety factor) and the decorative aspects (what works best with the structure of the place; what works best with paintings, objects, and texture; and the effect of light on color and vice versa).

Making the Most of Daylight

Although many people tend to think of artificial light as the counterfeit of daylight and the two as separate issues, an effective lighting system which will provide comfortable light at all times means that a balance must be struck between the two, the one discreetly boosting the other when necessary. To do this successfully it is important to understand the limitations of daylight as well as its qualities. It has, of course, all the advantages of variety: variety in intensity, in almost hourly as well as seasonal changes; and variety in color, from intense blue to overcast grey, from the clear light of early morning to the bluish dusk of evening, from the burnished light of high summer to the bright white cast up by snow. During each phase the interior of a building will look subtly different. That is why small windows should be left as uncluttered as possible to make the best of what light there is, why large windows should have screens or shades or blinds or nets that can filter any superabundance, and why it is useful to see a room in as many different lights as possible before deciding on a color scheme and furnishings.

However, it ought to be remembered that daylight does not have great qualities of penetration, although the low angle of the sun in winter gives deeper penetration at certain times of day than in summer. In most average rooms about 1 percent of the available daylight outside will reach the parts of the space furthest from the window, as opposed to as much as 10 percent near the window. In rooms with windows at both ends, light will fall off towards the middle. For large periods of the year, demanding visual tasks like reading, writing, drawing, or sewing can only be done close to a window, and many rooms in buildings with a narrow frontage, or in buildings surrounded by other buildings, will have poor lighting at all times of the day. This means that a good many rooms will always need the boost of artificial lighting for some purposes, and that many dark central areas in deep buildings used for service rooms

Center and above: *The differences of mood in a room full of bright sunlight and a room with well-manipulated artificial light are particularly well illustrated in these two shots of a Manhattan apartment designed by Mark Hampton. By day, light pours through the windows, dappling the walls, splashing the carpet, streaking through the leaves of the plants. By night, light filters down from the wallwashers and directional spots inset into the ceiling, mellowing the colors of the furniture, picking out the objects and sculpture. The floor-to-ceiling relief between the windows, which gives solidity as well as impact to the room, is by Louise Nevelson.*

Overleaf left: *More directional spots and wallwashers light up the paneled walls massed with pictures in this English dining room, leaving the dining table to a very much gentler light.*

Overleaf right: *A vaulted corridor, hung with art in two straight lines, is beautifully and dramatically lit by lighting designer Ralph Bisdale.*

such as kitchens, bathrooms, and storerooms, as well as halls and passageways, will need constant artificial light.

Again, this raises its own problems, for during the day the eye will have become so adapted to the high level of natural light, either from outside or from bright rooms, that in order to remain comfortable in dark inner areas it will require an equally high level of electric light. That is to say, a higher level than is usual at night, when the eye will have adapted again to the lower normal levels of artificial light all around. This means that ideally—and I stress *ideally*—there should be either a separate lighting system for perpetually dark rooms with a separate day/night switch, or some form of dimmer control on the existing system whereby the level of light can be controlled.

What Works Best Where

Quite clearly, any lighting system must first of all be dictated by practical considerations like the function of each room, since the aim should be to make each space as comfortable, easy to use, and safe as possible. Methods of lighting for cooking, washing, shaving, eating, writing, and reading all need a different approach, although rooms such as kitchens and bathrooms and passageways and halls have fairly static lighting requirements. Living rooms in particular need to be extremely flexible, since in just one general area there will probably be a need for reading lights, perhaps a desk lamp and a light over a dining table, lights to illuminate pictures and objects, and general diffuse lighting.

Once plans have been made for each room and the furnishings decided, work out whether the space will be used more by night than by day; what type of lighting is needed (direct, indirect, concealed, background, very bright); whether any more electrical outlets, switches, or dimmers are needed and if so, where (for example, if an outlet would be useful in the

middle of a floor, could it be done?). And think what style of lights would be best for each area. If spots or downlights are to be inset into a ceiling or at any great height, make sure that the bulbs will last a reasonable length of time and are easy to change and that the fixtures can be cleaned easily.

When the principles have been settled, it will be a great deal easier to make a final choice.

The Comfort Factor

Comfort in anything is always variable, and perhaps the best that can be said in a lighting context is that light should never be uncomfortable. Of course, one can get used to poor lighting —one can get used to anything—but ideally it should not be a strain to carry out any visual task or occupation. Glare should be reduced to a minimum, which means that reflected light, which gives the least glare, should be used as much as possible for general illumination. And in order to avoid glare, lighting fixtures, when lit up, should not be very much brighter than their backgrounds. Nor should a light source be too close to the object that must be seen, because the brightness of the light will raise the adaptation capacity of the eyes to a point at which the less bright object will be more difficult to see. This sounds complicated, but it makes sense.

A painting, for example, should not be hung next to a bright window unless there is some additional booster light available, either from another window at right angles or from artificial light. In fact, the position of all pictures should be chosen care-fully and quite as much from the lighting viewpoint as from the aesthetic, especially when the pictures have glass fronts that pick up reflections.

Light and shade should be balanced. An evenly lit room can be boring at night and often curiously depressing, whereas areas of strong light where it is needed and dark shadow where it is not can be dramatic and interesting and still be comfortable. The whole point of good contemporary lighting is to have pools of light, with spots of accent light wherever they are useful.

The Safety Factor

There are enormous numbers of accidents in the home and thousands of deaths each year as a result of falls, particularly in the winter when it is darker. When assessing a home for potential accident areas, walk around it at dusk with the house or apartment unlit, remembering that eyes deteriorate with age so that the average sixty-year-old needs twice as

much light as the average thirty-year-old, and that what seems tolerably safe to a healthy adult might not be so for the elderly or for a small child—who might also be afraid of the dark. If these factors are borne in mind, possible accident areas should soon show themselves.

Stairs and corridors should be well lit at all times with light on the floor to show changes in levels or surfaces, and light on the walls to show switches and door handles. When starting the lighting plan from scratch, the ideal would be either to have a night circuit of low-level lights in these areas, controlled by a dimmer switch that can turn them down to the right level at bedtime, or to have a separate circuit of miniature lights that could be left on the full twenty-four hours if desired because they consume a minimum of electricity. Although the latter is more expensive to install, it is convenient. Both types should provide a deterrent to burglars and prowlers.

There are also far too many accidents caused by a disregard of common-sense safety rules: by the failure to replace old and faulty wiring; by loading too few outlets with too many appliances; by the careless use of appliances near water; or by the thoughtless placement of cords leading from wall outlets to table or floor lamps.

To be safe as well as good, a lighting system should be neat, adequate for all present needs, and flexible enough to provide for unknown requirements in the future.

The Decorative Aspects

Once all the practical aspects of lighting have been planned for, the decorative aspects can be considered. By decorative aspects, I mean the way that lighting is used to enhance or define a space, improve proportions, show off a texture, set off angles, objects, and paintings, and create an atmosphere, as well as the look of the lights themselves.

The following observations are useful to remember:

Light washing walls, either from wallwashers or from lights set in plug-mold strips, will make a given space seem much larger.

Low lamps and lamps placed at a low level with the light coming from underneath will make a high ceiling seem lower and the feeling of a room more intimate.

Uplights set close into a corner will define the parameters of a room. The same uplights set underneath glass shelves or side tables will add considerable sparkle, and if they are placed behind plants they will cast intricate shadows on the wall as well as glossing up the leaves.

Be careful about the angles of light sources like spots and downlights. Textures can be completely flattened by bad positioning of light sources, beautifully brought out by good. For example, a textured wall covering is accentuated by a ceiling-mounted downlight positioned close to the wall, but deadened by a spot trained full upon it.

The lighter and whiter the surfaces in a room, the more they reflect the light. A dark-walled room will look surprisingly light with a white or off-white carpet and ceiling. And a general diffusing globe pendant hung in an all-white space will give a higher level of light than the same fixture in a darker-walled room.

Far left and above: *Extraordinarily interesting lighting, again by Ralph Bisdale, shows how the most prosaic rooms—which these spaces are not—can be transformed by colored filters, good light positioning, and spotlights shining through rotating wheels of colored lenses. Designs and patterns for walls can be created in an instant, projected onto the blank surfaces, and changed again in a minute. This way, one need never get bored with wall decorations, since new effects can be created as soon as one's mood changes. The results shown here are examples of real decorating with light.*

70

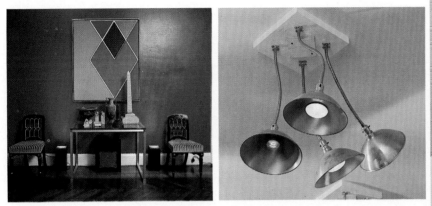

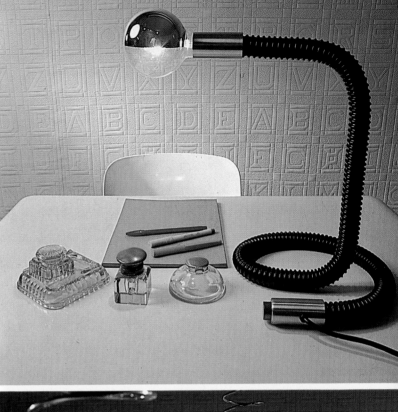

During daylight hours, most windows will direct the light coming in onto the floor, which, if it is pale, will reflect the light upward. When a floor is dark, it will reflect less light and the room will naturally seem darker.

At night, the scene will change because light sources are inside the room. If their position is well chosen, they will give direct light to ceiling and walls. Direct downlight on its own and shining on a dark carpet will be dramatic, certainly, but not bright enough for any sort of work.

Then too, quite different colors are reflected from different surfaces. When people are choosing clothes and fabrics in a store, they are likely to take them to a source of natural light to judge their "true colors," but they should take equal care to examine them in an artificial light as like as possible to the sort of night light that they use. Two fabrics that seem identical in color by day can look quite different at night, and even more peculiar under fluorescent tubes. Most reds, for instance, are emphasized by artificial light, while blues and greens tend to be diminished.

The color of bulbs will change the feeling of room colors. For example, white bulbs cast a yellowish light but pink ones give a pleasantly mellow effect. And plain white walls can be refurbished practically at will by putting different-colored bulbs in two or three sockets, or by using colored filters over downlight, spot, or wallwasher fixtures.

Lighting Different Areas

The following summary of the information given so far, plus tried and tested methods, might be helpful, even if it seems repetitive. Look back over the illustrations for other examples of the points raised.

Living Rooms

Sitting, talking, entertaining, listening to music, reading, writing, and watching television are the normal accepted activities in most living rooms, and therefore the best kind of light is a good measure of general or diffuse light with a play of light and shade. There should be adequate working light

Far left: *A good-looking articulated reading lamp.*

Center: *(Left) Uplights wash this wall with light. (Right) Articulated factory lights with colored bulbs for differing effects and moods.*

Above: *An elegant desk lamp from France, and a new French spring light for easy reading.*

where necessary, and well-controlled highlighting for the more interesting display of art, plants, objects, and arrangements.

Most lighting designers agree that the best sort of general light is the reflected variety—light that bounces off a wall—because it gives the least glare. This is obtained either from indirect sources like more or less concealed uplights, or from light concealed behind coves, or from wallwashers of one kind or another; or from direct lighting like table and floor lamps.

Whatever happens, do not let general light be all at one level of brightness. Our eyes see by means of contrasts, and nothing makes a room so flat, even boring, as bland light. Dimmers are a great help here with their easy-going control of intensity. And dramatic light can be provided by a mixture of judiciously placed downlights and uplights, with highlights from spots.

Reading lights should be at a reasonable distance behind anyone reading, or if the light is a downlight, about a foot in front of the book or work; otherwise, the light on the page will

Above left: *Candlelight is the most mellow of all light. In painter Hélène Fesenmaier's London kitchen, gently assisted by light on the working surface, it makes the room look marvelously welcoming. The working light is subtle enough to be unobtrusive yet strong enough to be practical.*

Above right: *A perfect battery of lights is tucked up in a canopy over the central island work surface in an English kitchen. Peripheral lighting is provided by the inset downlights edged down the side of the room, washing the walls with light.*

Far right: *Sometimes it is impossible to inset lights in a ceiling for one reason or another. Here two surface-mounted downlights bear down on another island work surface, slick and curved and very white in contrast to the old dresser.*

be too bright. For writing, light should fall over the left shoulder of a right-handed person and vice versa. Alternatively, a portable desk lamp or adjustable wall-mounted light should throw light onto the work.

Looking at television in an otherwise dark room is a strain. As a light near the viewer will reflect in the screen, a dimmed light behind the set is best if the set is on a shelf. If the set is free-standing, use a downlight or a floor lamp shining at the wall or down to the floor.

Dramatic lighting can be provided in storage units and on shelves or in alcoves. Collections of glass and ceramics look their best in front of a translucent wall of light (made by fixing vertical strip lights to the wall behind the shelves and concealing them with panels of pearly plexiglass, acrylic, or glass), or with a spot shining down on them from an angle. Single precious objects like a piece of sculpture, or even a plant or arrangement of flowers, are best served by a single downlight set above them, and other shelves can be lit up the sides by baffled vertical strips. Objects on shelves can be picked out with tiny portable spots, and deeply recessed sections of wall units can be similarly treated.

Conventionally, paintings are lit from above by so-called picture lights, but they are better lit by spots fixed to the ceiling or walls, and better still by specific spots for the purpose, such as the parabolic variety with inbuilt transformers, or framing spots which can be specially adjusted to the size of the picture. These particular spots also make a dramatic job of lighting foliage, plants, or objects. An entire wall of paintings can be beautifully lit by plug-mold or a wash of light from recessed strips. This has the advantage of staying beautiful however much the paintings are juggled about.

Kitchens

A kitchen should have good general light plus booster light for any precise activity like studying cookbooks, chopping, assembling ingredients, and washing dishes. Most kitchens have a ceiling light—often a strip of fluorescence—and little else, but this can be harsh. Well-placed general diffusing lights fixed flush to the ceiling, or spots, or a mixture of wall-washers, downlights, and spots, make good background light, stepped up with strip lights concealed under high-level cupboards to shine down on the work surface. Fluorescent lights should be the "de luxe warm white" variety because these make food look appetizing, which is more than one can say for most fluorescents. If at all possible, storage cupboards should be lit inside as well.

Halls, Corridors, and Staircases

So many halls have only one ceiling outlet, which is usually dreary and inadequate and quite often unsafe. The ideal is to have a series of downlights and wallwashers with supplementary lighting for mirrors, telephone, telephone books, and so on. Hall closets should certainly have an incandescent strip set behind a baffle just inside the top of the interior, or else an angled light on the ceiling outside, to avoid a constant irritating grope in the dark for coats.

If it is not possible to conceal the wiring required for these lights, attach the fixtures to a track, which, as I have explained, can be worked from a single outlet. If installing a track is difficult for one reason or another, run more cord from the original outlet and loop it across to another area, suspending the cord and extra light from a ceiling hook.

When stairs are properly lighted, there is a distinctly noticeable difference between tread and riser. The best way to achieve this is to have a strong light above the stairs and a softer one below. If the lights are on a dimmer switch, they can be turned down to an acceptable level and left on all night with very little waste of power. This is especially useful in households where there are small children or elderly people. Alternatively, but more expensively, a separate night circuit of miniature lights can be installed. A cheaper solution would be a single low-wattage bulb in a well-chosen position.

Dining Areas

Candlelight has still not been bettered for dining, but make sure that the candles are either above or below eye level, not flickering directly in the diners' eyes. Candlelight combined with a discreet downlight in the ceiling above the center of a round table, or at either end of a rectangular table, especially if the secondary lights are on a dimmer, is better still. Pendant lights with opaque shades cast a pleasant light downward, but they should be on a rise-and-fall fixture and so placed that they do not throw light into people's eyes. The serving area should be lit separately, perhaps by a spot or wallwasher, or by concealed strip lighting above.

74

Far left, above: *Hanging candelabra over a pair of dining tables in Mrs. Hannah Rothman's London room are discreetly helped by downlights recessed above the chains. The effect is very subtle.*

Far left, below: *Angled spots in a study designed by Mark Hampton wash a series of glass shelves set against a translucent panel. The displayed objects show up beautifully with this treatment.*

Above: *A dark wall with an eclectic collection of prints massed against it is lit by miniature spots, which pick out the individual pictures rather than bathing the entire wall.*

Left: *Directional spots bathe a display wall in light of just the right intensity.*

Bedrooms

Bedroom lighting usually needs to be as flexible as that in the living room: soft enough to be relaxing; bright enough to see to dress by; good enough at the dressing table for putting on makeup; well placed enough for comfortable reading in bed. Bedside-table lamps should be high enough to shine on a book, but not so high as to disturb anyone else. Small wall-mounted, adjustable spots or angled lamps are another good idea. Dimmers should provide all the variation needed for the main lighting.

Light above a mirror used for putting on makeup is not a good idea because it casts shadows under the nose and eyes. Lights side-positioned to shine outward rather than on the mirror itself are better. The same applies to long mirrors: the light should be directed on the viewer rather than on the glass.

Children's Rooms

All outlets should be childproofed, at least in small children's rooms, and lighting fixtures should be kept well out of reach. A dimmer is useful for children who are afraid of the dark; alternatives are one low-wattage bulb or the separate night circuit of miniature lights discussed earlier. Do not forget that older children will want to read in bed and probably to do homework in their rooms, so provide adequate reading lights in good positions.

Bathrooms

Small rooms may well only need one ceiling light and lights on either side of the mirror if it is to be used for shaving and

Far left: *Interesting cubes of light like some glowing Art Deco decoration flank a well-designed washbasin and dressing-table surface set back to back in this Californian bath-dressing room.*

Center: *Light set into the gathering at the top of the lace bed hangings cascades down onto the beds in a London bedroom designed by George Powers.*

Above: *Rounded, good-looking bulbs like these are much the best sort of light for shaving, if set in a strip along the top of a mirror.*

putting on makeup, or just above it if only for shaving. It is irritating to have a baffled light over a mirror only to see the lighting fixture reflected in the mirror behind. Prevent this by inserting a smaller baffle between the bulb and the glass. Downlights are effective in bathrooms, too, and one over the bath is worth considering.

Furnishing with Light

Up to now I have discussed general lighting and its possibilities without going into the use of light as an integral part of the architecture and furnishing of a room. I have not touched on the more elaborate methods of defining spaces; the creation of whole walls of light, or the ways of making seating or tables or seating platforms appear to float. Then there are the complete sound/light/air systems giving light, air conditioning, and hi-fi from the same series of tracks, and the sort of moving patterns and images that can be achieved in endless variable effects by lighting projectors, or spotlights shining through rotating wheels of colored lenses. It can all cost a lot of money, but there again, lighting like this is an art form in itself, and a particularly exciting one.

Light walls might seem light years away for most people, and yet they are comparatively easy to install instead of windows with depressing views or as a backing for a series of shelves or a background for display. To disguise a dreary view or an ugly window, install strip lighting or spots on the old wall and conceal the fixtures about a foot behind sheets of translucent white or off-white plexiglass fitted into a wood frame or frames that can slide on runners attached to ceiling and floor or remain static. Standard panels of plexiglass come in widths of up to 4 feet (122 centimeters), but they can be specially ordered in any size. Alternatively, it is possible to install panels of refractive glass between two rooms, or a room and a corridor, which will diffuse both daylight and artificial light in due season.

Paths and ribbons of light made from the plug-mold strips described on page 60, or simple strip lighting sunk into a recess and again covered with a translucent plexiglass or acrylic, can edge their way around the bottom of seating platforms or the top of conversation pits to particular effect. Cleverly placed tubes of neon can be amusing, especially in the context of a painted wall.

Other fascinating—and I mean fascinating—effects can be made by shining spots through any chosen object to cast intriguing shadows on the wall, especially when the spots shine through the rotating wheels of colored lenses mentioned above.

All three of these pictures show the effect on the same room in London of different-colored filters and lighting projectors, which proves what an art form this sort of lighting can be. Spotlights shining through rotating lenses pick up the vase of flowers on the table and cast an exaggerated version of their petals on the wall. Note how the painting changes color always, from grey-green to aquamarine and blue to rosy red. And how the mood changes from calm to interesting to festive.

4. Color

Color is the most malleable, the most exciting, the most immediately noticeable, and the cheapest element in decoration. It also arouses the strongest emotional response. The only problem is getting to know how to use it. Some people are born with a good, sometimes even an inspired, sense of color (one child of mine was recoloring wallpapers for fun at the age of four, and she was always maddeningly right). The rare few have so sure a sense that they can carry a color around in their head and match it absolutely. Most of us, however, have to develop such a sense. Although words are a poor vehicle for conveying all the possibilities of harmonious coloring, certain rules that are pointed out in this chapter, combined with the illustrations, should instill at the very least an incipient color sense.

Color

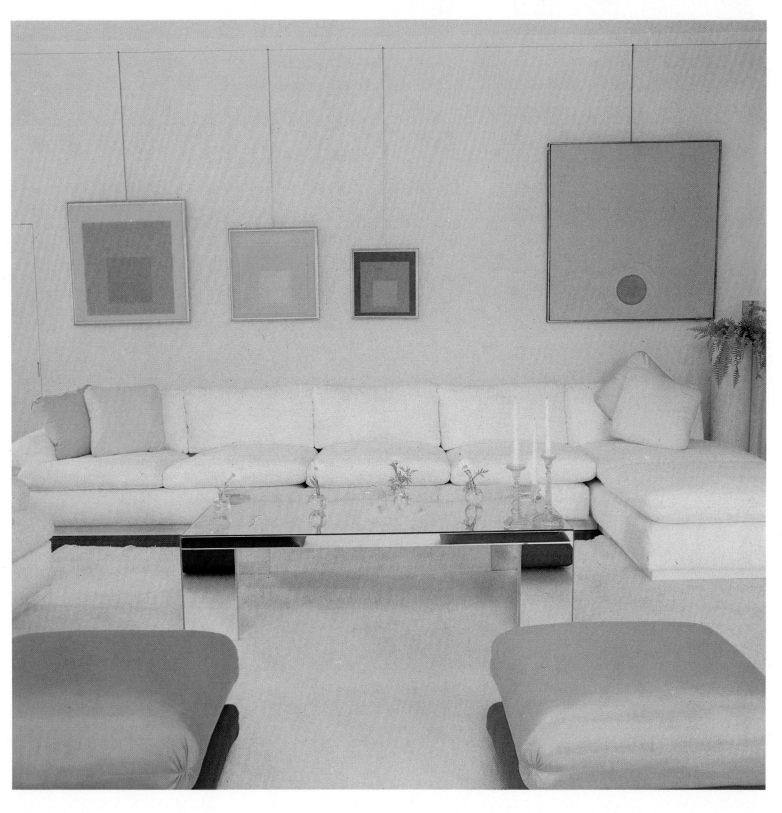

Chevreul, in his great nineteenth-century treatise *The Principles of Harmony and Contrast of Color,* noted that once certain rules had been absorbed, painters used colors to better effect. The same must be true in decoration. Words like "principles" and "rules" immediately begin to sound conventional and weighty when applied to as ostensibly lighthearted a subject as color, but I would make a deliberate distinction here between principle and convention, for the one is interesting fact and the other mere habit and safety.

I also want to stress these principles because, although there has been an almost aggresive color revolution over the last twenty years, with color for the sake of color and idiosyncrasy the only law, there has equally been a monetary revolution that makes the doctrine of expendability less attractive than it was. Mistakes, or something that is fun today and tedium tomorrow, cannot be remedied so carelessly or so lightly any more. Getting the right harmony and contrast from the beginning is important.

Preceding page: *Clear, cool colors in the pillows match the art in this otherwise all-white, glass, and mirror apartment in Manhattan belonging to the Arne Naesses.*

Left: *Purples running into blue-greys are set against white and stone in the Avray Wilsons' peaceful English country house, deep in rural Gloucestershire.*

Above: *Brilliant paintings stand out from white walls with a near-three-dimensional intensity in this dining room designed by Mark Hampton.*

Color Definitions

When a ray of sunshine or white light shines through a glass prism, it separates, and if the image formed (which is called the prismatic spectrum) is thrown upon a white screen some distance from the prism, it will show six colors arranged in the exact order of a rainbow. Three of these colors are simple, or primary: blue, red, and yellow. They cannot be produced by the mixture of other colors, but they can vary in intensity. The other three—green, violet, and orange—are compound, or secondary or binary, colors and are mixtures of the simple colors in pairs:

Blue and red produce violet.

Blue and yellow produce green.

Red and yellow produce orange.

All other colors are variations of these basics, depending on their proportions. For example, by increasing the quantity of blue in the mixture of blue and red, we produce indigo; by increasing the quantity of blue in green, we produce aquamarine.

The following definitions of color terms are elementary and worth remembering:

Normal colors The colors of the spectrum: red, orange, yellow, green, blue, violet.

Binary or secondary colors Compounds of two primary colors.

Complementary colors The complementary color of a primary color (such as red) is the secondary color composed of the two other primaries (green).

Luminous or warm colors Yellow, orange, red, light green, and the light tones of somber colors. Orange is the only secondary color that cannot become cold, because it is composed of two luminous colors, orange and red. When yellow predominates in green, it is warm; when blue predominates, the green is cold.

Somber or cold colors Blue, violet, and the broken tones of the luminous colors. (Broken tones are those containing all three primary colors.)

Noncolors Black and white.

Normal grey A mixture of pure black and white, in various proportions, producing a variety of tones from white to black.

Colored greys Normal grey to which a primary or secondary color is added.

Tertiary colors Colored greys. Russet is really red-grey. Olive is green-grey. Citrine is yellow-grey.

Pigments Material colors or paints.

Left: *Mushroom pink and subtle off-white in walls and ceiling blend with a variety of soft colors in accessories, paintings, and pillows in the apartment of Fleur Cowles and her husband, Tom Montague Meyer, in London's Albany. The buildup of color is harmonious.*

Above: *Green and white shag-pile carpet up the stairs is an impressive contrast in texture to glossy paint in the same green and white in an English country house renovated and decorated by architect Max Clendinning. Part of the ceiling is picked out in a darker shade of green to give a feeling of depth.*

Tones The series of gradations of a color from its greatest intensity to its weakest. For example, cream, tan, and brown are all tones of orange.

Hues The changes produced in a color by adding another color. The original color must always be in the ascendancy; otherwise, it becomes a hue of the color added to it.

Tints The tones of a color produced by the addition of white.

Shades The tones of a color produced by the addition of black or colors that are close together in the rainbow spectrum.

Contrast The result of using complementary colors that are widely different. Contrast colors are usually known as accent colors in room schemes.

Harmony The result of using colors that are close to each other in warmth or coldness; for example, a monochromatic scheme composed of a light tone like cream, moving through middle tones like beige and orange, and ending with a deep tone like dark brown.

Left: *The deep blue-greens and blues of Provence are reflected in the mirror as well as in the view in this sheltered outdoor eating area in Van Day Truex's French house. Whitewashed walls and bleached beams act as a cool foil to the intensity of the natural colors splashed all around.*

Above: *A clear green sofa, the green leaves of plants, and a green view framed by the window seem especially striking against the white of walls and floor in the Bernard Sterns' old chateau in the South of France. The wooden monkey perched on the sofa arm and the collection of decoy ducks are nicely beguiling extra details.*

Right: *Harmonizing colors are squared off to handsome effect in this color chart prepared in Germany. The chart is actually a painting by Johannes Itten, a Bauhaus color theorist.*

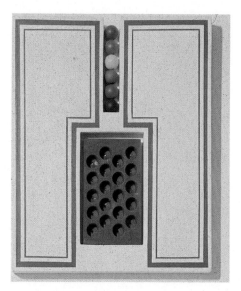

Monochromatic scheme One basic color in a variety of shades and textures. Most monochromatic schemes benefit from the addition of contrast or accent colors.

Neutral color A safe basic that any accent color will go with: white and off-white; most of the browns from beige to dark through camel and nutmeg; greys from pale to charcoal. Most neutrals take about two accent colors.

Color will change radically according to the circumstances under which it is viewed. For example: if red is put near blue, the red appears yellower. Near yellow, the same red appears bluer. Next to green, it appears purer and brighter. Next to black, it seems duller; next to white, lighter and brighter; and next to grey, brighter.

If a dark color is placed beside a different but lighter color, the dark color appears deeper and the light color appears lighter. This is the result of contrast of tone. A color is also greatly intensified by gloss: look at butterflies' wings, the feathers of some birds, the different textures of petals.

Colors are much modified by the shape and form of an object and according to light and shade, so that there are many tones of the same color.

Both the tone and the hue of a colored object are changed by the quality of light.

Interestingly, if we look for a few moments at a given color, the eye, spontaneously and unconsciously, calls up the complementary to that color, which, since it is now added to the first color, makes it appear duller. The effect is the same as if a quantity of grey had been added.

If you look at two regular stripes of the same color but of different tones, or at two stripes of different colors but of the same tone, they will look quite different than if they were viewed separately. Take the example of blue and yellow stripes: the complementary of blue, which is orange, is added by the eye to the yellow so that it appears redder and more brilliant; violet is the complementary of yellow, and so will be added by the eye to the blue, making it appear indigo.

Far left: *Primary and binary colors in an indoor game theme used as art on an Italian wall.*

Center: *A harmonious monochromatic scheme in a house on Fire Island designed by Horace Gifford. The light that pours through the skylight by day is duplicated at night by downlights set all around the perimeter of the cut-out ceiling circle.*

Above: *Noncolors—black and white—in a stylish room designed by Joe D'Urso for the Bruce Simons' interesting duplex in an old New York building.*

A Color Sense

Finding the start to a color scheme is often the most difficult part of furnishing. A single item, a rug or a painting, a piece of china or a particular fabric, might well suggest a room more or less in detail. I took my own sitting room from an English painting by John Bratby of peonies, vivid splashes of pink and green, against a brick wall. This suggested to me green walls; a pink, green, and white carpet; and window shades or blinds of pink and orange Indian cotton with accent colors of orange and mustardy yellow. But if no color scheme suggests itself immediately, what then?

When the mind seems blank about a scheme, try emotional response. Take a color, any favorite color—yellow, for example—and think of it in depth. Think of everything floral and yellow, from the palest creamy yellow of honeysuckle or freesias to thick, creamy velvet roses through narcissi to daffodils to crocuses to the centers of daisies. Or try straw and dried hay, cream and sand, the gold of stripped and waxed wood floors, lemons and melons and honey. It is all very evocative and should help to build up a good monochromatic scheme in no time, especially when the colors are translated into the look of the textures that will also go to make up a room: wood and wool, cotton and vinyl, paint and paper, all of which will give differing depths and surfaces.

Think of country or forest or sea colors. Take note of color combinations that are pleasing in museums and art galleries, exhibitions and libraries, and other people's homes. Study paintings in detail and see how color is laid against color, tone upon tone. Cut out photographs from magazines of rooms that look good. If such pictures are systematically clipped out over a period, kept together, and then looked at all at once, the same balance of colors will tend to repeat itself. This will indicate as nothing else does the colors that are comfortable for the collector.

90

Far left: *Clean-cut white Lucite cubes, the pattern on the chair, blue and white china, and glass are set off with precision in this predominantly red and black scheme in a roomy New York apartment belonging to decorator Mark Hampton.*

Center: *The bright stripes of color in the painting seem particularly clear and striking in this otherwise black and white room designed by Joe D'Urso for the Lockers' Long Island vacation house.*

Above: *Chrome-yellow walls and ceiling edged in white and spiced with brown were put together by Irish designer-architect Max Clendinning.*

Putting Schemes Together

Thinking up color combinations for a room is one thing, finding the right balance is another, and preparing schemes for a whole home is the most difficult exercise of all.

There are several permutations for achieving an interesting balance. One way is to keep most of the room in one color, or shades and variations of it, by using that color—say, white or off-white—for walls, curtains or shades, floor, the major seating such as a sofa or unit furniture, and one or two chairs if the room is big. Use one accent color for another chair, or a pair of chairs, and a third for pillows or flowers.

Another permutation would be to keep walls, curtains, and most upholstered furniture in one color, to use another color for the floor, and to add a third color in accessories which can be juxtaposed with variations of both the other colors. Or use the major color for walls and smaller pieces of furniture and add the accent colors in larger furniture, pillows, flowers, and art. It is, of course, important to vary surfaces and textures in these colors as much as possible, to make a play of light and shade and pattern. Always look out for the meeting points of floor and wall finishes, for corridors and open doors to adjoining rooms, to see what colors, textures, and patterns work well together.

In a small apartment or house, the space will seem much larger if more or less the same colors are used in different juxtapositions throughout, especially if they are rooted to the same general floor covering. Strong or warm colors like red or orange will make walls appear to close in and the space seem smaller. Cool colors will push the walls out. A long corridor will appear less so if the end wall is painted or covered in a warm color, and a high ceiling can be brought down by painting it dark.

Left: *Max Clendinning worked out this warm brown, red, and blue scheme for a London library. The room was turned into an octagon with leftover space used for deep inset bookshelves, and then outlined by the cut-out blue border on the carpet and the blue strip edging the shelves and the fireplace wall. These crisp lines are softened by the red circle on the ceiling and the red and blue painted arches above the shelves.*

Above, left to right: *Wild flowers and grasses in specimen vases are delicate accents of color in a mainly black and white room designed by Joe D'Urso for Mr. and Mrs. Bruce Simon. In designer Mark Hampton's own apartment in New York, the hall is a build-up of red with a white trim merging into strong black and white next door. The Arne Naesses' kitchen in their New York apartment is in bold red and yellow cooled with black and russet tiles and natural wood units. This basically black and white kitchen, designed for Sir Anthony and Lady Nutting in London, is accented with the brilliant red and yellow of the utensils.*

Rooms facing north will look more cheerful if warm, luminous colors are used. Rooms that are constantly filled with sunlight will do better with cool colors or a noncolor like white. The whole balance of a room will be changed by altering an accent color here and there; by adding a new cover to a chair, or swapping covers; by changing pillows or cushions; by importing a large plant or a new painting or rug.

Function must obviously play a large part in the choice of color. Halls and corridors can be as dramatic and lively as desired. Bedrooms are very personal and can be as idiosyncratic as is compatible with rest and calm. Living rooms should be a background for people, and generally speaking, they are best with solid-color neutral walls spiced with accent colors. Dining rooms should clearly be good backgrounds for food; kitchens, cheerful; play, study, and family rooms and family bathrooms, ditto. Master bathrooms, spare-room bathrooms, and powder rooms can be original, eccentric, and experimental since they are either purely personal or less subject to common use.

Left: *Natural textures and peaceful monochromatic colors are accented only by paintings and flowering plants in a country house designed by Chuck Winslow. The stripped wood stairs match the faded wood ceiling, garden door, and floor surround.*

Right, above: *A muted blue seating unit and cushions echoing a particularly pretty rug are set against ivory-painted walls in a town-house living room designed by Chuck Winslow. The over-all effect is cool and gentle.*

Right, below: *The colors of the Oriental rug show clear and strong beneath the glass table top.*

Far right: *Blue and orange handworked tapestry chairs repeat the orange of the room behind the the blue door and window surrounds and the blue vase of dried grasses in a distinguished room in southern Spain.*

94

5. Texture & Pattern

Colors are so radically changed by differences in texture and pattern that a monochromatic, or one-color, room can be as lively and as memorable through its subtlety as a more vividly contrasting room. Therefore texture and pattern need to be considered as seriously and as evocatively, if not so emotionally, as the whole process of color-building. I say evocatively, because the name of a known texture immediately conjures up an almost tangible surface. Just as I showed in the preceding chapter that thinking about one color can evoke many depths and variations, so too will I show in this chapter how different textures engender their own imagery.

Texture & Pattern

Preceding pages: *A wall of green-painted paper cups designed by Louis Muller and William Murphy provides another unexpected textured surface in this room.*

Above: *A white tiled floor, a deep-piled rug, the hard-surfaced plastic of Saarinen chairs and table, and the thick surface of the paintings all add up to a tactile room in the Bernard Sterns' house.*

Right: *Deeply comfortable seating, a patterned rug, hard, clear plexiglass and glass, the soft glossiness of leaves, and the stiff prickles of cacti all meld and contrast with each other in this very satisfying collector's room in California.*

Anyone who is interested in thinking in textural terms—which is really the only way to get a grip on the subject—should take a little time to consider the following:

boarding	chain	lace	plexiglass	steel
brick	corduroy	leather	quilting	stone
burlap	cork	linen	rope	suede
cane	denim	marble	rush matting	travertine
cashmere	felt	patent leather	silk	tweed
ceramics	glass	plaster	sisal	wood

If these are thought about in turn, it is practically possible to feel as well as see the varying textures. Pick out some of them and imagine how they would look appropriately distributed among floor, walls, ceiling, and furniture. Contrast their qualities; weigh up their varying depths. For what seems to be the right—though not necessarily the most conventional—surface, used in the right place, can give a most satisfying pleasure.

Contrasting Textures

Obviously, some textures are more in keeping together than others. Clearly rough goes with smooth and matte with gloss, but what rough with what smooth, what matte with what gloss, is a question of taste and appropriate place. For example, rough brick walls would look considerably better contrasted with a smooth tweed or linen, a burlap or hessian, or a cotton than with a silk. And while velvet walls do not look especially good with plexiglass or Perspex furniture, they undoubtedly look good with lacquer. There are no real rules—only sensibilities.

I have talked before of the advisability of collecting samples to make sure of their effect together, and this applies to textures as much as to colors. Shop around. Bring back samples of wall coverings, tiles, carpeting, matting, fabrics, vinyls, paint surfaces. Do not forget the differences you can make with painted surfaces, whether they are matte or shiny, lacquered or glazed (see "All About Paint," pp. 130-36). Juggle them all about and try them in varying juxtapositions before making a final choice.

100

Above: The Cadbury-Browns, both architects, converted this old warehouse in London's Soho to be their studio, offices, and pied-à-terre. On the top floor, approached by a ladderlike stair, a beautiful spoked ceiling crowns a collection of different textures, some of them reflected in the old mirrored overmantel, rescued from the demolition crews, which now acts as room divider as well as room enlarger. Sculpture, plants, leather, and a fur throw make nice patterns on their own and complete an inviting room.

Center: Bare boards and white-painted concrete contrast with a Chinese paper lantern and banners of black and white fabric, as well as with the black and white octagonal table and the huge bust on a white plinth, in this handsome Californian space.

Remember that even when a room is finished to all intents and purposes, the introduction of yet another contrasting texture, like yet another accent color, might make all the difference to its liveliness and interest. One often does not see this until some chance incident points it out—a coat thrown over a chair, for example, or a basket left on a floor. But suddenly the quite unthought-of color or surface seems so right, so delineating of all the other colors and surfaces, that one cannot imagine why it was never thought of before. But this is what decoration is about, after all: the relaxed and gradual accretion of possessions and experience.

102

Above: *Rough stone walls are contrasted with rush matting, a soft cotton coverlet with cane chairs, wool curtains with stripped pine and pottery, in a bedroom designed by Hilary Green.*

Right: *An early cast-iron stove set against a wall of planks, a trug of logs, a rough wooden structure nailed to the wall and filled with twigs, and dried leaves set alongside a couple of spare grids all add up to a rural still life, an effective composition for displaying the natural pattern of textures.*

How to Contrast a Pattern

It used to be a convention never to mix patterns, and it was a convention because it made things safer and easier. But when one thinks of it, pattern in a room is formed as much by possessions as by fabrics. Books with their varying colors and jacket designs; the way pictures and prints are hung on a wall; the arrangements of objects and of storage units; the jagged edges of leaves; the play of light and shade; the shapes of different pieces of furniture: all these things form patterns in their own right and without question. When the fact is considered, one fabric pattern more or less can hardly make too much difference as long as the scale, tone, and proportion are right.

Scale, tone, and proportion: these are important. Large patterns that look interesting and diverting in shops and stores are often more suitable for a public than a private setting, unless one possesses a very sure sense of scale. Similarly, it is useful to remember that very small patterns often meld into one color when actually used for curtains as opposed to hanging in show lengths.

A play of pattern, however, can be very effective, varying as it does the whole balance of color. Properly used, it will often give added depths and thus space to a room. I have mentioned in the chapter on space that small-scale repeats in upholstery or soft furnishings of a larger pattern on a wall or curtain or shade can give a sense of perspective, and this should be remembered in the present context.

The same pattern in two different colors can look good, and so can the same pattern reversed—say brown on white predominating, with white on brown predominating.

Very similar patterns in the same colors can be used together with effect, as in curtains and carpet, with plain or textured walls.

Patterns with the same feeling if not design can also be used together effectively: vividly striped North African or other ethnic fabrics with heavily patterned Oriental rugs; minipatterns of all sorts with small geometrics; small Liberty prints with nineteenth-century designs in the same colors.

Left, above: *A battered cane packing case serves as base for an occasional table, making a satisfying contrast to the Oriental rugs and camel fabric in Chuck Winslow's New York apartment.*

Left, center: *Kinetic sculpture, Oriental rug, and North African pillows form a patterned point-counter-point in the Dykers' study.*

Left, below: *Wallpaper matches quilting but contrasts with the chevron rug and the very rustic chair in designer Chuck Winslow's apartment.*

Above: *Three different patterns in rug and pillows plus flowers, objects, sculpture, and furniture form a warm and memorable composition in this apartment designed by Mark Hampton.*

And do not forget the subtle effect of sheers printed with the same pattern as the curtains, or with an allied pattern, either a simplified version in one color on white, or in white on white, or in toned-down versions of the main colors.

All this may sound irritatingly nebulous when read, but look at the illustrations for examples. Here again, the same advice about collecting samples holds good. Find patterns that appeal. Juggle them around again: look at them against existing furniture, walls, and objects and in different lights. It is the only way to learn.

106

Above: *Green and white fabric, greens and white in upholstery and walls, the green of plants and foliage, all intermingle into one intricate pattern in a deliberately indoor-outdoor room in California.*

Right: *A diagonally striped carpet, horizontally striped louvered doors, vertically striped blinds, and floor-to-ceiling rows of books fuse together into a composition of different angles in this room designed by Nicholas Hill. The only softening counterpoint is the round shape of the bay tree.*

6.Floors

Floors are clearly the bottom line of any room. They anchor a scheme, steady it, hold it all together. They are also walked on, sat on, lain on, and generally take a tougher beating than any other surface. Adding up the floor area to be covered in even the smallest house or apartment can come as something of a shock, which is hardly alleviated by the thought that whatever is put down will necessarily be a permanent part of the domestic scene for years and years. All the same, the exercise need not be too shatteringly expensive. Many existing surfaces like wood or stone or tiles or even elderly carpet can be titivated, painted, bleached, waxed, stenciled, or dyed and generally brought back to shape for considerably less expense than putting down a new floor. This chapter goes into all the choices.

Floors

There are so many different types of flooring, so many qualities to compare, so many textures to choose from, so many technical terms to sift and comprehend, so many patterns, so many colors, that one could be forgiven for dismissing all the technological triumphs and longing for the good old days when the choice veered from marble or mosaic to bare boards or brick to bare boards or mud.

Then again, the choice of flooring depends very much upon the structure of a building. For example, concrete floors allow any kind of hard flooring, like random-length strips of wood or parquet blocks, planks or wide strips, composition tiles, and marble, brick, or slate. But suspended wood floors mean that care has to be taken about superimposing any other heavy material because of the weight problem. Carpets and most vinyl floor coverings, on the other hand, can be put down on any surface, though it is easier to lay carpet on wood, because concrete or tile floors need plugging first.

To help the uninitiated, I have set down one guide to flooring terminology and ingredients, whether soft or hard, and another to help in deciding what goes best where. But before looking at them, there are some other basic points to consider.

Basic Flooring Facts

Do not make any radical decisions on floor coverings before studying existing floors carefully. They might not even need to be covered. Old parquet and timber floors in reasonably good condition—that is to say, without gaps, splits, and frayed and splintered ends—could just be polished and have rugs laid on top with some nonslip backing to underlay the rugs. But if the surface is worn, they can be sanded down— either professionally, or by hiring a sander with a dustbag attachment, which is cheaper—then sealed or polished. Or they can be painted with floor or deck or marine paint, or stained, or stenciled. A clear seal will bring out the grain and color of wood. A white seal will produce a bleached and pleasantly cool look.

Staining can produce a remarkable renovative effect. There are wood-color stains and colors like blue, red, green, orange, and yellow in varying tones. They are either water-based or spirit-based; the latter type contains oil, so if the floor is going to be sealed after coloring, make sure that the sealer is compatible with the stain or an unholy mess will result. I know: I once ruined a glossy dark green floor of which I was rather proud by using, in ignorance, the wrong finish. I ended up with a horribly scarred surface like blotched nail polish, which I

promptly had to carpet at great expense. And even though the story had a happy ending in that I probably liked the carpet better, I now find it safer to use water-based stains, which can be thinned down and paled, mixed to make different colors, and sealed with impunity. In fact, they must be sealed, or they will eventually wash off.

When planning any sort of flooring, remember the vistas that are constantly opened up in a home. Doors that lead off corridors and hallways are often left open. Glimpses of upper stories can be seen up stairways, and it is commonplace to have vignettes of one room from another. In order that the given space will always flow naturally, make sure that floor coverings are coordinated at least in color. And of course, a a small space is greatly helped by the spread of one color throughout, though that one color need not be of uniform quality. Where different textures or colors meet at doorways—say, carpet with tiling, or brown with apricot—the effect is neater if a threshold strip is inserted between the two. This is practical, too, since it will protect the edges of the materials as well as delineating the contrasting areas.

Chapter opening: *Mark Hampton bleached out half the strips of the otherwise conventional parquet floor in one of Carter Burden's rooms in his Manhattan apartment. The result is a hard floor of great distinction, which makes a handsome base for his collections.*

Preceding pages: *George Powers covered the hall floor in this budget apartment (left) with a rich wood veneer which cost very little and looks amazingly opulent. Slim white tiles continued up the baseboards in a London corridor (right) exaggerate the narrow space.*

Above: *A great patterned rug on parquet separates the sitting room from the dining area in a long, light Californian room filled with plants.*

Right: *Mark Hampton has many original ideas for floors. Here, he has set a tiled area into a conventional wood floor as if it were inset carpeting. Flowering plants in low pots define edges.*

If the decision is for carpets, they should be as expensive as can be afforded, especially in hard-wear areas, even if it means a substantial increase in the furnishing or decorating budget. It is possible to make do on most things, but there cannot be much compromising upon carpets, which offer more value, wear, sound and heat insulation, and, it is hoped, dirt absorption than any other furnishing element. It is much better to start off with the minimum coverage (paint or stain with rugs or floor-weight felt with rugs) until carpet of the right quality can be afforded than to put down inferior-quality carpet, which will cost twice as much in the long run since it will almost certainly have to be replaced after all too short a period.

It is important, too, to buy a good foundation, or padding or underlay, as an adjunct to all carpets, except for the kind with a heavy foam backing, which is best with a layer of newspapers underneath. Padding forms a cushion between carpet and floor and evens the wear, as well as absorbing sound and cutting down on heat loss. There are basically two types: felt and rubber. Felt, made usually from a fiber mixture, is less springy than rubber, but still effective. The best rubber padding is corrugated to give it extra resilience and to make it safe with underfloor heating. (Do not, on any account, use ordinary foam-rubber padding with underfloor heat, as the foam might disintegrate.) All padding must be put down with care, making sure that there are no gaps, creases, or folds, all of which would show through the carpet. On stairs, it is sensible to wrap pads of felt over the edge of each tread. However tempting it may seem, old carpet should *not* be used as padding: it is simply not the right weight or texture.

Finally, carpets should not be allowed to get too dirty. Although good wool is comparatively dirt-resistant, the looks and usefulness of any carpet will be prolonged by regular cleaning. Vacuum all carpets at least once a week and shampoo them with a proprietary cleaning preparation at least once or twice a year, or whenever they look grubby. Avoid overwetting. Carpets may also be cleaned professionally if the cost does not seem overwhelming.

Much the same rules about quality apply to all other floor coverings: vinyl or vinyl asbestos or matting; haircord or woolcord; ceramic, terrazzo, or quarry tiles; wood or cork. Whatever the final choice of material, put down the best quality affordable and clean it regularly. Old dirt is obstinate dirt. It also destroys the fiber or surface.

Left: *Shaggy white rugs on square white tiles in the Avray Wilsons' French house set high up in the hills behind Grasse with views to the blue sea of the Riviera. The contrast of textures with the white cotton of the sofas and uncurtained windows enhances the feeling of calm, uncluttered cool.*

Above: *Four views of different carpeting. The carpet in the town house (top, left) designed by Chuck Winslow picks up the pattern of the fireplace tiles. Charcoal industrial carpeting covers the floor in the Lockers' Long Island house (top, right), designed by Joe D'Urso. An Oriental rug anchors the working area in Chuck Winslow's own New York apartment (bottom, left). Large white, pink, and green octagons designed by Billy McCarty (bottom, right) expand the space in a long, narrow London drawing room. The carpet is a Brussels weave, which takes very well to crisp geometric designs.*

This being said, it is obvious that some areas are going to get more wear than others: stairs, halls, passageways, and living rooms get rougher use than bedrooms; holiday houses and guest rooms get less use (on the whole) than permanently lived-in spaces; adults rooms usually get quieter treatment than children's rooms. Wet surfaces, as in kitchens, bathrooms, and utility rooms, take more of a beating than the dry areas in a home.

Carpet Language

The various fibers used in carpets are wool, nylon and other man-made fibers, jute and sisal, and mixtures of some or all of these.

The term "pile" means the tufts or loops of yarn above a carpet's backing. They form the surface of a carpet. The various pile textures are:

Low pile, plush, or velvet A short, dense, and deep smooth finish.

Twist A sturdy, hard-wearing finish, less prone to shading than the more luxurious smooth plushes and velvets.

Shag A luxurious long pile. The average length of yarn is 1 inch, but it can be 2 inches. It is best in living rooms or bedrooms. It is not especially practical for stairs because heels can get caught in the pile, and the shag will get grubby quickly since stairs pick up more dirt than flat surfaces. There are special rakes to keep the pile in shape.

Loop or bouclé The pile is formed by loops of yarn. It looks good, but can snag like sweaters.

116

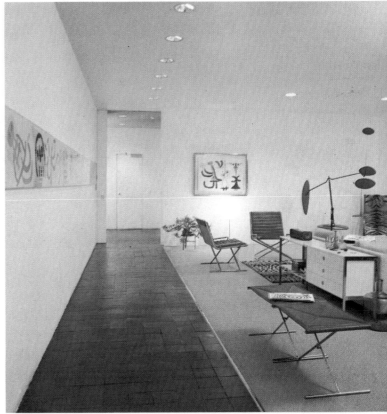

Far left: *A close-up of different carpet textures with sisal, coconut, twist, bouclé, and velvet pile.*

Center: *Sisal matting contrasts with a large square of creamy fur rugs and white enameled furniture interspersed with red in an English room.*

Above: *A throughway of heather-colored tiles runs through the reception rooms of an apartment belonging to Mrs. Hannah Rothman in London. The Italian coir matting is divided from the tiled "path" by a long strip of metal that ties in with the furniture frames and at the same time defines the perimeter of the sitting-room area. Ward Bennett helped with the design, which turned two medium-sized apartments into one great flowing space.*

The different carpet weaves are Axminster, Wilton, Brussels weave, and cord. However, there is often some confusion as to the exact description of the first two. Briefly, they are both smooth-piled and woven on a loom, which means that surface pile and backing are woven together for strength and durability. But the size of an Axminster loom allows greater variety of color in patterned carpets, while in Wilton, the number of colors in any one design is limited to five. The colors not appearing in the surface pile are carried along the back as in a Fair Isle sweater to form, in this case, an extra pad of fiber that cushions against wear; hence Wilton's greater reputation for hidden value. Axminsters are usually patterned; Wiltons are usually plain.

When the surface pile is looped instead of cut, it is known as Brussels weave. It has a neat, crisp appearance and is a good texture for clear-cut and geometric designs. Cord is woven in the same way as Wilton carpet and is similar to Brussels weave in that it has an uncut pile, which gives it its recognizable looped appearance; it is an effective construction for cheaper fibers that would otherwise become flattened. Woolcord is made from wool; haircord, from animal hair.

Tufted carpets are nonwoven and are made by needling individual fibers into the base material, which is then coated with latex bonding to anchor the tufts. The pile can be cut, looped, or mixed, and good-quality tufteds can last as long as woven carpet. The cheapest of them should be used only in light-wear areas.

"Broadloom" and "body carpet" are terms for widths. Broadloom is woven on a loom more than 6 feet wide, and common widths are 6 feet (1.83 meters), 12 feet (3.7 meters), and 15 feet (4.58 meters). Obviously, the more nearly a room's measurements approximate these widths or their multiples, the more economical on carpet it will be. Body carpet is made in narrow strips, 27 inches (68 centimeters) and 36 inches (91 centimeters) wide, and is generally used for stairs, passageways, and awkwardly shaped rooms, although it is easier to get subtly shaded colors in body carpet and the denser smooth piles.

To my mind wool is the best carpet ingredient, since it is comparatively dirt-resistant, takes dyes well and truly, and is soft to the touch. Wool reinforced with 20 percent nylon makes some of the hardest-wearing, most expensive carpets on the market. But it must be admitted that some of the man-made-fiber carpets, though harder to the touch and less subtle in coloring, nevertheless have strong wearing qualities too. Jutes, haircords, and sisals make tough, neat-looking, and very reasonably priced floor coverings which, although they are

Above: *Brussels-weave carpet in another geometric pattern covers the bed platform in a bedroom designed by Chuck Winslow. The effect is both neat and nicely luxurious with the dark walls.*

Below: *A handsome Portuguese rug softens the cool stretch of tiles in a leafy roof-terrace room belonging to Mrs. Hannah Rothman in London.*

Right: *A sophisticated circular rug in a pattern of squares coordinates with a pile of differently patterned cushions and pillows, and contrasts well with the slatted bamboo ceiling.*

118

coarse to the touch and inclined to be slippery on stairs, are a handsome base for modern furniture and often serve to unite and harmonize a mixture of furnishing periods.

Coir, or coconut, and rush matting are also good-looking in their own right and, in spite of their coarseness of feel, a far better substitute for good carpet than is bad carpet, however superficially alluring. In any case, many people prefer the coarser texture, savoring the contrast it makes with furniture and wall coverings.

Carpet tiles are a practical idea because they can be moved around stress areas to avoid undue wear and worn ones can be replaced. They are usually made from animal-hair mixtures or cord and are also reasonably cheap. Because they can be changed around or replaced so easily, they are good value for rough-wear areas and corridors, quite apart from fairly temporary accommodation, from which they can be removed with much less hassle than conventional carpeting.

Hard Floors

The field of hard floor coverings is not quite so complicated as that of carpets and matting, but it is just as extensive. The point to remember about hard floors is that although they are handsome, and much more practical in hot climates, natural textures like brick, slate, ceramic tiles, and quarry tiles are both very expensive and tough on the feet. On the other hand, they are worth their weight in gold in country halls, houses by the sea, and basements. And in hot climates, even marble,

Far left: *Coarse but neat sisal flooring is effective in a great sweep and as a background to a mixture of possessions and furnishings of different periods. It seems to have a uniting influence.*

Center: *Gleaming hexagonal Provençal tiles are another excellent uniting background, as they are here for a disparate collection of glass bells, family photographs, and nineteenth-century furniture in this small room designed by Mark Hampton for Carter Burden. Here they also lead directly out onto a terrace overlooking the river in a romantic way, and give continuity between inner and outer areas divided by a glass wall.*

Above: *Narrow white tiles are seductively cool on a landing in Mr. and Mrs. Bernard Stern's old chateau in the South of France.*

mosaic, and terrazzo do not seem an insane extravagance. Mosaic, incidentally, can be made of glass or silica mounted on paper for easy laying, as well as of the traditional clay or marble.

Good vinyls, although many of them are substitutes for natural materials, are nevertheless well worth considering since they are also warmer, softer, quieter, easier to lay, and cheaper. Inlaid vinyl sheet flooring comes with backings of asbestos, felt, or latex foam. The first is for basement floors; the other two, for any floor eighteen inches or more above ground level. The latex-foam backing is good for "softening" a concrete or wood floor and makes a good sound reducer. Sheets come in rolls of 6, 9, and 12 feet (1.83 meters, 2.7 meters, and 3.67 meters). Tiles, which are easier for the amateur to handle, come in 9-inch and 12-inch (23-centimeter and 30.5-centimeter) squares. Both sizes can make distinguished-looking floors if plain sheets of tiles are bordered with stripes or different-shaped tiles (rectangles or half tiles instead of squares, for example), or inset with contrasting patterns or motifs, and they are without doubt practical for halls, kitchens, and bathrooms as well as general living areas.

Vinyl asbestos tiles are cheaper than vinyl and are good for hard-wear areas: halls, corridors, washrooms, and utility rooms. Since they come in good solid colors, they can also look striking in living rooms, especially if used in diagonal or conventional stripes. Some manufacturers offer tiles that are cut so precisely that the seams are virtually invisible when the tiles are laid. Cork, if it is used in conjunction with vinyl or a polyurethane sealer, is also good for kitchens, bathrooms, and children's playrooms. In the last area, heavy rubber tiles are good since they are happily sound-deadening, although they get scuffed easily by rubber soles and heels and are made slippery by spilled liquids.

Above: *Industrial factory flooring separates the kitchen island from the rest of a New York loft (top left). A studio floor was surfaced with coats of white marine paint (top right). A battered parquet floor was stained a cheerful orange to brighten basement gloom (bottom).*

Right: *Painter Frank Avray Wilson completely disguised a parquet floor with a blue-green abstraction.*

Overleaf: *Russet quarry tiles continue from the living room out to the plant-filled terrace.*

Floor Coverings: What Goes Best Where

Area	City	Country	Beach/Hot Climate
Halls and passageways	Best-quality patterned or least dirt-showing plain carpet; carpet tiles. Wood with rugs . Vinyl tiles.	Tiles, preferably in brick, slate, quarry tile, or stone. Failing that, vinyl or vinyl asbestos. Marble for luxury. If wood already, add rugs.	Ceramic or quarry tiles; marble, mosaic, or terrazzo for luxury. Composition tiles for economy. Keep wood if existing. Narrow white stone tiles.
Staircases and landings	Best-quality carpet as in hall and preferably the same.	As city. Or good wood stairs can be stripped, as can old stone. But uncovered stairs are not practical for old people and young children.	Stone and stripped wood are cooler than carpet and do not harbor sand. Or paint with floor paint or stain.
Living rooms	If nice wood, leave bare and polished, with rugs. White tiles of whatever variety and rugs look handsome. Shag is luxurious and good for sitting on. Coconut, haircord, and jute are good backgrounds for a mixture of furniture. Try two colors of vinyl asbestos for inexpensive good looks.	As city, plus the alternatives of rush matting or old brick or stone floor with rugs, if lucky enough to have such a floor in situ.	Ceramic, terrazzo, marble, mosaic, wood, vinyl, composition tiles—anything but carpeting.
Dining rooms and areas	Carpets in a kitchen-dining room or living-dining area are best avoided, in my opinion, because they harbor food smells and stains. Use wood, polished or stained, or any sort of tiles. If a soft covering is needed for acoustical reasons, have a rug which can be cleaned and aired easily.	As city, with the option of matting if it suits furnishings.	As city and country.
Kitchens	Practical comfort is important. Cork with vinyl is ideal, or sealed cork, or nonslip vinyl. Quarry tiles and brick are handsome but hard. Vinyl asbestos is efficient.	As city; but brick and quarry tiles and slate, though hard, have the virtue of looking natural and being easy to mop down after dogs and muddy shoes.	As city and country.
Utility rooms	As kitchens, or try vinyl asbestos tiles where there is much spillage.	As city.	As city and country.
Powder rooms or cloakrooms	Carpet for women's, tiles for unisex and children's. Carpet should be water-resistant, like a nylon mix, rather than best-quality.	Almost certainly tiled. Nonslip ceramic would be handsome; otherwise quarry, vinyl, or vinyl asbestos.	Nonslip ceramic tiles would be ideal; or same as country.
Bathrooms	Carpet or nonslip ceramic tiles. Foam-backed man-made fibers are often better than wool in this area because they withstand water better, and some can be taken up and put in washing machines. Beware of dark colors with talcum powder. Cork with vinyl is also good.	As city.	Any sort of tile that is suitable in price.
Main bedrooms	Carpet if possible. Shag is particularly luxurious. Smooth-pile wool is comfortable too. If carpet is too expensive, use heavy quality felt and rugs by the bed, or matting and rugs.	As city, but old and polished wood floors look good with rugs; so does rush or coconut matting.	As country, but ceramic tiles are cooler in hot climates; or bare boards and rugs.
Spare bedrooms	Carpet. Best quality need not be used as little wear involved. Heavy felt with rugs is a cheap alternative; so is woolcord.	As city.	As main bedrooms.
Children's playrooms	Cork and vinyl-sealed cork, vinyl, rubber tiles, chipboard. Must be hard-wearing and nonslip. Rugs by beds if bedroom as well.	As city.	As city and country.

7. Walls & Ceilings

The imaginative treatment of walls gives as much fillip to a room as a face lift to a fading woman—except that wall decoration lasts longer and is, in most cases, rather cheaper. Once again, the initial problem is what to do and how to do it. Basically, walls can either be painted, papered, or covered with fabric, but choice should be guided by position, condition, proportion, and shape of rooms, as well as by existing furnishing items, and then tempered by the budget. Ceilings, too, can make an enormous difference to the look of a room, and there are many treatments to be considered, most of them listed here along with the various fertile ideas for walls.

Walls &
Ceilings

Of the three basic ways to cover a wall—with paint, paper, or fabric—painting is virtually the cheapest. But to paint with any sort of lasting efficiency presupposes that the walls are first of all in good condition.

If there are any stains on wall or ceiling, make sure that the cause has been discovered and remedied. If not, it is imperative that the cause be discovered: it will almost certainly be damp. Rising damp requires professional advice, but condensation problems can be overcome by applying an undercoat of anticondensation paint to the walls, or by superimposing plasterboard fixed to battens or thin wood uprights and treating it with a preservative.

Shabby old plaster or plasterboard will need checking. If it is merely uneven and cracked, patch up the cracks with liquid plaster, smooth them down with sandpaper, and cover them with lining paper. If it is damp, parts of it might need renewing. Sometimes the whole wall will need to be stripped and replastered, or replasterboarded. It is important that new plaster be allowed to dry thoroughly before decoration starts.

128

Preceding page: *Ceiling, moldings, cornice, arches, and walls are arrestingly picked out in paint in a hall in London worked on by designer Billy McCarty.*

Above: *The smooth curved wall and staircase in Van Day Truex's house in the South of France almost forcibly make one stop and contemplate the beauty of their structure, the interest that walls can hold.*

Right: *Striped tiles are cleverly used on the diagonal for walls and steeply sloping ceiling in an English bathroom. Placed like this, they unite all the difficult angles and make the space seem larger, at the same time bringing out the interest of the structure. The stripes are softened by the broad-leaved, variegated plant and the shining round of the mirror, which looks rather like a porthole against the tiles.*

Latex or emulsion paint, which consists of synthetic resins and color pigments suspended in water, stands the best chance of staying put if an obstinately damp wall simply has to be neatened, but do not on any account paper walls before they are as dry as bleached bones.

Old latex or emulsion paint should be washed with water and detergent before being repainted with new latex or oil paint. Old oil paint should be sanded down to get rid of all shine and form a base for the next layer. Old paper can be painted over if it is still in good condition, but first make sure that its colors are fast. Try a small area: if the color runs, or if the paper is in a poor state, it will have to be stripped off and the exposed underwall thoroughly washed to remove old size or paste.

Old woodwork should be washed and sanded, but if there are several layers of paint on it already, it is advisable to strip the old paint off; otherwise, the new paint will tend to chip.

All About Paint

If decorative ideas are scarce, if a room has become too familiar to inspire, if children are at the messy, scribbling stage, if the given space is small or dark, or if the accommodation is a short-term rental, then my advice is to paint the walls white. There might be a distinct preference for it anyway — there often is. And certainly white is an excellent background for a disparate collection of objects, or vivid splashes of color in accessories, or the elegant cool of whites on white.

If ideas are hard to come by at first, unadulterated white will bring out a room's shape and make a neat white shell of it, and it will soon be obvious what needs warming, what disguising, and what exaggerating. For short-term residents, white is the sort of cheap, neat antidote to possible squalor to which no landlord could fairly take exception. And parents of scribbling children won't need to go into fits about infantile ravages since white can be touched up so easily.

Leaving white aside, the transformations that can be effected by simple paint and color are interestingly diverse. To take a few examples:

Faults can be disguised and proportions changed — at least visually — by various tricks. Raise a ceiling by painting it a lighter color than the walls and keeping the carpet a light tone as well. Lower a ceiling by painting it darker.

Dull spaces can be banded or delineated with color. Keep a simple light background and paint baseboards or moldings

Center: *Deep beige walls are picked out in a darker pinky-brown, the exact color of the seating units, in a London room by Liberty's. The ceiling is painted the same pinky-brown, and this simple paint treatment alters the feel of an otherwise ordinary boxy room. Tall glossy-leaved plants add accent color, as do the pillows in pinks, dark reds, and pink and white.*

Above: *An ordinary slip of a bathroom is given some distinction by a bordered door surround composed of two strips of burlap binding with a painted stripe between the two. Time and cash outlay for this treatment are minimal for the result.*

in a contrasting shade. Paint two or three bands of different colors in different widths, starting from the baseboard. Or form a false cornice or cove by painting a stripe or two immediately under the ceiling. This can be continued down corners to the baseboards and around doors. Do draw the stripes first, though, and with precision.

Anyone with courage and sufficient sleight of hand—or a willing house painter or a good stencil kit—can create various graphics designs on the walls. Or if not graphics, free-flowing bands of color in varying shapes. Sometimes, as in 1920s and 1930s style, the shape of a bedhead or a mirror or a storage unit might be delineated over the object proper and then exaggerated with a contrasting edge of another color. And shapes drawn down a wall can spill over, say, a chest of drawers.

A feeling of paneling can be conveyed by sticking rectangles of contrasting tape on a plain painted wall.

So-called eyesores—a confusion of unboxed pipes, off-center doors or windows, too many breaks in ceiling levels, as up a tall staircase—can best be disguised by painting the area in a dark color so that everything melds together. Crispness can be regained with a light carpet, or white or off-white soft furnishings. Again, on the principle of "If you can't hide it, brazen it out," a confusion of pipes can actually be picked out and made to look like found objects and interesting in their own right, which indeed they often are.

Paint can be manipulated in many different ways to produce a variety of finishes and textures. Terms like "lacquering" or "enameling," "stippling," "combing," and "scumbling" mean commonplace techniques to decorators, but are often just unexplained words to the amateur. To clarify what is meant by the various terms, the techniques are described below.

Lacquering or *enameling*, in this context, is not strictly lacquering, but the finish is similarly deep, rich, and durable. The surface must be prepared with particular care and a good undercoat painted on. A perfect job consists of six or more coats of eggshell or satin gloss paint, each of which must be allowed to dry thoroughly, then carefully rubbed down with steel wool before the next layer is applied. If a very shiny finish is preferred, all the coats could be of high-gloss paint with a final coat of varnish.

Glazing is a hard, almost transparent colored finish that is often used in hot climates, where it seems particularly appropriate. For example: a glazed ceiling in aquamarine above a white tile floor seems to keep a room perpetually cool.

132

Left: *George Powers has made interesting bathroom walls from panels of the sort of beaten, obscured glass often used for bathroom windows. The floor and sunken bath are molded out of firm foam rubber, and the hexagonal shape of the tub looks well with the tall beaten-glass strips with their aqueous greenish-blue reflections.*

Center: *This Californian bathroom has mirrored panels edged in wood, which reflect the plants and foliage that fill the room, making it seem more greenhouse or conservatory than bathroom.*

Above: *This corridorlike hall was so dark and dismal even when painted white that Liberty's, who decorated it, decided to cut their losses and paint it a distinguished shiny black edged with glossy white. Black and white and grey graphics and prints were massed on the walls, and since the sand carpet was a given, the color was repeated in the Chinese bamboo chair. In contrast, the room next door blazes with light.*

Glazing can equally be used for whole rooms. It is best to
have two people working, one to paint the first coat—which,
if for aquamarine, might be sky blue—and the other to super-
impose a transparent or semitransparent coat of green. The
whole is normally finished off with a coat of varnish.

Stippling is one of the best finishes for a large area because
it softens and breaks up surface monotony as well as hiding
any brush marks. It can also be used for doors and other woodwork. It is done with a brush called a stippler, which is dabbed
against the last coat of wet paint. The groundwork is prepared
in the ordinary way, and the stippled coat mixed rather thicker
than usual. The stippler has to be pressed firmly and gently
in position—not jabbed, because that would produce uneven
work. Again, it is best to have two people on the job, the first
to apply the main coat of paint and the second to follow with
the stipple brush.

Good-looking effects can be produced by using contrasting
colors in the two top coats of paint and stippling the finishing
coat with a dry brush to expose a portion of the coat beneath.
Obviously, the colors should be chosen carefully, and the
ground coat must be impervious to the stipple coat (i.e., quite
dry), or a ghastly mess will result.

For example, supposing walls were to be stippled ripe
apricot. It is really almost impossible to produce a clear,
glowing impression of the fruit with a commercial paint color,
but if walls are first painted red with an orange cast, then
painted a buff color and stippled almost immediately, the two
colors will merge to produce a lively depth and glow. Try a
light green ground with a darker green stippled top coat;
a somber green with emerald or vice versa. Various blues,
from cobalt to Prussian blue to ultramarine, will all look good
on a white or pale blue ground. And the various browns
stippled over white or cream will give a useful palette of
umbers and tobaccos, cinnamons and nutmegs. Even if the
job is to be done by a professional painter, it is a good idea to
experiment with color permutations first. Try them out on
various primed boards (that is, boards painted with undercoat)
and compare the results.

Combing is the technique of making a good, coarse texture

134

All the pictures on these pages are details of one totally painted room in England. Walls, ceiling, bed bases, and floor are all dedicated to a fantastical zoomland with sun rays, clouds, stars, planets, and planes winging their way over the entire area. A cloud-shaped wooden structure over the angle of the beds holds recessed angled spots, and more cloud-shapes cut out of white-painted wood act as a continuous bedhead with integrated shelves. Pillows and coverlets follow the same theme. Storage is supplied by drawers under the beds.

with the help of a steel, rubber, or leather comb. The comb can be used on different colors, in varying degrees of thickness of stripe, with a wavy motion, or by doing a second lot of combing at right angles to the first. And there are many other variations.

The background is painted first and allowed to dry. The top coat is then put on and while it is still wet, the comb is passed through it in a chosen pattern. Again, it is a good idea to experiment. Paint a board black and when it is thoroughly dry, overpaint it in white and comb it, trying out a number of different patterns.

Scumbling is a finishing technique in which the colors superimposed on the ground coat are heavier and more opaque, and the effect is produced by brushing or wiping off parts of the scumble color to reveal the coat beneath. The scumble coat must be thick (many paint stores sell a special mix for this purpose) so that the color will not flow and obliterate the markings. If a special paint cannot be found, a thickening agent such as eggshell varnish must be introduced.

Different surfaces will be obtained according to the tools used, which can vary from a well-worn brush or a stippler to a crumpled wad of cheesecloth or tissue paper. Nothing very grand is involved, nor does it take any particular skill, but it must be done quickly. Like all the other methods, scumbling should be practiced on board first, if only to determine what will look best, or what to suggest to the painter.

Trompe-l'oeil and Wall Paintings

There has always been a tradition of *trompe-l'oeil* in decoration —that is to say, painting that cheats the eye into seeing all kinds of false vistas, perspectives, and scenes. Latterly, there has been as well a revival of wall painting and murals, which were the main forms of wall decoration among the ancient Egyptians, Greeks, and Romans and in the European Middle Ages. There are professional and amateur painters who run the gamut from serious scenes to wall graphics to sensuous jungles thinning out to single trees, with stems of leaves and scudding clouds in between. Some wall paintings are all fantasy; some are merely humorous (see "Humor in Decoration," pp. 238–42); some are painted with the intention of visually enlarging a space, or at least dignifying it.

136

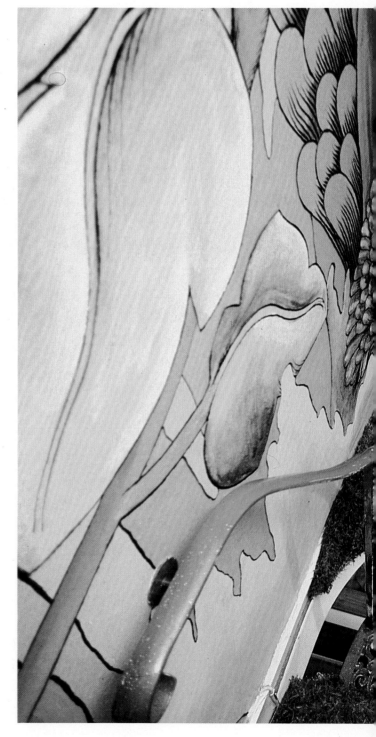

Paint lends itself to fantasy. On the left and at the top are spaces painted by Stan Peskett, two for Julie Christie in London, the third for a New York office. The child's room above has a medieval-castle bed set in a rural English landscape.

Wall Coverings

If paint is extraordinarily versatile, wall coverings, from papers to the most luxurious fabrics, are great disguisers and quick to set a mood. They will cheer up a dull room, hide uneven cracked walls, help to change the feeling, style, and proportions of a place, and give a proper unity where none existed before.

There is such a choice of both patterned and plain papers, from cheap machine-made to expensive hand-printed, as well as separate borders, friezes, and different scales of the same pattern to be used together, that the difficulty is more one of narrowing down the choice than of finding one that is suitable within a price range. If walls are to be papered without professional help, it is worthwhile looking at the prepasted or self-adhesive varieties that need only to be dampened and then set in place. Happily for the amateur, there is a good twenty minutes' grace for retrieving mistakes, such as crooked edges, before the adhesive sticks irredeemably.

Lining papers are a help in achieving a good finish, if walls are in bad condition. The heavier the lining, the better it will hide any defects. Hang it horizontally and be careful to join it—that is, stick it precisely edge to edge—so that no bulge will show through the paper proper.

Tough papers for walls in bad condition are anaglypta and Lincrusta. Anaglypta is made from cotton fiber embossed with some sort of texture or pattern and can—indeed, should—be overpainted. Lincrusta is made from layers of linseed oil welded to a backing paper and embossed with textures such as burlap or tiles. It too can be painted.

Vinyl wall coverings are waterproof and tougher than washable wallpapers, because they are made from polyvinyl chloride with a backing, rather than paper with a plastic coating. They can be scrubbed (with slight, not heavy, pressure), as opposed to being gently washed. They are an excellent choice for bathrooms, kitchens, and playrooms, and possibly passageways, or anywhere that walls are likely to be touched a lot, but they must be stuck on with a fungicidal adhesive or a disagreeable mold will form underneath.

Foil or silver or copper Mylar papers come plain or with overprinted designs. Because of their shine and reflective quality, they give an illusion of space. They are also practical for bathrooms, although walls underneath do have to be in perfect condition or the foil will discolor badly.

Embossed and flock papers go in and out of fashion and certainly in their traditional form have little in common with

138

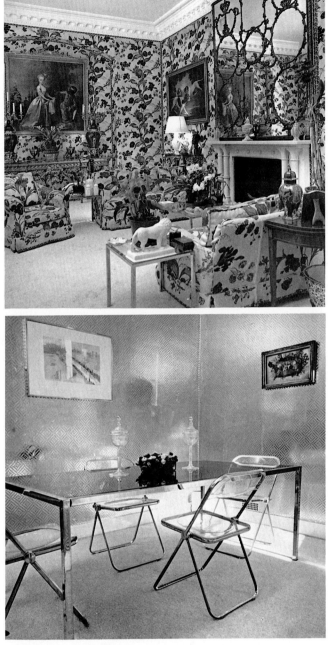

Center: *Wallpaper in an old colonial design is taken up between the ceiling beams in this sixteenth-century English farmhouse. The blue and red on ivory are repeated in blue and red stripes on the ivory window shades.*

Above: *Fabric designer Michael Szell has used one of his cottons on walls and furniture, and even glazed as a surround to the carpet, in his own London drawing room.*

Below: *Diamond-patterned silver Mylar acts as a space-enhancer on walls and ceiling of a small dining room. All the furniture is transparent.*

modern furnishings. Flock has a long history and a velvety pile and is much associated with the nineteenth century and overstuffed rooms complete with antimacassars. However, a modern version uses it for cloud and sun or landscape effects and zany spray-on patterns, and turns the old staid reputation pretty well upside down.

Wall fabrics in general, though often more expensive than papers, have much to commend them. They cover imperfections, neaten up mediocre proportions rather more efficiently than papers, have good sound and heat insulation properties, and will last for years and years—long after paint has become chipped and discolored and paper grubby, torn, and faded. They can be Scotchgarded against undue dirt, spot-cleaned, and often vacuum-cleaned, are more fireproof, or at least fire-retarding, than paper, and all in all pay for themselves over and over again. They also come in great variety. If the long-term convenience can be accommodated to economic planning, then wall fabrics deserve very serious consideration.

Of course, given the right adhesive and a skilled hanger, just about any fabric of reasonable weight and texture, from cottons to velvets, can be stuck onto walls, and if it cannot be stuck it can be battened, as long as the fabric is not stretched or distorted. To stick fabric to a wall successfully, apply the paste to the walls and not to the fabric. Cover any frayed edges with a braid of some sort.

Battening—which gives an upholstered, soft look to walls as opposed to the flat look of stuck-on fabrics—is achieved by fixing battens, or thin strips of wood, horizontally just below the ceiling or moldings and just above the baseboards. Add vertical strips of wood over 6 feet (2 meters) long and then staple the previously seamed fabric to the wood. If paintings and prints are to be hung on the walls, it is important to figure out where they are to go beforehand and to make sure that battens are fixed in those areas. When the fabric is up, these battens can easily be felt, and hooks or nails hammered through in seconds. For a professional, comfortably uphol-stered look, fix Dacron padding between the strips first, then stretch the fabric and tack it to the battens in much the same way as canvas is stretched on a frame for an oil painting. Cover the tack marks with lengths of braid, which should also be used around the top and bottom of the fabric and around the doors and windows.

A comparatively cheap and certainly a most effective fabric to use for battening is matching bedspreads, especially the inexpensive Paisley-like designs in rich colors from India and the Far East, and the subtle stripes. Bordered bedspreads give

Left: *Tartan fabric is stuck between the beams on walls and ceiling in a room designed for Blooming-dale's by Richard Knapple.*

Above: *The room at the left has a thick woolen wall covering with stripes to match the apricot carpet. The room on the right, designed by Chuck Winslow, is covered in neat camel wool edged in pale grey and white and looks particularly calm and peaceful with its lounging platform and desk set across the angle of the corner (an excellent space-saving device).*

Below: *(Left) The walls in this London sitting are covered in green felt stuck directly onto the plaster. It has proved its practicality as a wall covering. (Right) A detail of Michael Szell's drawing room also shows the red-fabric-covered walls of the hall.*

an even greater paneled effect. But both bedspreads and walls have to be measured and the patterns matched with extreme care to ensure symmetry of result, because in my experience the bedspreads vary enormously in minor details, however similar they may seem in the store.

There are other ways of covering walls with fabrics, like shirring them from poles fixed around the room, and I go into this method in more detail in the next chapter. But the ready-made, ready-prepared wall fabrics—the paper-backed burlaps or hessians, simulated suedes, felts, corduroys, shiny patent-leather-like vinyls, thick woven wools, jute, silk and vinyl "silk," moires, Japanese grass cloth, and cork—provide an enormous choice of textures already.

Rich, warm coverings like wool, felt, and suede—and, of course, carpeting continued up the walls as well as on the floor—can make a room look comfortably furnished however sparse the furnishings. In plain, strong colors they make a good foil for a collection of paintings, books, or objects. The Italians now market matching floor and wall-weight coverings, which are perfect for those who like to turn otherwise undistinguished rooms into nice, warmly lined boxes to act as a comfortable framework for their possessions.

Other materials for covering walls include mirror (which I have dealt with in chapter 2, "Space"), acrylics, match-boarding, tongue-and-groove boarding used vertically, horizontally, or diagonally, and, of course, ceramic tiling.

Pepping Up the Ceiling

Ceilings are often left to look after themselves, given a coat or two of paint but generally just accepted as large blank surfaces that are difficult to get at and tedious to decorate. Yet up until the late nineteenth century the ceiling was often the most richly ornamented part of the room, and at various stages through history it has been richly painted, beamed, covered with plaster reliefs, or intricately corniced with the plaster molding fixed between ceiling and walls that was so common in eighteenth- and nineteenth-century buildings of any pretension.

In fact, ceilings need never seem blank and boring. They can be brought into the wall coloring to make a smooth box of a room, painted lighter or darker, or divided from the walls by a false cornice of braid or a painted line or border, if no original molding exists. If original moldings do exist, pick them out in white if walls and ceiling are both in one color like blue or ocher; or in two colors if the moldings lend themselves to the treatment; or in a darker or lighter tone of the general coloring.

142

Center: *This beautiful drawing room in Fleur Cowles Meyer's apartment in Albany, off Piccadilly, in London, has an exquisite ceiling and is an excellent example of the sort of elaborate treatment that was given to so many buildings in the eighteenth and nineteenth centuries. Mrs. Meyer has had all the intricate moldings and cornices subtly picked out to show them to their best but not overstated advantage.*

Above: *This room in a sixteenth-century English farmhouse was low and dark, so the ceiling and walls were painted a warm nutmeg with the beams picked out in white. It is very far from the conventional black-and-white treatment of such houses, but many people forget that the period was actually rich in color. In any case, this particular treatment certainly lightens and brightens the room, makes the ceiling seem less lowering, and generally makes the space more memorable.*

Some designers paint patterns up the walls and over the ceiling, or paint ovals or other shapes on the ceiling alone in a simplified twentieth-century version of earlier grandeur, and it is quite possible to work out or stencil such designs oneself. Work out a pattern to scale first and then measure and draw it out on the appropriate space, filling in the color when it is absolutely right.

Again, ceilings can be covered with wallpaper or fabric in exactly the same way as the walls, or they can be lined with ceiling planks with textures like weathered wood, or with matchboarding, or tongue-and-groove boarding, or acoustical tiles, or light decorative tiles. Another interesting treatment is to repeat the floor motif on the ceiling by painting on a simplified and muted version of the carpet design, or copying a simple tile pattern.

From the practical point of view, ceilings can be treated and renovated in much the same ways as walls. Old wallpaper should be stripped off and flat paint washed. Stains should be treated with aluminum primer before the area is lined with paper and repainted. It is almost always a good idea to line ceilings before painting, because however well and neatly cracks are filled in, they have an irritating habit of reopening. The lining should hide this.

It is, of course, interesting to alter ceilings structurally. The existing plaster can be stripped away altogether to expose the ceiling beams or joists, which can then be bleached and waxed or stained or painted, and filled in with wallboard. This will add considerable height to a room. Alternatively, the wallboard or plasterboard can be omitted, leaving the floorboards above exposed; these can then be waxed, painted, or stained. As I explained in the chapter on space (pp. 46–47), ceilings can also be lowered, or rounded, or curved, or lowered in different areas by using wallboard or plasterboard for straight surfaces and plaster on expanded metal for curves or undulations. But the latter method is necessarily complicated, however well worth the complication the result turns out to be.

Suspended-grid systems are a simple means of lowering a ceiling. They consist of metal rails suspended from the ceiling to support ceiling panels of acoustical material like polystyrene or fiberglass. In this way, air-conditioning ducts, unsightly wiring, and plumbing can all be concealed, as well as a good hiding place created for a strongbox for valuables (just lift a panel for access). Again, suspended grids can be the basis for an illuminated ceiling. Mount regularly spaced fluorescent lights on the existing ceiling and place a suspended-grid system below from wall to wall. Translucent plastic panels can then be fixed to the system, and the light will shine softly through.

Above: *The dark ceiling in this cool London room acts as a steadying antidote to the crisp color.*

Below: *Max Clendinning totally altered a run-of-the-mill ceiling with brilliant paintwork moldings.*

Right: *Mirrored walls and ceiling in Manhattan.*

Overleaf: *A wall of louvers doubled by mirror by architects Louis Muller and William Murphy.*

8. Fabric

Fabric is of the greatest cosmetic help in decoration. We cannot all live in naturally beautiful spaces or make the variety of structural alterations necessary for exciting space, but fabric—along with paint or instead of it—can transform uninspired walls and ceilings, disguise bad proportions, and be of inestimable help in cheering up a rented house or apartment that cannot be changed in any other way. It can pep up dark corridors and halls, jazz up windows, soften awkward shapes and corners, and hide a multitude of sins. It will turn a dreary square box of a room into softly draped luxury, and change hard edges to sumptuousness. The list of the other uses of fabric is surprisingly long, from the revitalizing of upholstery to the aggrandizement of beds. And anyone armed with determination and skill with a staple gun can achieve almost overnight transformations. Many of these uses are described and illustrated here.

Fabric

Most of the credit for the improved general standard of decoration in the later half of this century must go to the variety of fabrics now available, and the imagination with which they are designed and subsequently used. As I discussed in the last chapter, many of these can now be used for wall coverings as well as for upholstery, bedcovers, curtains, shades, or blinds. Even denim appears almost as much on walls as it does on legs. And with the help of adhesives, it is possible to paste up almost any thick cotton, cotton union, shiny cotton ciré, linen, corduroy, chenille, or velvet, which is quite a choice of textures. For best results, make sure that the adhesive is applied to the walls and not to the fabric.

As printing and other techniques improve, there are correspondingly more innovations. There are huge choices in printed and jacquard-weave velvets. Many fabrics have their own matching or coordinating sheers, which are a great
150

improvement on the old white nets, and it is often possible to print the same pattern, or a simplified version of it, on two or three different textures which can be used together or in adjacent rooms. A wall fabric, say, can be printed in a simplified version of the curtains in a bedroom, and the same pattern can be printed on curtain fabric for the adjoining bathroom.

Other fabrics have coordinating braids, trims, and fringes, as well as a plain color taken out of the main patterned fabric for upholstery or wall coverings, so that it is easy to achieve all kinds of improvisations on a theme. Cottons come pre-quilted for bedcovers, ciréd, or made shiny, for walls, Scotch-garded for dirt resistance. Other fabrics can be printed in any color combination in any one of a choice of designs. This valuable service, provided by a growing number of innovative fabric houses, does away with the exhausting search after the exact color to match something that has already been chosen.

Preceding page: *A Chuck Winslow design for coordinating fabric and wallpaper used in a room in Glen Lajeski's country house in New Jersey.*

Left: *A silky bedhead wall contrasts with quilted cotton on the bed and with the rough bark of a spiky indoor tree in a Californian room.*

Above: *Shiny black glove leather covers the mattress and pillows on the dark-grey-carpeted and curved banquette in Calvin Klein's New York apartment. The conversion of a basically conventional set of rooms to a space that flows almost uninterruptedly from one end of the apartment to the other—give and take a few easily maneuverable walls—was masterminded by Joe D'Urso.*

Fabrics for Windows

On the whole, almost any fabric can be used at a window, though clearly some fabrics are more appropriate for particular rooms and particular climates than others. But just because chintzes, light cottons, and silk taffetas or gauzy silks are conventionally suited to bedrooms, there is no reason why flannel, tweed, or coarse woven wool should not be used. Heavy textures, plain colors, wools, tweeds, and velvets are thought good for living rooms; but these rooms can just as well be a riot of flimsy textures. Cottons are normally used in hot climates and thicker materials in cool, but since illusion plays such a large part in almost all decorating exercises, the textures can easily be switched around. Successful and idiosyncratic decoration is rarely if ever achieved by sticking to rigid rules, but rather by using firm preferences with assurance or panache.

There is, however, one very practical rule for curtains (which, along with shades and blinds, are treated as a subject by themselves in chapter 9, "Windows"), and that is that it is far better to use a great deal of very cheap material, smartened up with a border of trimming like cord or braid if need be, than a skimped quantity of a more expensive and beautiful fabric. Most fabrics also look, hang, and last better if they are both lined and interlined. If the sheer look of unlined curtains is specifically wanted in a delicate room scheme, or in conjunction with shades, use an interesting texture such as coarse linen, softly printed voile, embroidered muslin, or filmy silk taffeta. If possible, ensure that any sheer curtains chosen are three times the width of the window, with deep hems—say, 10 inches (25.4 centimeters) deep.

Do remember how useful fabric shades or blinds can be at small windows, or at windows positioned close to a corner with little space for hanging curtains, or in rooms where the crisper, more clear-cut look of blinds would be better than the soft bulk of curtains. They give a finished look to a room when they are used in conjunction with curtains or with dress curtains, and can give added light and sound insulation as well as interest to an otherwise architecturally undistinguished space.

Roller shades usually need a rather light, easily rolled fabric, though it is possible to get a variety of fabrics specially laminated. Roman shades, which are raised or lowered by strings on either side, can be made in literally any material, even velvet, as long as it is not too thick to roll up and pleat evenly. When this type of shade is pulled up, it forms its own pelmet, which gives it an added softness of line.

Preceding pages: *Peach marble Martex sheets have been used to cover the bed platform in this living room by day, spare bedroom by night. The chairs are covered in quilted cotton in creamy white.*

Left: *Filmy white curtains are tied back at either side of a pillared and stepped anteroom, piled with patterned pillows, in the Naesses' apartment.*

Above: *White tweed curtains tone in with white woolen walls in a London apartment designed by Liberty's for Portman Estates. The curtains are lined with a small black and white print that contrasts with the totally different-scale black and white Marimekko tablecloth.*

Below: *White cotton bedspreads edged with lace and plain white cotton curtains add softness to a pristine black and white room in the Bernard Reises' Manhattan house.*

Upholstery Fabrics

There are rather more rules, all of them sensible, to observe in the choice of upholstery fabrics. Primarily, the use to which they will be put should be determined from the beginning, as well as to what extent they will come into contact with those insidious destroyers of any pretension to elegance, namely, children, dogs, cats, food, drink, ballpoint pens, mud, cigarettes, cigars, pipes, sun, and grease. Living rooms take greater wear and tear than bedrooms; people who entertain or have young children are likely to need much tougher fabrics than childless recluses; and dining chairs take more of a beating than occasional chairs. This all sounds elementary, but the simplest precepts are forgotten time and time again in the first rush of enthusiasm for a fabric or a finish.

The toughest-wearing upholstery fabrics are cotton, canvas, denim, cotton rep, twill, and corduroy, which are all cotton-based, and linen union, which is linen mixed with cotton and the most traditional slipcover material. Wool is an excellent but softer upholstery fabric and is the basis for tweeds, wool reps, jacquards, and some good shaggy textures.

Acrylic has made a tremendous difference to pile fabrics and velvets, since it makes them washable. Nylon mixed with wool gives greater toughness, and nylon on its own has been especially useful for stretch covers. Interestingly, the American man-made-fiber industry production capacity exceeds eight billion pounds of fibers annually.

Upholstery fabrics will last a good deal longer if they are given regular weekly attention. Vacuum them thoroughly, turn the cushions on chairs and sofas if possible, spot-clean as and when stains arise, and remember to keep the manufacturer's instructions for care and cleaning for any special blend of synthetics. This is important, as they vary.

Far left: *Red and white toile de Jouy on the walls contrasts with another red and white print in curtains, dressing-table cover, and seating in a children's room in Mark Hampton's apartment.*

Above left: *Shiny tan glove leather covers a sofa in Diana Michener's Manhattan brownstone. The rangy indoor tree acts as a casual screen for the otherwise uncovered windows. The sofa color picks up the outer border of tan in the Oriental rug and in the Oriental throw on the back, and the honey color of the parquet.*

Above right: *Thick white cotton edged with red is used for bath curtains, window shade, and small screen dividing off the toilet in a room designed by David Hicks. Walls and bath panel are covered in a burgundy red felt, and a geometric carpet is diamonded in both the reds and white. The general effect is fresh, elegant, and highly comfortable.*

Leather, of course is a splendid upholstery material and looks as good when old as new—better, I think. If it is fed regularly with a good leather cream, it keeps supple and comparatively scratchproof. The only real snag is its price. Suede is even more expensive and certainly needs greater care. Before buying any piece of suede upholstery, it is essential to see that it has been properly treated to withstand grease and water. On the other hand, Ultrasuede and Supersuede, the man-made versions, look almost as handsome and are extremely practical since spots and stains can be rubbed off in an instant. They are not cheap but are worth every cent.

Synthetic leathers are sometimes quite good-looking and are certainly cheaper, but they can be uncomfortably sticky in hot weather if made from polyvinyl chloride (PVC). Polyurethane simulated leathers, however, are fine and soft and appear to have none of this stickiness. Both types can be wiped clean with a damp cloth dipped in mild soapy water, and then dried carefully. As with all fabrics, any stains should be taken care of immediately before they have a chance to sink in.

Fabrics as a Disguise

I have discussed wall fabrics and ways to use fabric on walls, like sticking it on or battening it to give a soft upholstered look, without going into another way in which fabric can be used to disguise a room, its proportions, its faults, its awkward shape. This is by shirring fabric on rods fixed beneath the molding, cornice, or cove, if any of these exist, or just below the ceiling if they do not, and again just above the baseboards.

Because yards and yards of fabric will be needed, the cheaper it is the better, and remember that fabric has to be used wherever there would normally be paint or wallpaper— that is, above and below windows, above doors, everywhere. This means either looping back the material over doors and windows with tiebacks, or fixing rods above doors and above and below window frames as well. Although this method is undoubtedly extravagant in fabric, it at least does away with the need for curtains, and it is a reasonable idea for a rental or fairly temporary accommodation, since it can all be taken down and reused when necessary. The fabric can simply be gathered onto the poles or rods, or hung from rings as from a curtain pole, or looped straight from the rods if the material is fairly firm and heavy.

Another temporary but no less effective solution is to attach fabric to walls with a staple gun and double-sided Scotch tape, the twin magic tools of set builders and photographic studios.

Left, above: *Diana Phipps, who shows amazing ingenuity with a staple gun, covered the window embrasure at one end of her London dining room with Indian crewel fabric in blue and white trimmed with two different kinds of braid.*

Left, below: *Shirred sheet fabric tents and also disguises a too-high ceiling in this bedroom.*

Above: *Green and white cloths, pillows, and upholstery vie with the massed plants and tangle of greenery in this Californian room.*

One gifted and volatile woman of my acquaintance changes
the moods of her house almost as often as her own, or perhaps
to suit them. Anyway, it makes for attractive, comfortable,
and comforting rooms even if the finish is occasionally a little
rough—and only occasionally at that. All it needs is good
ideas, energy, and perseverance—with perhaps a head for
heights thrown in.

Fabrics on Beds

Beds can assume too much importance in a room unless they
are treated carefully, which means covering them with some
subtlety. If a room is small and single, try to have a bed
covered in a fitted spread, preferably a tuck-in one over a
straight valance, of the same color as the walls, or at least the
curtains or shades. Adding a long bolster or squab, or a long
and a short one at right angles if the bed is against a corner,
plus small pillows or cushions, can make the bed look much
more of a sofa, and it can double as a seating unit.

A double bed in a small room can be minimized by a cover in
the same color as the walls or carpet, and minimal but comfortable bedheads can be made from two matching pillows or
squabs slung on a brass pole suspended behind the bed.
A bolster in the same fabric as the bedcover or the valance
always finishes off a bed well. Alternatively, try covering two
pillows with matching or coordinating fabric and leaving them
on top of the bedspread.

160

Left, above: *Fresh white and green sheets designed for Martex by Hanae Mori are used to close-cover the bed as well as make it up and also shirred to cover a corner screen. The effect is good at considerably less cost than that of conventional fabric.*

Left, below: *Scraps of material have been appliquéd onto white cotton to form a lovely tree-of-life pattern on this bed. The pattern seems particularly apposite in juxtaposition with the bedhead.*

Above: *More sheet designs (this time by Gloria Vanderbilt) have been used for bed, pillows, tablecloth, and curtains on this comfortably furnished porch. The two patterns coordinate well.*

Below left: *A small-flower-patterned cotton is used for a full tester with curtains, bedcover, bedhead, tablecloths, and screen and even to cover the dressing table in a bedroom by David Hicks.*

Below right: *The tester or canopy is attached to the ceiling to act as a support for curtains. The same fabric has been stuck onto all the walls.*

If a room can take it, beds look handsome resting on, or set into, platforms of various descriptions. The bases could be polished, lacquered, or painted wood, or covered in carpet, or made from plexiglass so that the bed appears to float. Cover the mattress in neat Supersuede, Ultrasuede, or suede proper, or felt, tweed, or fur, or plain heavy quilted cotton. The sides of the platform—if it is big enough—can act as bedside tables, or as a base for a television and hi-fi.

Four-posters—or at least the idea of four-posters, especially in fairly traditional rooms—have always been attractive. By their nature they fill in all that air space over a bed with no trouble and give an enclosed, built-in, elemental look to what is almost always an awkward piece of furniture left to itself. They look handsome in steel as well as wood or brass, sometimes completely plain and unadorned except for a bedspread, sometimes with a valance around the top to match the spread, sometimes with side curtains coordinating or contrasting with the spread. These side curtains can billow in a luxuriance of some light, flimsy fabric like voile or batiste or cheesecloth or gingham, or they can be neat and tailored in straight-lined heavy fabric. In any event, the "feel" of a four-poster can be obtained just as well, often more softly and decoratively, and certainly more cheaply with fabric alone.

A ply canopy or tester, for example, can be attached to the ceiling over the bed, or cantilevered from the wall behind it, and covered with fabric. This canopy can then act as support for four sets of tied-back side curtains, which again can coordinate with the fabric used to cover the canopy, the spread itself, or a mattress valance. The curtains can be unlined, self-lined, or lined in a contrasting fabric. Alternatively, a

162

Far left: *Zandra Rhodes, the dress designer, changes the mood of her bed and indeed her whole living space with a staple gun, different fabrics, and ingenuity whenever she feels like it or has the time. On this occasion, six or more variously patterned and colored but toning cottons go to make up the tented, curtained, and cushioned bed. The substantial-looking pillars are actually made of the sort of cardboard tubes that carpets or bales of fabric are rolled around.*

Center: *Philippa Naess's bedroom in New York is all white with flashes of blue and red. The curved bed is covered in thick white cotton and the bedside table in another fringed candlewick bedspread. She has cleverly used a corner to inset an alcove with mirror and glass shelves, which makes the room seem deeper than it is as well as giving it an added sparkle.*

Above: *White and beige figured cotton is used to curtain a bed all around in an ancient Italian villa in the Veneto said to be by Palladio. The same fabric covers the bed base and mattress and has a parchment effect against the vaulted stone walls and battered rosy-brown herringbone brick floor.*

half-tester or canopy can be attached to the ceiling or canti-levered from the back wall with just one pair of side curtains up by the pillow and perhaps a back curtain hanging behind the bedhead. This treatment is cheaper but still looks substantial.

Other effects consist of hanging a shirr of fabric on its own behind the bedhead; hanging a straight panel of fabric; or looping a length of fabric over a central dowel or bracket fixed some feet over the bed and then over a pair of brackets fixed at bedside-lamp level, or just above them on the wall.

A long length of fabric can be used as a sort of baldachin, like the canopies over altars and pulpits in churches. Bring the length up behind the bed and shape it over a rod suspended from the ceiling about 2 feet (61 centimeters) out from the wall. A variation of this is to do much the same thing, but to continue a longer length of fabric in a casual loop to another rod suspended over the foot of the bed and from there to the floor.

On the whole, most bedspreads benefit from being quilted, unless they are very tailored or made of firm fabrics like leather or suede, or a ticking, tweed, or corduroy. Quilting resists wrinkles and creases, makes most fabrics seem more substantial, glosses over any irregularities in the bedding underneath, softens the whole effect, and folds easily.

Pillows and Cushions

Pillows and cushions are an instant reviver, accent adder, and extra comforter for bedrooms and living rooms. A heap of small pillows will make any kind of seating or a bed look particularly luxurious. Large, plumped-up floor cushions provide extra seating—or all the seating—and can be covered in almost any fabric from cotton to corduroy, from velvet to old or cheap Oriental rugs or Kelims. When a room seems to need just one extra splash of color, add a cushion or two.

164

Far left: *Orange, brown, and honey-colored pillows or cushions, together with the wall hanging, add the required splashes of color to a monochromatic scheme in a London penthouse belonging to Mrs. Hannah Rothman.*

Center: *Diana Phipps turned the balustraded balcony at one end of her London sitting room into a gaily cushioned tent. The actual tenting is made with striped cotton curtained on the outside with tied-back brown velvet draped over a pole.*

Above: *Pillows certainly do not have to be in soft fabrics or exotic colors. The group at the bottom of the stairs in this Fire Island house, designed for Felipe Rojas-Lombardi by Earl Burns Combs, look and feel like stuffed sacks, being made out of hessian or burlap. They are amusing, decorative in their own right, and very useful as extra seating. They also fit well into the soaring space, which is full of natural textures and neutral colors in deliberately low key with the constantly changing sea-view.*

9. Windows

There is a good deal more to a window than a source of light or air, a base for curtains, and a view, although one would not necessarily elucidate this fact from a sampling of average homes. Quite apart from the treatment of the window—the decision whether to leave it alone to stand on its own merits, or to put up curtains or shades, screens or louvers or shutters—do not forget the decorative potential of the window frames themselves. There is no reason why pedestrian frames in an existing building should not be imaginatively treated and titivated, as long as they fit in with the general design of the room, for they are, after all, part of the background. Extra trims of wood can be added to make frames more substantial; frames and surrounds can be stained to match the floor, perhaps, or painted and left to stand on their own; a window with an especially pleasing view can be treated like a painting in a frame; and with a little judicious thought, windows with or without a view can be treated as a focal point for an entire room.

Windows

There are several factors to get straight before deciding on any sort of window treatment. Do not forget, for example, that windows are just as visible from the outside as from the interior. Therefore, do not decide to lengthen a window or alter the structure in any way before making sure that the elevation of the building will not be unduly affected. Consider the effect of any treatment as it will look from the outside, by night as well as by day. If the window is not overlooked or is particularly beautiful, does it need to be covered at all? The point could be raised here that this is all very well on a fine summer's evening, but what about a howling, lashing night in winter? Even then, optional shades or blinds can be fixed to provide a screen of some sort when necessary without detracting from the window. An alternative could be to position a light or candles of some sort near the panes, which would look glowing from the outside, at the same time making it hard to see in as well as providing a screen from the elements. Beautifully shaped windows—slits, the small circles known as *oeil-de-boeuf*, or bull's-eyes, ovals, arches, and inset or engraved glazing—might just as well be left untrammeled, since they will not show more than a glimpse of the outside whatever its inclemency.

What is the light/view factor of the windows in question? If they are small and deep-set, they will need to be kept uncluttered, which obviates curtains. If they are large but are still needed to give maximum view, a place will have to be found for curtains (if they are used) at the sides of the frames. It may be that light is needed more than view, or that the view needs to be blocked altogether, or, if a window is on a ground floor overlooking a street, that the view in must be excluded at no cost to light filtration. Sheers are the obvious answer here, used conventionally as curtains, or stretched less conventionally on light wooden frames. Other solutions are café curtains, half blinds, tinted acrylic or plexiglass screens, tinted glass, pierced wooden screens, trellis, or covering half the window with mirror, which is especially useful in small bathrooms. These methods are all detailed later in the chapter, but they should be considered in the planning stage.

168

Preceding page: *The view of New York from this window is so panoramic that no kind of decoration is needed.*

Far left: *Colored panels form a Mondrian-like screen for the large window in this London basement dining room. By night the window becomes a strong focal point, the frame for a large painting.*

Center: *Mark Hampton mirrored the reveals of the windows in Carter Burden's New York apartment to take full advantage of the river view and to catch the maximum light and reflection from sky and water. Bordered Roman blinds provide a screen at night without detracting in any way from the view by day.*

Above: *There is no possibility of being overlooked in this house in the remote French countryside, and in any case, the windows are so simple and beautiful in their own right, the view so undulating, that it would be a shame to screen them.*

If the enhancement of light and view is desirable, consider
covering the reveals of windows with mirror. It gives immense
added zest. Bead the edges of the mirror glass to prevent
sharpness or ungainly lines.

Apart from questions of light, view, and looks, how prob-
lematical are the windows? How do they open, inward or
outward? How are they set in the wall? How should pivot,
French, arched, corner, and dormer windows and those with
odd-shaped or sloping tops be treated? How should skylights
be covered if light has to be prevented from entering? All
these points must be thought of and answered.

If windows open inward, mount nets or sheers onto the
windows themselves for privacy, stretching them on
expanding wire from top to bottom of the frame.

If windows are set in pairs, treat them as a single unit with a
curtain on one rod drawn back at either side, or with a
permanent length of fabric set in between. If blinds or
shades are used, make sure they are symmetrical.

Above: *Always consider what a window looks like
from the outside as well as from the interior of a
room. Sometimes the dressing of an outside window sill adds as much to the façade as interior
dressing does to any indoor decoration scheme.
This window, complete with cat and assorted
plants, is beautifully tended.*

Right: *An interior window leading out to a porch
in a London house gains its decorative effect from
its vivid green framework and from the plants and
sculpture that can be seen set out on the wooden
shelves beyond.*

If windows are uneven, treat them as a pair if they are to be curtained, or if they are set close together. If blinds or shades are used, they could be matched to the walls to minimize their awkwardness. Blinds or shades could be used in conjunction with a pair of long curtains to turn them into a deliberate unit.

If windows are set right up to a corner, either use one curtain drawn or looped back, or forget about curtains and use a shade or blind.

Pivot windows are always a problem. However they open—horizontally, vertically, or mid-pivoting—fix sheers or café curtains onto one half, or use two layers of café curtains or two of sheers. It is impossible to fix blinds or shades if you ever want to open the annoying things. Whatever is fixed will have to open with the window.

French windows can also be a problem. If all the doors open, treat them as a single unit with curtains drawn to the sides, or with blinds set above the frames, if that is possible, so as not to impede the door opening. If there is an inward-opening single door, try a door-sized curtain on a hinged rod that will swing the curtains clear of the door, or fix the curtains on an expanding wire to the frame itself.

Arched windows are handsome, so try not to conceal the arches. Mount curtains on an arched wire and loop them back with tiebacks. If the light or view should not be obscured during the day, it might be necessary to forgo the arch at night instead. In this case, fix curtains to a rod set well above the arch. If the view can be lost without remorse, fit a perforated panel or screen within the arch.

A pair of corner windows can be awkward. If there is very little space between them, make sure that any curtain rods extend beyond the outside edges so that curtains can be well drawn back on either side only. Vertical louver blinds or screens are the only other solution. All other blinds or shades would snag at the corners where they met.

Dormer windows are best with blinds or shades only, or with sheers attached to top and bottom of the frame.

Oddly shaped and sloping-topped windows should be treated like normal windows, using the highest point to carry the horizontal line of curtain rod, pole, top of blind or shade, or shutters.

Skylights can be curtained by sheers fixed onto the frame, or by roller, Venetian, or matchstick blinds mounted on a special fixture.

Above: *French windows leading out to a garden in this bedroom designed by Bloomingdale's, New York, are headed and bordered with a closely patterned fabric to contrast with the plain curtains and plain slipcovers on the chaise and stools.*

Right, above: *Tiny windows set into the thick walls of the Avray Wilsons' English farmhouse make a setting for a collection of green glasses.*

Right, center: *Another window in the same English bedroom was simply left with its original white shutters.*

Right, below: *Windows are set deep into the thick, curved walls of this old house in France. Since curtains or shades would have been impossible to fix and seemed irrelevant anyway, rows of plants have been used for decoration.*

Far right: *Carpeted platforms brought right up to the window, massed with pillows and cushions, and used as seating would only have interfered with curtains or any elaborate window dressing, so the owners of this sitting room chose to leave the windows bare, relying on the variation of texture and pattern and color for any decoration.*

172

Whether it is decided to curtain windows, or to put up blinds or shades, or to use a combination of both, the following guide might be helpful.

Curtains

In my view, curtains should almost always be floor-length and should only just touch the floor, not sweep it, although there are times—when there is a deep sill or a window seat or a deep radiator and no room to extend curtains out to the sides— when there seems no other solution but to hang them to the sill. It is often a moot point whether to hang them from the ceiling, just above the top of the frame, or flush with the reveal of the window, but this really depends on the room available and on one's sense of proportion. If it seems impossible to hang long curtains, and blinds or shades are not wanted or are difficult to fix, a good-looking alternative is to hang café curtains from a rod slung across the window halfway down if they are single, or at the top and halfway down if they are double. This is a useful method for awkward pivot windows.

The fabric to choose will depend upon budget; upon whether it is necessary to keep out noise and drafts; upon whether the morning light must be kept out or the curtains used as a decorative screen; and upon one's personal taste in pattern, plain fabric, color, and texture. The only real rule to remember is that curtains must never look skimped, so that it is better to buy a generous amount of a cheaper fabric than a too-careful quantity of an expensive one. If curtains are lined and interlined, they will look expensive anyway. Do not use heavy or very large-patterned fabrics for short curtains or shades. When buying any patterned material, always take into account the pattern repeat—that is, the length of each run of pattern before it starts again. As all curtain lengths must match, it may be necessary to buy an extra length of pattern for each curtain.

As patterned fabrics can be difficult to deal with, it is safer to keep to a plain-color fabric to match or contrast with walls or to go with upholstered furniture in a room. It can always be bordered with a contrasting color or edged with a pattern from the room for extra distinction. Pattern on pattern can, of course, be very effective, but such combinations demand experience and sureness of judgment.

Preceding pages: *A close-up of the window with its panoramic view of New York used as the opener for this chapter. The room, with its contrasts of texture and pattern, was decorated as a special office by Philippa Naess.*

Left: *Black and white festoon blinds have the look of curtains in this Boston bedroom. Lengths of the same fabric are simply wound around the bedposts.*

Right, above: *Straight curtains are turned over at the top and bordered in Van Day Truex's house in Provence.*

Right, below: *Sharp triangular pelmets in a bedroom in Mark Hampton's Manhattan apartment.*

Above: *A pair of differently shaped windows (left) are treated as a single unit behind looped-back Liberty print curtains. (Right) Chuck Winslow shirred these curtains over old drainpipes.*

Below: *(Left) Painter Gerta Conner matched bed canopy to French-headed curtains in this tiny bedroom. (Right) Bright yellow curtains are hooked onto a slim brass pole and backed by a filmy printed muslin in the Avray Wilsons' house in the South of France.*

Right: *Very thin striped cotton curtains, almost transparent in the California sun, are crossed over and looped back at a high level over a series of dramatic windows and glass doors. The effect is almost theatrical, with the windows acting as a backdrop for the long dining area underneath. Note the nineteenth-century cast-iron stove standing on the rough cobbled floor in the foreground.*

178

The sort of heading to use is always a vexed problem. Headings are the pleats or gathers at the top of curtains. When curtains are homemade, they can be gathered onto special tapes which are widely available for the purpose from stores and fabric departments. There are really only two basic types of tape: one for pencil pleats and gathered headings, the other for pinch pleats. When the pencil-pleat tape is sewn to the top of the curtain, a drawstring is pulled, then hooks are threaded through at intervals to be attached to the previously fixed curtain rod. The pinch-pleat variety has no drawstring. Long hooks are drawn through the back of the tape which then fold the fabric into single, double, or triple pleats according to preference or the fabric chosen.

Pinch pleats are usually easier to make than gathered headings. Use deep pleats for long curtains, shallower ones for short. Light curtains, sheers, and nets look lighter with pencil pleats. Gathered headings have to be very deeply gathered if they are to look interesting, although ordinary gathering looks well enough under a pelmet or valance in a traditional room. A happy alternative to gathering is deep smocking, but this is best left to professional curtain makers, (who do not use tapes anyway), because it is quite a difficult undertaking.

I have said there are only two basic types of tape, but there is also a lining tape which has two decks for hooks, one for the curtain proper and one for the unattached lining. Although curtains with separate linings do not hang as well as those whose linings are sewn in, they are practical because the side of a curtain nearest the window always gets dirty first, and separate linings can be removed easily for washing or cleaning. They are also cheaper to make.

Curtains can either be suspended from "invisible" rods which display the chosen heading and nothing else, or they can be hung from poles or rods that are meant to be seen. These can be bought in brass or in wood, or silvered, or stained, or painted, or covered in fabric. If only short, slim poles are necessary, wooden dowels can be found cheap at most hardware stores and wooden doorknobs can be screwed on to make effective ends. These can be painted, stained, or varnished to taste. If very heavy curtains are planned, it is possible to buy brass or wooden rods with a cording set fixed inside, which obviates the need for constant pulling and handling. Curtains can be looped or hung by rings from poles of all sorts, in which case tapes will not be necessary. This treatment is advisable over radiators, for it will allow warm air to escape rather than trapping it behind close folds of fabric.

If invisible rods are used, curtains can be finished with a buckram valance covered in fabric, which can be either straight and simple or shaped according to the feel of the room.

Curtain rods should always be wider than the window frame so that the curtains can be drawn as much to the side as possible. They come in every shape, size, and variety for mounting onto ceilings or into walls, for fitting into bays or round arches or onto the underside of window frames. There are double rods and single rods, tension rods for lightweight curtaining and for people who move around a lot and can so take their rods with them, extendable rods (which are also useful for people on the move), hinged rods for French windows and glazed doors, ultra-slim rods for easy bending and shaping. It is just a question of explaining the purpose to the salesperson and getting the proper advice.

Left: *Another view of the curtains shirred over old white-painted drainpipes in a country room in New Jersey designed by Chuck Winslow. The table-cloth and wall covering match the border on the curtain fabric, and the bleached wood ceiling gently repeats the pale wood of the slender Victorian chairs.*

Above: *Liberty geometric-print curtains in dusty pink and white are French-headed onto an invisible rod and backed with a coordinating sheer in pinks, beiges, and white. These, together with the matching tablecloth and pink cotton walls, all anchored by a dark red carpet, cast a roseate glow over the room.*

When calculating the amount of material needed for curtains, decide on the width and length and heading preferred. Standard gathers need fabric one-and-a-half times as wide as the rod chosen. Pencil pleats need two-and-a-quarter times the rod width, and pinch pleats depend on the number of pleats per pinch and the width of the fabric. Allow a turn-over for the heading and a generous turn-up for the hem to allow for shrinkage. A sensible idea is to double the hem over so that it acts as a weight to hold the curtains in place. If the fabric width is not wide enough for the curtains—and it very often is not—allow 2 inches (5.1 centimeters) for each side seam.

Blinds and Shades

Fabric shades or blinds have one great advantage over curtains: they are much cheaper because they use much less fabric. They have other advantages: they show off the fabric design better than any form of gathered curtain since most designs are best seen flat; they take up less light and space when drawn up; they look neat in recessed, corner, dormer, and narrow windows; and they look especially good in conjunction with curtains or dress curtains (which are for show and softness, not for pulling) or sheers.

Fabric shades are usually divided into roller shades and Roman shades, although there are also the more complicated and elaborate festoon shades, which look much as their name implies and work on much the same principle as the simple Roman variety.

Roller shades are quite easy to make. The kits are readily available and consist of a spring roller, a base batten or strip of wood for the bottom fixings, and competent instructions. The rollers normally come in standard widths and can be cut to fit any space exactly. So buy the size that is nearest in width to the space, or just wider (not just narrower). The best fabric for these shades is any firm, light cotton that will roll easily. Holland, unfortunately, is hardly ever for sale to nonprofessionals, and although most professional shade makers can laminate almost any lightweight fabric so that it will roll as easily as holland, it is usually part of their service and not for sale as a process.

When measuring for fabric, decide whether the shade is to hang inside the window recess or outside. If shades are to be hung inside, it is most important that they fit the glass exactly, or they will hang crooked and look as stingy as skimped curtains. Shades fixed outside the recess should extend at least 2 inches (5.1 centimeters) to each side of the window, or they will be sucked in. Brackets to hold the shade can be fixed

from the ceiling, inside the window recess, just above the window frame, or sideways from the top of the frame onto the walls at either side.

If possible, the width of the shade should be less than that of the material chosen, because seams can be distracting and any extra thickness can impede smooth rolling up. Do not turn in side seams, but cut them with pinking scissors or oversew them. Press them as flat as possible, and press any other inevitable seam. Allow an extra 1 inch (2.5 centimeters) at each side to take the brackets and pins and an additional 12 inches (30.5 centimeters) to the normal length or drop of the shade for a good fixing at the top and a generous pocket for the batten at the bottom.

If this sound complicated—and I happen to think that almost any sewing instructions sound complicated however easy they are in practice—do not despair, for apart from the necessarily more expensive custom-made products of professional shade makers, there are enormous ranges of ready-made shades available, and these can be made more individual by sewing or sticking on borders of lace or braid or ribbon or strips of another fabric used in the room. If shades are used in conjunction with curtains, use one of the colors in the curtain fabric for plain shades, or trim a plain shade with strips of the

184

Preceding pages: *Thin-slatted Venetian blinds (left) in a Bloomingdale's room, and thin vertical stripes on simple roller shades (right) in a room by George Powers.*

Above: *The group of shades on this page are all painted and fit well into dormer or deeply recessed windows to form wall decorations.*

Right: *An elaborate Roman shade or blind hanging in accordion pleats.*

curtain fabric. Again, shades can be painted with views or designs and used as canvases; I have even seen the exact daytime view reproduced on canvas for night use. There are also shades with self-laminating surfaces to which any fabric can be pasted.

Roman shades are pulled up by strings or cords into accordion-like pleats so that they form their own pelmet, so to speak, when fully drawn up. They can be made in literally any fabric and look softer than the roller variety, but like those can be mounted from the ceiling or on the wall or window frame. If the window is very wide, it is best to use two or more smaller shades, depending on the expanse of glass, rather than one large, heavy one. In fact, a group of them look interesting when hung at different levels. Like roller shades, they can be bordered at will.

If Roman shades are to be homemade, measure fabric as for roller shades but do not allow the extra 1 inch at each side for the pins and so on. Instead, allow 2 inches (5.1 centimeters) extra material at each side for the side seams, and an extra 10 inches (25.4 centimeters) to the normal length or drop of the blind for turnings top and bottom. This type of shade is normally lined either with self fabric or any lining material. The other materials needed for this job are enough ½-inch (1.3-centimeter) tape to run down each side of the shade, with another two lengths in the middle, or more if necessary, because the tapes should be spaced between 8 and 12 inches (20.3 and 30.5 centimeters) apart; 1-inch (2.54-centimeter) tape to finish the top of the shade; one vine-eye for each vertical tape; half-inch brass rings or their metric equivalent to go every 8 to 12 inches (20.3 and 30.5 centimeters) along tapes, and thin nylon cord to go up each tape, across the top, and down again to the fixing cleat; a wooden batten about 2 inches by 1 inch (5.1 by 2.54 centimeters) to fix the shade at

Far left: *The bright patchwork border of a roller shade weighted down with a slim brass rod forms a lambrequin of deep scallops in this kitchen.*

Center: *Painted cats on painted walls considerably enliven the roller shades and, of course, the English dining room-cum-kitchen with its polished cork floor and handsome wood fittings.*

Above: *Fresh blue and white roller shades fit neatly into the recesses of a pine-framed window in a nineteenth-century London terrace house converted by architect Bernard Hunt and his wife.*

the top, a batten or wooden dowel to weight the shade at the bottom, and fixing cleats to attach to the window frame so that the cord can be wound around them when the shade is drawn up.

Matchstick or Pinoleum shades are made from very thin strips of wood woven together with cotton and are usually in natural pine or stained green, but also look smart sprayed white. They are comparatively cheap and can be used with or without curtains. Pulled down on a bright day, they let in an attractive filtered light. They can either have the same spring mechanism as a roller shade or be drawn up more simply on strings.

Bamboo shades are made from strips of bamboo in varying widths, from matchstick to half a broom handle, attached to each other in much the same way as matchstick or Pinoleum shades. They come in natural or sprayed white, or, if they are made from the burn-marked outer peel, can have a pleasing tortoiseshell look. They are not as cheap as matchstick but look more distinguished.

Wooden slat shades are made in much the same way as matchstick shades but are coarser and can be used as screens as well as blinds. They are expensive but they give a warm, light and an architectural look. They control light effectively as well as aesthetically, although they can be noisy when the window is open and there is a through draft.

Venetian blinds have slats in varying widths made from plastic, metal, or wood; the slimmer the slats, the better they look. Like wooden slat shades, they can be clattery in a through draft but control light well and with cheerful effect. They must be cleaned regularly.

Vertical louver blinds pivot open and shut and can be fixed or drawn back. They make good room dividers as well as appearing to make an extra wall of the window when they are drawn. They are made of vertical strips of canvas, man-made fiber, white shade cloth, wood, raw silk, sheers, chrome, or brushed steel. They look particularly handsome in the latter

Far left: *Handsome black-lacquered openwork shutters improve the proportions of two otherwise quite ordinary windows in a London room designed by American designer George Powers for a client.*

Center, above: *Old shutters in a Victorian house in London converted by Jack and Liz Lambert were painted with huge red circles to memorable effect.*

Center, below: *Thin matchstick shades form a ceiling canopy as well as a window covering in an English bedroom by Hilary Green.*

Right: *Folding mirror shutters between windows, then screens at the glass in a Bloomingdale's room.*

188

Overleaf: *Openwork panels completely cover a bay window (far left) in a London house. A painting is hung on the central panel. (Left) The designs on this window look like stained glass but were actually traced with glass paint that will not wear off. (Center) Tinted glass mirror panels run at right angles to tinted glass windowpanes in a room designed by Richard Knapple for Bloomingdale's. (Right) Shutters in a nineteenth-century London house, picked out in white and apricot, look just like paneling when open. When shut, they form a band of apricot at the sides of a white roller shade painted with peacocks and exotic foliage.*

two, when they reflect both light and view, but they are cheaper and more common in white shade cloth and none the less good-looking for that.

Pleated shades come in vinyl or fabric and look like a fan. The vinyl versions are crisp and can be sponged down. The fabric versions can be made in sheers or in heavier lined materials as required.

Shutters and Screens

Many older houses have retained their shutters, and if these are still in existence there is hardly need for curtains or shades as well. They can be painted with designs or in two or three tones, or the panels can be picked out in different colors. It is quite possible to buy new unfinished shutters in sections, which can be painted or stained, or have them made up from hardboard. The louver shutter is really the twentieth-century favorite. It is made of wood, which can be left natural or painted or stained, and is useful for disguising badly proportioned windows, or for making dull windows look rather gracious and semi-colonial. Louver shutters can be hung horizontally or vertically or a mixture of both, and used in small sections or large.

Screens of all sorts can be made to slide clear of windows, or fitted into the window recess, or hinged with piano hinges so that they fold flat on top of each other. They are particularly useful for disguising a dull or unsightly view.

There are a variety of ceiling tracks available on which different materials can be mounted for use as sliding screens: sheers of all sorts, tinted or smoky acrylics or plexiglass, lengths of firm fabric or simple matchstick, old-fashioned garden lattice, pierced hardboard panels, or grilles. Equally, any of these materials can be used as fixed screens.

Other Window Treatments

Windows in kitchens or bathrooms that are not overlooked, or corner windows that are of a different proportion from other windows in the room, can all be made more interesting by putting glass—or occasionally wooden—shelves across them and massing these with plants or a collection of glass or china or all three. Evergreen creeper grown up the outside of a window with an otherwise dreary view is an effective screen —if a rather greenish light can be borne. A tiny window can be surrounded by shelves of books and objects as in a frame, and a shuttered window with shutters inset with panels of fabric can be surrounded by a framework of more panels inset with fabric to make an imposing montage.

Ordinary glass can be removed and replaced with panes of tinted glass which exclude a view in, filter light, and make the outside view seem like an early aquatint. Occasionally, an old piece of stained glass can be inserted into a windowpane, or it might fit the frame of the pane exactly. New stained glass or etched or sand-blasted glass can be commissioned, and designs and painting can be executed with special glass paint which will not wear or wash off.

Windows facing onto gloomy back walls can often be covered with opaque glass or blinds or sheers and lit from behind, as can any sort of grille. Plants in baskets set at different levels can be suspended from traverse rods across windows to make a glowing window garden. Tiny windows can often be enhanced by a narrow-stemmed vase with a single flower, an old jug or glass, or a small plant: it is all a question of generating ideas.

10. Storage

One of the major difficulties in any family home—or in any home, come to that—is the neat but adequate storage of impedimenta, from clothes to books, kitchen utensils to toys, records and cassettes to bills and receipts, general household paraphernalia to sporting equipment, and then some. However sparse possessions are to begin with, they tend to grow with the years, and whether this is for reasons of thrift or prudence, security, sentimentality, or sheer laziness is of little account. What is of account is that storage space, or space for storage space, be given some concise thought as well as a concise budget from the beginning. Then, too, it is of particular importance to integrate storage areas into the background of a room. Build storage space in wherever possible, or at least make it look like a deliberate part of the room, not an afterthought. Follow up on some of these suggestions.

Storage

Anyone planning on finding solutions to various storage problems should think about their needs in depth.

How much can be spent, if not now, over the years? (This is an impossible sort of question, but it does at least serve to get the subject in context with the rest of household planning.)

Should everything be enclosed? Some people prefer to shut everything away. If not, what can be seen? What can be left out satisfactorily? What will look good on display apart from books, objects, pots and pans, and possibly towels on bathroom shelves (if the occupants can be trusted not to rumple them too much).

Is there anything against having the same sort of storage system in different rooms? The advantage in this is that it provides continuity in a small space. Many ready-made storage systems have enough permutations to take care of all requirements.

Is a move anticipated in the next few years? (One out of five Americans, after all, are supposed to move every year.) If so, this will affect decisions on movable (free-standing) or fixed storage.

Are there any specific ideas on storage in general? Can clothes, books, papers, or toys be stashed in one of the wire-basket systems-behind-doors like the Swedish Elfa system? Or would it be preferable for them to be stowed in traditional drawers, cupboards, and filing systems?

What sort of storage will be needed in which rooms? Bedrooms, kitchens, living rooms, children's rooms, studies, utility rooms, and bathrooms need storage facilities as a matter of course, but where are the general impedimenta going to be kept? Tools, suitcases, sports equipment, barbecue grills, light bulbs, the household necessities that can be bought more cheaply in bulk?

If storage walls are decided upon as the neatest way of stashing away a multitude of different objects in a living

Far left: *Subtly lit glass shelves fitted into the recesses of the wall provide storage as well as display space and enhance rather than alter the proportions of this room by Max Clendinning.*

Center: *Bookshelves and cupboard storage are fitted all around the walls and on either side of the long window in this Manhattan apartment. The platform that runs around the perimeter of the room, with steps leading up to the shelves, gives the whole a pleasingly integrated feeling.*

Above: *The wall of books and storage in Jack Ceglic's converted Soho, New York, loft is made from industrial shelving components but looks as expensively built-in as the most elaborate custom-built shelving. The wall is lit both by spots suspended from the ceiling and by downlights and small spots fixed just in front of or on the shelves. The television fits inconspicuously below.*

room—hi-fi, records, cassettes, drinks, papers, desk, books, magazines, and so on, how far will this affect the proportions of the room?

If built-in cupboards are desired, where can they be fitted to best and most inconspicuous advantage? What corners and recesses could be used? what old fireplace taken advantage of? Can cupboards be fitted around a window with a dressing-table surface in front of the windowsill? (This last is often a splendid way of saving space.)

How much conventional storage will have to be bought and how much can be improvised? Cane baskets for drinks, for example; ordinary open shelves on brackets; cloakroom racks on wheels or castors for clothes; filing trays inside cupboards for socks, tights, underclothes, and shirts; lidded window seats; an old bureau or dresser with invaluably capacious drawers for periodicals, games, toys, and papers; chests of drawers which act as coffee tables as well as storage for incidentals.

Can existing storage and built-in cupboards be improved or better organized in any way?

196

Above: *Storage is very much a good-looking entity in its own right in these two rooms, and in the Bloomingdale's model room above, designed by Richard Knapple, it is an exciting focal point achieved by clever shaping and a subtle variation of lighting between storage and seating spaces.*

Right: *A ceiling-height cylindrical structure holds drinks and living-room paraphernalia, which can be shut off from view by curved doors on runners. When shut, the structure melds in with the sweep of the dashing cut-out walls in this English room designed by Max Clendinning. Open, its red-lacquered interior provides a striking contrast to the shining cool walls in the rest of the space.*

These questions, and others that will undoubtedly stem from them, should at least help to clarify needs and wishes before the stores are scoured for designs that will suit pocket, taste, and space. It is, of course, impossible to draw up a blueprint for successful storage which will suit everybody (although it is helpful to show illustrations of other people's solutions). The only certain facts are that more space should be allowed for the purpose than could be imagined, and that any sort of storage should be as much in sympathy with the basic feeling and proportions of a room as is tenable.

Fitting Storage In

Whether storage is to be custom-built, improvised, or bought ready-made, it must be fitted into a room as neatly as possible. Take a detached view of the space and take particular note of proportions, architectural elements, and details. In an old building, bedrooms with high ceilings and fine moldings might be best—or at least most inexpensively—served with good-looking free-standing cupboards or wardrobes. Vast old pieces, too large for modern room measurements, can often be bought gratifyingly cheaply.

If there are convenient recesses or spare walls in a large room (and if the room is large, a whole corner sectioned off will make a fine storage area), the ideal is to ensure that built-in cupboards reach to ceiling height and that any moldings and baseboards are matched along the fronts. Few things spoil the proportions of a room so much as an unsightly gap between the top of a wardrobe and the ceiling, quite apart from the dust trap that is caused. The attention to detail involved in the continuation of the room's moldings makes all the difference between storage as part of the background and storage as an unfortunate intrusion.

To be really unobtrusive, custom-built cupboard fronts can be made to seem part of the walls, or even paneled like the

198

Far left: *Smoky plexiglass bookshelves topped by amber wineglasses and balanced by a large cylindrical glass vase full of shaggy white daisies look cool and neat in the white-tiled sitting room belonging to the Avray Wilsons in the South of France.*

Center: *Storage, doors, baseboards, and moldings in stripped wood and a mahogany casing and dresser in the bathroom all add to a discreet sense of opulence in Mrs. Joyce Menaged's London apartment designed by Billy McCarty. Note the depth and perspective given to the space by the ancient figure on a plinth set in front of the long mirror.*

Above: *American designer George Powers put bright yellow doors on all the cupboards set into the grey brick walls of this English kitchen. Bought from the same manufacturer who made the yellow stove, they give a sense of unity as well as cheerfulness to this thoughtfully planned working area.*

existing door or doors, and either painted or covered with paper or fabric. On otherwise flush doors, thin reeding or molding around the edges and sides will prevent any covering from tearing or fraying. If there is a choice of doors on ready-made units, the plain painted variety can be fitted into the existing surroundings better than laminates and veneers.

Whether cupboards are bought or built as good-looking objects in their own right, they should still incorporate some feeling or some detail of the rest of the room, whether it is in color or trim or general proportion. Louvered doors look light, but it is preferable to buy half rather than full louvers to prevent too much dust entering the slits. Paneled doors can be inset with a color or fabric that matches the walls, or with the same caning as a chair. A wall of pine paneling or long panels covered in felt or burlap or hessian or other fabric can hide rows of shelves and drawers, baskets, and hanging space.

In very small bedrooms, it might be best to put up cupboards in the corridor outside rather than curtail sleeping and dressing space still further. Or a bed can be built-in in conjunction with cupboards, with drawers underneath the bed and wardrobes on one side, or both, depending on the length of wall available. A smallish room that must hold a double bed can have the bed inserted into a wall of cupboards with the top cupboards continuing over the bed so that it lies in its own recess; if need be, the door to that room can also be integrated into such a wall of storage. If dressing tables are incorporated into storage as well as hanging space, drawers, and shelves, a room will look peacefully uncluttered; it is often possible to build such storage around windows, leaving the rest of the

Far left: *Old chestnut armoire doors on a newly built closet and similar wood doors on a low dresser harmonize with the antique bed and the general ambiance in Mr. and Mrs. Bernard Stern's restored and revived chateau tucked away in the South of France.*

Center: *Irish architect Max Clendinning has particularly ingenious ideas about storage and space in general. Here, an all-black (or more or less all-black) room has a storage structure built in at the top of the bed to provide a substantial bedhead as well as shelves and cupboards at different levels.*

Above: *Floor-to-ceiling shelves set neatly into a wall between windows and supporting beams make the windows seem deeply recessed and at the same time provide an effective housing for the warm-air grille below. The wooden surround of the shelves also harmonizes well with the floor and the walls.*

Above: *Both these photographs, taken in Paul Goldberger's Manhattan apartment, show excellent storage fitted unobtrusively into rooms full of nineteenth-century character and detail.*

Right: *Wardrobe doors edged with mahogany match the ceiling and walls in Mrs. Joyce Menaged's London apartment.*

Overleaf: *Storage behind a bed (above) and stepped down in an interesting pattern (right).*
202

room clear. Again to save space, a bed can be set up on a neat platform of surfaced and carpeted drawers, or right up on top of low cupboards.

Recesses on either side of a fireplace in a living room are a natural place to build shelves. But the uprights of built-in shelves all around a room might form new recesses for windows and doors, giving the impression that they are built in rather than the shelving, so integral a part of the walls do they become.

Free-standing storage systems or sturdy shelving systems make good room dividers between dining and sitting areas in a living room, or eating and cooking areas in a dining room–kitchen, or work and play areas in a kitchen–playroom or family room. Used in these ways, they make maximum use of space and light without looking superimposed.

It is a commendable idea to want to level up appliances in a kitchen and to stow equipment like a small refrigerator for drinks, or a television, in with the books, objects, and hi-fi in a living room, but one must remember how deep the deepest piece of equipment might be and establish a mean from that if everything is to be flush. Televisions and refrigerators, in particular, have an inconvenient habit of not quite fitting in otherwise beautifully worked-out systems of shelving and cupboards, and often have to be placed elsewhere. For this reason, too, always remember to check the availability of appliances specified for inclusion in the various ready-made storage systems.

There are cases when, say, an efficient German system that seems to encompass every possible domestic permutation, claims to fit any wall, and is itself internationally available will specify electrical equipment that is not—or not easily. So check and check again.

Organizing the Space

Although, as I said, it is impossible to draw up a blueprint for storage that will suit everyone, there are certain common-sense methods for organizing the space at one's disposal that should be kept in mind, but often are not, with all the welter of other things to plan and decide. For easy reference, I have divided them into sections by rooms.

Bedrooms

Items to be stored   Suits, trousers, jackets, blazers, dresses, long dresses, skirts, underclothes, ties, scarves, shirts, sweaters, handkerchiefs, hats, handbags, shoes, suitcases, personal papers, cosmetics, jewelry.

Their disposal   In an ideal wall of storage behind cupboard doors there would be slots for all these things with not an inch of wasted space, and if there were space in the rest of the room, a pedestal desk for papers. If, as is more likely, the space available is divided into hanging space with cupboards above, a shelf or two, and separate dressers or chests of drawers, then suitcases and whatever happens to be currently out of season in the way of shoes, handbags, and so on can go in the upper spaces and the smaller and foldable items on the shelves and in drawers. If a dressing table is not included in the storage wall, a separate one could be used as desk-dressing table with drawers for papers as well as cosmetics. Another space-conserving idea is to leave sufficient kneehole space between two or three chests of drawers set side by side and run a separate top over them that can act as both a writing and a dressing-table surface.

   If there are few drawers but many shelves, wire baskets are a good idea for keeping underclothes, shirts, and similar items tidy. Stacking plastic drawers can be inserted into any excess hanging space for shirts and sweaters.

204

Bathrooms and Linen Cupboards

Items to be stored Toothbrushes, toothpaste, soap, talcum powders, shaving materials, bath essences and salts, cosmetics, washcloths, towels, bathmats, toilet paper, cleaning preparations, medicines, first-aid equipment, sheets, pillowcases, blankets, bedspreads, down quilts or comforters.

Their disposal If there are children in a home, medicines and razor blades are best stored separately in a locked cupboard. A cupboard under the basin is a good place for storing spare supplies of soap, toothpaste, toilet paper, and shaving equipment; or if there is room to install a vanity unit, this will hold these supplies as well as cosmetics. On the whole, bath beauty products are decorative, so they can be displayed on open shelves along with plants—which thrive in the steamy atmosphere—as can neatly stacked towels.

An ideal linen cupboard should be big enough to hold at least two sheets per bed (the other two will be in use), two pillowcases, and a spare bedspread, as well as at least two towels per person, table napkins, and spare blankets, comforters, and down quilts in the summer.

206

Left, above: *A triptych mirror framed in cran-berry red fronts a bathroom cabinet in another English room designed by Max Clendinning. The towel rails are suspended unusually high on the dark blue walls.*

Far left, below: *The wide sunken bath and basin almost distract from the clever storage in Arne Naess's smart brown bathroom-dressing room. Mirrors conceal cabinets, and a whole corner of the room (not shown) is sliced off to form walk-in closet space.*

Above: *Wood cabinets in a 1930s vein topped with a cloudscape in William Waldron's London house.*

Left: *A stained-glass-fronted armoire in an Art Nouveau-ish Californian bath-dressing room.*

Overleaf: *A mahogany cabinet holds towels in this palatial mirror-columned room designed by Bloomingdale's.*

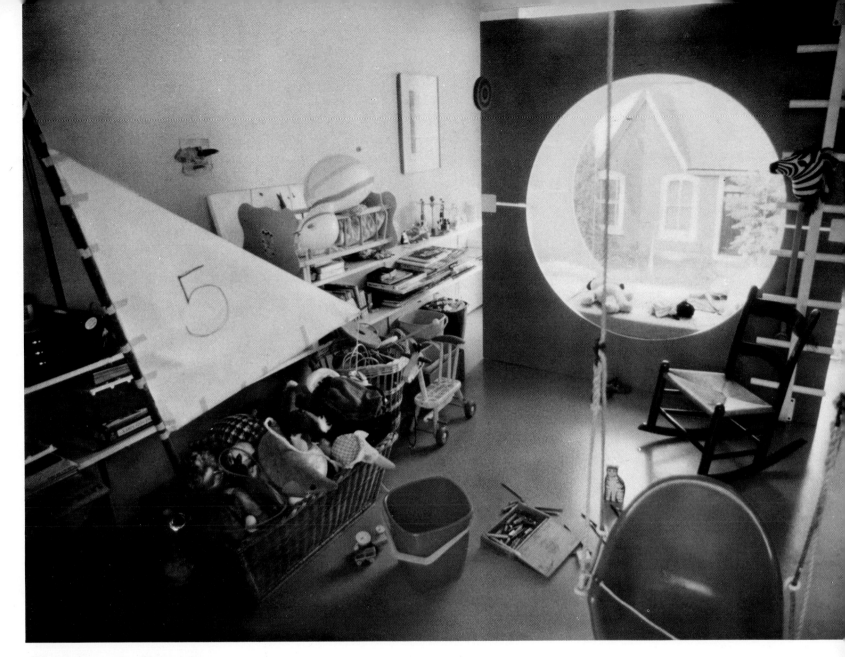

Children's Rooms

Items to be stored Diapers, underclothes, outer clothes, shoes, toys, books, games, sports equipment.

Their disposal Since children's needs and equipment change as fast as they grow, it is much wiser to provide them with adult-sized storage space from the beginning, or at least from five or six years old. (Before that, all their clothes and belongings will lie flat.) By all means, lower shelves and clothing rods to put them within easy reach of the child and raise them by degrees as the child grows. But so-called children's storage is an unnecessary extravagance.

Deep drawers under a bed or bunks are often quite adequate for a child's wardrobe until such time as clothes are better hung up, and can go on being used for underclothes, shirts, sweaters, and jeans. Or a wardrobe can have double hanging space on one side, with rods set one above the other, and divided shelf storage on the other side, with room for shoes and boots and schoolbags underneath.

Left: *This is not a children's room but a Soho, New York, loft belonging to British designers Jim O'Connor and Pamela Motown. However, the idea of suspending clothes from crossed strings tied to a handily available pipe is one that would appeal to children. The open shelves holding a miscellaneous collection of toys and clothes turn necessary storage into a decorative display in its own right. Even the service pipes have been painted in brilliant colors and used as struts for the criss-crossed cords.*

Above: *Baskets, shelves, and tea chests of various sizes are stacked with toys and books in a splendid children's room belonging to Mr. and Mrs. Meyer in Toronto. The dividing wall with its huge circle cut-out acts as an extramural gymnasium with its swinging rope and athletic-looking white ladder.*

Toy, game, and book storage are another matter. It is often better, and certainly tidier, for a child not to have immediate access to every book and toy owned, so storage need not all be low-level. Toy storage should be roomy and enclosed, with shelves for books and games and the more fragile or decorative toys. Shelves should be deeper than normal bookshelves because children's books are often wider and deeper. Chests and deep wooden boxes—which can be used for other storage later—are useful for toys. Or a row of cupboards can be used to store toys and later be converted back for clothes storage. Some extra cupboard space for sports equipment and the clutter that always accrues is desirable.

A sensible unit in a child's room would be two or three chests of drawers set side by side with a separate top over them, as suggested for bedrooms. These can be cheap if bought unfinished and then stained or painted. The top surface can be used for playing games, painting, model making, and homework, and can be wiped down very easily.

212

Above: *All the pictures above were taken in graphic designer Ian Taylor's London house. Cut-out clouds in thin, white-painted plywood fixed on sky-blue painted walls complete with birds, butter-flies, airplanes, rainbow, and sun can be used as files. Crinkly paper shelves hold an amazing collection of Disney characters, and an ordinary pine dresser has been lacquered white with lozenge-shaped flashes of brilliant color. It is all marvelously imaginative.*

Right: *A child's room in Mr. and Mrs. Arne Naess's Manhattan apartment has a built-in bed complete with steps up and over, which can be used for play as well as for seating and storage, and—best bonus of all—a tunnel that burrows under the whole space. The floor is ordinary vinyl sheeting in bold blazer-colored stripes. The actual bed is almost incidental to the inventive play area.*

Living Rooms

Items to be stored   Records or tapes, cassettes, hi-fi equipment, television set, books, objects, movie camera and projector, slides, films, filming screen, drinks, glasses, files and work papers, stationery, typewriter, sewing machine, magazines, telephone directories, tape recorder.

Their disposal   All these items can be stored in a well-designed wall unit or room divider, or in shelves with cupboards underneath. Baskets underneath shelves can hold drinks. A separate desk can hold papers and files.

All other household impedimenta—cleaning equipment and materials, camping and sporting equipment, barbecue grills, bowls and stands for flowers and plants, picnic baskets and insulated containers, folding tables—should be stored as neatly as possible in cupboards in hallways or corridors, on landings, or in utility rooms or attics. The space under the stairs makes good storage and can be enclosed, except where there are open treads. So does the space left after old fireplaces or old-fashioned stoves have been removed.

Above: *Plain wooden shelves like an elegant grid system hold display objects at one end of this large living room with its spoked ceiling designed by Richard Knapple at Bloomingdale's. More storage is provided by the woven cane chests and the generous baskets. The natural textures fit subtly into a room that is in itself a composition of neutrals and varying textures.*

Right: *Staggered glass shelves set above an antique chest hold an impressive collection of wooden statuary and other old wooden objects in this cool Spanish living room, which opens out onto a white-painted and balustraded balcony with a heavily beamed roof. This striking display of dark woods set on strong horizontal lines works well in contrast to the Thonet bentwood rocking chair on the wooden balcony outside.*

Kitchens and Dining Rooms

Items to be stored Pots and pans, casseroles, mixing bowls, kitchen knives, cutlery, plates, dishes, cups and saucers, soup bowls, glasses, dry and packaged foods, jams and marmalades, staple foods, table linen, baskets, candles, matches, string, bottles of oil, vinegar, and wine, jars of herbs.

Their disposal This depends very much on what sort of a cook the occupant of the kitchen is. Dedicated cooks will usually need everything, or a great deal, within easy reach: wooden spoons and forks will be stashed in earthenware jars; casseroles will line the tops of units; saucepans and cooking pots will be stacked within reach of the stove; lids will be nearby on wooden racks; kitchen implements will be hooked on a pegboard; cooking knives will be suspended from convenient magnetic racks; cutlery, table linen, matches, and string will go in the drawers; and crockery, glass, and serving dishes will be stacked on shelves, with cups, mugs, and jugs hung from hooks. On the whole, the width of shelves is more important than the depth, since it is neater to stack things one deep than to have to grope to the back of a cupboard. Dry goods should be stored in cupboards, vegetables in a rack or in the crisping box of the refrigerator, and perishable food in the refrigerator and, if there is one, the pantry. Bottles can rest in baskets, and bread and fruit baskets can be stacked.

Many people, however, prefer to have almost all their kitchen equipment behind (they hope) dustproof doors. There is a large choice of units on the market which will suit them.

216

Far left: *Beautifully made built-in cupboards and shelves put most everything out on display in a subtle green-blue kitchen belonging to Diana Phipps in London. Racks of wine, storage jars, and a whole batterie de cuisine are within easy reach of the various working areas in the room.*

Center: *Wine is neatly stored in one side of the tiled central island unit in the Arne Naesses' Manhattan kitchen. Sensible wood storage units are placed all around the periphery, and open shelves hold items that are in constant use. The tiled surfaces everywhere are eminently practical.*

Above: *Floor-to-ceiling louvered cupboards have shelves for food and general impedimenta as well as housing the large refrigerator and freezer in this New York State house. A V-shaped island unit is fitted with drawers and cupboard space and has a very useful run of working surface.*

11.Detail

An eye for detail is the factor that lifts competent decorating to the memorable level, and as such, it should
clearly be cultivated. It is the ability to place and
arrange objects in a compelling way, grouping them so
that they are seen to their best advantage. It is a
knowledge of balance: the juxtaposition of texture and
color, form and scale, height and width, solidity and
lightness. Equally, it is knowing what architectural
elements to use with what style; how to make subtle
variations on one color; what to light and what to leave;
when to spoof and when to stop. It embraces humor in
decoration, the sympathetic hanging of paintings and
prints, and green-fingered indoor landscaping. But
above all, it is the gift for making personal, idiosyncratic touches to the completed framework of a room,
the feeling for the detail that makes the difference.

Detail

An eye for detail may sound esoteric, but it can be developed with observation and practice, and once developed, it makes all the difference to any given interior. In one sense, it means a heightened awareness, a joyousness in the showing off of a possession, a satisfaction from extreme simplicity, the ability to savor one perfect flower. In another—as in the most sophisticated designers' work—it is a smoothness, an attention to the smallest detail of finish, a conscientiousness, an assurance, as comforting and assuaging as the soft click of a Rolls-Royce door, however irrelevant this may all seem to reality. All those deep-piled carpets, sumptuous fabric walls, brass edgings, tweed-covered Louis XVI chairs, and soft, soft leathers are not such an illogical jump from the bare stone floor and the single ravishing flower. For anyone with a true eye for detail has to have an understanding, an all-embracing observation, of what will give the most visual pleasure.

Architectural Elements

From the end of the Dark Ages on, any European who could afford it reveled in elaborately designed interior detailing, or in the architectural elements of a house, whether built in or superimposed. So did the Americans, as soon as they could. And although in this century architects and designers have, on the whole, concentrated on paring down those elements to their barest essentials, relying on the form and structure itself as decoration rather than on embellishments, the more eclectic of the general public have never given up exploring antique shops, country sales, junkyards, second-hand stores, and demolition yards for decorative elements from disparate cultures to incorporate into their homes.

Lately, too, there has been a brisk trade in well-detailed fiberglass columns, moldings, and balustrading, fibrous plaster pelmets, porches, canopies and fireplace surrounds, instant oriel windows of glass-fiber-reinforced polyester with an antiqued timber finish, linenfold paneling ditto, and simulated marble fireplaces and surfaces which can look surprisingly handsome. In fact, some of these reintroductions in long-lasting modern materials, which the purist might well consider ersatz, have been given the imprimatur of approval by such august bodies as the restorers of the Prince Regent's Royal Pavillion at Brighton, England, and the Nash Regency terraces in London.

Quite apart from cultivating a working knowledge of old architectural elements and styles which can be put to work whenever the occasion seems appropriate, it is worthwhile assimilating facts about contemporary elements and finding

Preceding page: *A group of delicate old bottles on a country windowsill, dappled with sun and balanced by spiky wild flowers, makes the sort of deeply pleasurable little still life that the art of detail is all about. And as can be seen, there is nothing in the least complicated about it.*

Far left and above: *Beautiful intrinsic architectural details in an Italian palazzo. Look at the marble floors, the moldings, the elegant woodwork and doorcases, the fireplace, and the candelabrum. Details similar to these, or even parts of them, are covetously searched for all over the world today.*

out what can be done to titivate existing components. Of these, staircases are necessarily the biggest item, though not necessarily the most expensive, with fireplaces and doors the most often in need of refurbishing or replacement.

Staircases

Stairs themselves might be difficult to replace unless a home is undergoing large-scale remodeling, or is only on two floors, but the treatment of ancillaries like stair rails, banisters, and rods and the covering or noncovering of the treads make a great deal of difference to appearance.

If stairs are to be replaced whatever the upheaval—and I have known imposing great sweeps of stairs found in demolition yards to be installed in country houses without too much of a performance—it is often an agreeable surprise to find that some staircases are hardly more expensive than a good-quality stair carpet. And if the stairs are left bare, which new treads frequently are, the cost of the carpet is saved anyway.

Naturally, the amount of available space must be considered before a decision is made. Curving stairs take up more room than a straight flight. Although spiral stairs seem compact, remember that an area at least 6 feet (1.83 meters) square must be allowed for wide-enough treads—and also that the invaluable storage space to be found under a straight flight is lost.

New wood staircases with open steps need no carpet, but occasionally the newness of the wood might look raw in the surroundings. Since there is no real reason why wood has to be wood-colored, it often makes sense to stain it a bold color with a polyurethane stain. In our own very old farmhouse in the country, we had to replace the original stairs because they were both precipitous and riddled with worm. Pine looked brash against the rugged oak beams, but I did not want to stain the wood to match—which always looks rather makeshift I think. Instead, I decided on a brilliant red, which in a curious way fits in much more sympathetically with the feeling of the structure.

Prefabricated concrete spirals, too, can be painted with plastic paint in white or in red, black, blue, and yellow, and there are several steel spirals that seem like sculpture first, the means of ascent and descent second.

Far left: *A gently decrepit set of old stone stairs leading up from a courtyard in the South of France. Heads and small stone busts are tucked in among the moss and lichen and Provençal flowers as if they had been scattered there nonchalantly by some improvident chatelaine some centuries ago.*

Left to right: *A sculptured staircase seems only fitting among the superb collection of sculpture, paintings, and antiquities in the Bernard Reises' house in New York. The second staircase has a new balustrade rather in the the Chinese Chippendale vein. Shallow wooden steps in London are flanked by arched niches—natural repositories for sculpture and objects. The modern wooden steps on the far right are covered with fur throws for extra seating and lead up to an elegant spiral staircase in a house on Fire Island designed by Horace Gifford.*

Doors and Door Furniture

Doors, whether internal or external, make an immediate difference to the feeling and stature of a home. I have said that it is possible to buy all types of fiberglass porches, door cases, and pediments, and there is even a good and handsome line of colonial columns to support a colonial porch. It is equally possible to buy from a large range of ready-made doors, or to find old ones in demolition yards or at an antique dealer's who specializes in architectural elements.

Double mahogany doors can be elegantly imposing in a large but architecturally undistinguished apartment. And large, wide pivot doors that swing either way are just as impressive in a contemporary context. Paneled doors can relieve the flatness of a characterless box of a room, and suede- or leather-covered flush doors might add richness to an otherwise austere expanse of walls.

Again, a great deal can be done to doors cosmetically. The moldings of the door surround can be painted a different color from the door itself. A door can be surrounded by mirror or painted the same color as the walls with lighter moldings. It can be paneled with wallpaper or a wall covering, or painted in clear fondant colors in an otherwise all-white room. A good wood door like old pine or oak can be stripped and waxed, and a flush door can be brought into one with the walls if it is covered or painted the same.

Fireplaces

A working fireplace is one of the best assets a room can have. However efficient the heating system, however beautiful the contents of a room, nothing as comforting as flickering flames and sweet-smelling, smoldering wood has yet been invented. Whether these flames are contained by a steel frame or bricks or elaborately carved marble or chastely carved wood is a matter of what best suits the style and proportions of a room.

Consider carefully before doing away with any fireplace or any mantelpiece, unless it is hideous. If a building is in any degree old, the fireplace and its surrounds may well be original and will probably suit the proportions and feel of the room as nothing else will—with the exception of a superior version of the same period taken out of another house. Sometimes, of course, the original will have been removed already, and then the choice is either to try to find another as suitably of the period, whether an original or a good reproduction, or to

224

Above: *Beautiful old locks on a cupboard (left) in Hélène Fesenmaier's London house. An old cupboard door exactly matches the room door (right) in an ancient French house.*

Below, left to right: *A suede-wrapped door with a simple chrome knob in Bernard Stern's London house. Moldings picked out in black on a handsome front door in the Kensington district in London. A pair of elegant curved handles on either side of a garden door in London, which add interest to an otherwise plain pane of wood-trimmed glass. Matching handles on louvered double doors.*

introduce some classic-shaped fireplace of no particular architectural style. This last is often the best choice in rooms that have no especial character, or where the fireplace has an irredeemably unattractive surround.

A comparatively easy solution is to remove the existing fireplace, neaten up the aperture that is left, and either install a basket grate in the hole or plan to burn logs directly on the brick ground. Alternatively, once the old mantelpiece has been removed and the recess tidied up, it can be framed with wood, steel, or angle iron. Or the whole chimney breast can be stripped of plaster and the bare brick either left natural or painted white.

One effect worth thinking about is to take down the walls on either side of a fireplace, leaving a central grate between two rooms. The grate can either be knocked right through so that one fire is shared by the two ends of the enlarged space, or rebuilt so that there can be a separate fire on each side. On the whole this is the most satisfactory solution if smoke is to be avoided. The exposed chimney breast will usually form a striking shape in the room, and there is no reason why the hearth in this or any other remodeling should not be raised a couple of feet or more off the floor. Raised hearths can also be extended along a wall to form a long brick base to hold a television set, books, and piles of magazines and to provide extra seating space.

If it is difficult to carry out any structural alterations, and the mantelpiece is undistinguished rather than unattractive, it can always be painted the same color as the walls. This is an effective disguise—particularly if the walls are dark and shiny —and is a good way of integrating a late Victorian or early Edwardian mantel into an otherwise contemporary room.

Above left: *A simple black square with a white surround—the fireplace in Diana Michener's old brownstone in New York.*

Above right: *A gently curved Victorian fireplace, again painted white to blend in with the background so that nothing will detract from the patient collection of paintings and sculpture in the Bernard Reises' beautiful house in New York, hardly changed since they decorated it in the 1940s.*

Below left: *A simple old stone fireplace in France.*

Below right: *A fireplace in Van Day Truex's house in Provence.*

Far right: *A Victorian stove with foam "sleeping dogs," which look extraordinarily realistic.*

Finishing Touches

I have talked consistently of the need to make a good background first and to fill in the details afterwards, so it is logical to assume that the finishing touches to a background are of particular importance, whether they are to the walls, floors, windows, or the architectural elements. Only when these are satisfactory should one concentrate on the finishing touches given by the balance of the room's possessions.

If walls and woodwork are painted, the paint should be smooth and unbroken. Although good paintwork often passes unnoticed in the general sense of satisfaction given by a room (and this is how it should be, for in pleasurable decoration nothing should jar), bad paintwork is usually immediately noticeable and can subtly spoil the most exciting roomful of objects. Wallpaper must be hung with no bumps and lumps, the pattern repeats lined up, the edges cut straight and snugly fitting alongside baseboards, doors, and windows.

Above: *Natural stone embrasures are contrasted with smooth white stone walls and an even smoother white tiled floor in a French house. These architectural elements establish a perfect framework for an eclectic collection of decoy ducks, a stone urn filled with plants, an abstract painting by Bernard Stern, and simple Provençal furniture flanking a vivid green Italian sofa.*

Right: *In the same house (which is crammed with little vignettes of one sort or another at every turn), an old wooden cradle beneath a plant-strung window holds a collection of nineteenth-century dolls. Their jejune painted faces seem perfectly companionable with the medieval statues in the alcove and on the windowsill.*

Wall coverings should not fray at the edges; if they are inclined to, they should be edged and covered in some way, as with a thin metal strip, or a painted strip or beading of wood, or a braid or border of some sort. Seamed and battened fabric walls can have their seams disguised by vertical lines of braiding or cording as well as horizontal lines below the ceiling and along the baseboards. Plain colored wool or felt walls can be subtly delineated by running a trim of a slightly darker shade along the top of the walls underneath the ceiling, or cornice if there is one, and along the top of the baseboards and sometimes around door and window frames as well. Sometimes a plain colored wall (as I suggested on p. 130) can be nicely finished by painting baseboards or skirtings and moldings in a contrasting color.

Floorings should be smooth. Carpets should be tight-fitting and unwrinkled. The point where one carpet ends and a different carpet or kind of flooring begins—as in a room opening off a hallway or in adjoining rooms—looks best covered by a metal threshold strip. Hard floors should break at walls at the best-looking point. Tiles and block floors should not end with tiny fragments if avoidable; any borders on both carpets and hard floors should be planned with precision.

230

Above: *Stripped brick walls hung with paintings, copper pans, and an old wooden clock are a good textural contrast to the gleaming, polished tile floor, round wooden table, and old chairs of different shapes. Silver and glass shine, the wood glows, the plant in the white-painted Edwardian cast-iron stove flourishes. Every detail is right.*

Right, above: *Everything is beautifully balanced, and a lot is nicely wry, in Diana Phipps' exotic London drawing room. Walls are brown velvet edged with gilt picture-framing strips, arched bookshelves are neatly recessed, pictures and objects are well hung. One can spend hours in the room absorbing all the details and the humor.*

Right, center: *An indoor tree and an armoire strike a good balance in this Boston apartment. Note the relationship of soft and hard, low and tall, smoothness and texture.*

Right, below: *A good sense of scale in furniture is shown in this London kitchen-dining room.*

Curtains should just touch the floor; tiebacks should hold fabric gracefully, not in a bunch. Shades or blinds should fit perfectly, and not wrinkle at the bottom or hang slightly away from the sides of the windows (this is always a point to watch).

If it is at all possible, the tops of doorways and windows look best at the same level, and certainly doors should be the same height. If windows vary, at least make them seem level by fixing the tops of curtains, shades or blinds, or shutters at the same height.

Coming from the background to furniture and possessions: upholstery should be neat and smooth and usually piped or edged to hold its shape. Polished wood should be kept polished; marble, glass, plexiglass, and metal, unspotted and unsmeared. Table lamps usually look best if the bases are all one color, or at least variations of the same, and the shades one shape and one color (say, all brass lamps with off-white drum shades), and if they are all at the same level. I do not mean of the same size, but rather that a lamp on a desk, for example, should be shorter than a lamp on a lower lamp table so that their tops appear to be at the same level—which brings us once more to the whole subject of balance and scale.

It is important to balance one big piece of furniture such as a sofa against another such as a sofa table or desk or worktable. Balance a tall object or plant in one corner with perhaps an étagère or a range of shelves of a similar height in another. Offset the mass of an armoire or bookshelves on one wall with a large painting or group of paintings on the wall opposite. But do not choose a large painting or mirror that is actually larger than the object beneath it, or the effect will be top-heavy. Likewise, too small a painting or mirror on a large expanse of wall looks too much like an unfortunate pimple.

The same sense of balance and scale applies to groups of accessories. Keep similar objects more or less of a size, or since that is not always possible in any sort of collection, balance the largeness of one object with a heightened intensity of color in another. Size does not matter so much with dissimilar objects, where the fascination of contrast is the main objective.

Balance applies equally to color. Repeat the same color here and there in a room. The color of a chair at one end can be repeated in a painting or in pillows at the other. Colors in a patterned ceramic table lamp can be picked up in a plain ceramic lamp somewhere else. The tones of a painting can be echoed in the plain color of a carpet. These are small details that give the finishing touch to a home.

Objects and Sculpture

If furniture is what makes a room habitable and comfortable, accessories and objects are the embellishments, the elements that give it personality. But for a truly personal room the objects must be personal too, liked for their own sake, thought about carefully, collected or put together for some reason, not just any old thing chosen to fill a space, or perhaps because cane or wicker is in at the moment.

There are two quite different schools of thought on the possession and display of objects: the school for simplicity and the school for clutter. The offering up of one or two exquisite and interesting pieces, or an accretion of possessions and collections that can be called, rather aptly, memorabilia. The trouble about the first school is that the few beautiful objects really must be beautiful, or made to appear so. The difficulty about the second is that the clutter must be organized to display it to its best advantage. This involves a careful assemblage of texture and shape and color, for after all, it is creating a still life in just the same way as a painter or a photographer.

Collections of small objects should always be grouped together rather than scattered thinly around a room or house. Very small things like pebbles, polished beach stones, or shells can be put into goblets and displayed on window ledges or on shelves. Slightly larger objects, however different, should be grouped so that they have something in common like color or national origin, or alternatively, contrasted with larger things for the interest of the juxtaposition. Add a plant or a simple arrangement of flowers or dried grasses. If arrangements are grouped on low tables that are also used for practical dumping, leave appropriate spaces so that the composition will not be ruined for a drink, a cup of coffee, a tray of food, or an ashtray. Ashtrays, incidentally, are important accessories in their own right. Always see that they are both large enough and good-looking, whether they are of beautiful modern glass or plastic or chrome, or are simply a pretty old saucer or plate.

If arrangements are on a glass shelf or table, lighting them from underneath with an uplight is effective. If they are not on a transparent surface, try lighting them from above with a downlight or a spot to give extra brilliance.

Interestingly enough, serious or at least energetic collections of a diversity of quite commonplace or ordinary but unexpected objects often make for more memorable rooms than much rarer items, perhaps because one is less impressed by the effect of something one knows to be good than by that of

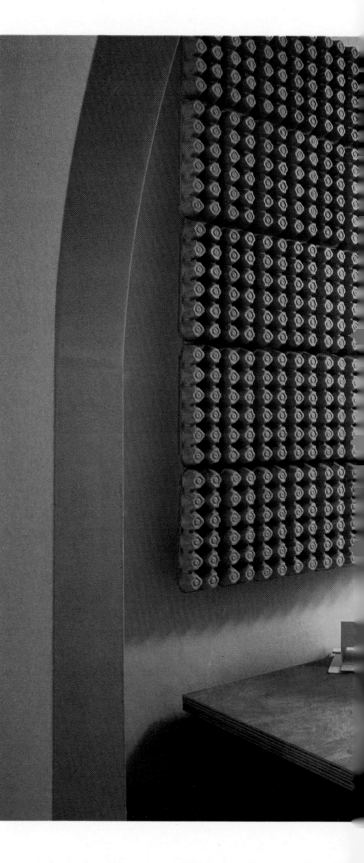

something one had not thought about. I can think back with pleasure upon massed assemblies of old irons, small boxes of every sort, snuffboxes, card cases, china toast racks, mugs, jugs, old commemoration plates, old bottles and pill jars, baskets, eighteenth- and nineteenth-century spectacle cases, old straw hats of all varieties, and old locks and keys, among other things. I personally collect farewell scenes, whether they are sadly depicted in paintings and prints or on nineteenth-century jugs and plates. I have filled a guest room with them, and they spill over into most parts of the house wherever there is an appropriate space. A friend collects ancient shoe lasts, and these march up the sides of the stairs, along hallways, and onto window ledges to great effect. Although the house is a very tiny and, one might say, very undecorated, one always remembers it with great affection.

Something sculptural, whether it is African or Oceanic, pre-Columbian or Chinese, classic figurative or abstract bronze, kinetic or a two-colored plexiglass composition, will always add to the distinction of a room. Mount small pieces on Lucite blocks; balance large pieces with plants again. Almost all sculpture looks better on some sort of plinth made to scale, whether it is lacquered, painted, or natural wood, marble, plaster, or plexiglass.

Hanging Art

There are varied schools of thought on hanging art just as there are on displaying objects. On the whole, they are divided into those who want to make room for their serious collections, and those who want to use wall space to its more decorative advantage. The first school are always thinking of a wall as a means to an end—a support, a background—and moving paintings around as their collection contracts or expands and their interests digress. But the second, who are thinking more of the walls, need to find some unifying factor for their disparate and often less than distinguished possessions.

A miscellaneous set of nondescript prints, for example, can be given a unity they otherwise lack if each one is matted with the same distinctive color—buff or bright yellow or red, whatever fits in with the room—and edged with a thin strip of

234

Preceding pages: *A splendid relief of egg boxes (left) in Louis Muller and William Murphy's apartment. Mirrored reveals on the windows (right) in the Dykers' apartment reflect both sculpture and the green tangle of luxuriant treetops down below.*

Above left: *A tablescape of antiquities, mounted for the most part on plexiglass cubes, in Mr. and Mrs. Bernard Reis's endlessly fascinating New York City house.*

Above right: *A more or less full-length portrait of good cook Felipe Rojas-Lombardi on—logically enough—the kitchen wall in Jack Ceglic's airy converted loft in New York's Soho district.*

Below: *An amazing collection of chamber pots.*

Right: *Every sort of glass on an Italian table.*

chrome or brass. Again, an oddly assorted group of works will
have a unity of their own if they share a predominant color:
all sepia tints, perhaps, or all black-and-white or all green.

In any case, try not to hang things too high or too far apart.
Do not fix anything so low over a sofa or a chair that people
will knock their heads on it, but always try to hang at eye
level (taking either standing or sitting levels into account).
When there is a large grouping, keep at least the central
pieces at eye level. But when the seating in a room consists of
low-level couches and pillows, there is no reason why some
paintings should not be hung very much lower than normal.
Obviously, vertical arrangements will make walls look taller,
just as horizontal arrangements will make them seem wider or
the room appear longer. Most artwork looks best hung against
dark walls. If a wall is strongly patterned, it is best to mount
prints and drawings on very deep mats so that the subject is
becalmed in an area of its own and does not get lost in the
surrounding background.

Juggle different sizes of pictures around to find the arrangement that works best with other arrangements in the room and
the wall space available. Decide on the over-all shape of the
arrangement and mark out the area on the wall in an imper-

Above and right: *Painted decoration and
figure in a room by English painter-designer
William Waldron, who divides his time and work
between London and New York. Another example
of his work (on the right), painting, folding painted
screen, et al., makes use of the turf-green carpet for
golf, the clubs permanently propped against the
wall when not in use. Note also the gigantic straw-
berry on the painted wood-and-glass stylized
flower table.*

236

manent way. Then lay the various items on the floor with each piece in the relation it will have to the others when on the wall, and taking up the same area. This will save a lot of unwanted pin and nail holes.

A lot of very small works can be hung together to balance a larger painting, or as a substitute for one. If one painting or print is much larger than the others, put it at one end of a grouping, rather than in the middle surrounded by smaller ones, which can give the impression of tailing off, and balance it at the other end with something else that is tall: a plant, a piece of sculpture, or a flower arrangement.

Posters can be preserved in special holders so that they do not curl at the edges, tear, or mark the walls too much. Balance them by size or subject or color. Or use them like wallpaper on a blank white wall, not necessarily filling up *all* the space but filling up enough of it to cover the blankness.

Wall hangings can be made from just about any piece of decorative fabric, from the bedspreads I mentioned above, whether modern or antique, to pieces of colorful abstract-design cotton. Hang heavy fabrics on a slim curtain rod suspended from hooks, or frame cotton and lighter fabrics in plexiglass or glass or stretch them like canvas over a thin wood frame.

Humor in Decoration

One of the nicest things to discover in any room is a sense of humor. Levity of any sort gives an obvious lift, strikes chords of empathy, and adds a lightness, or an irreverence, which is almost always beguiling. In fact, much of the inexplicably—or anyway, inexpectedly—stultifying effect of otherwise perfect detailing is caused by too self-conscious an approach. Decoration—like oneself—should not be taken too seriously. As I write that, I realize it must sound absurd coming from someone who spends much of her life both decorating and writing about decoration, but all the same, humor is quite as pleasing a quality to find in a room as it is in a person.

Humor can be injected in many ways. In some rooms, it shows just in the way objects are arranged: the deliberate repetition of themes and subjects in different scales or textures or periods, an association of ideas which is a kind of visual pun. To give examples: a large painting of pillows (as in one of the illustrations here) billowing over a group of the real thing on the floor; a toy King Kong perched on the Empire State building set in front of a serious photographic montage of the same building; make-believe birds set among leaves in a conservatory; stuffed owls on a shelf juxtaposed with a painting of the same subject.

238

Center: *Abstracts, pop art, and early drawings jostle together in enviably easy harmony on the staircase in Carter Burden's New York apartment.*

Above: *Another tableful of antiquities in the Reis house, with even the windows seeming sculptural.*

Below: *An eclectic tablescape of objects sharing a similarity of color and size, set on a tawny marble top and equally balanced by a plant.*

Overleaf: *Marvelous articulated wooden models lounge in molded plastic chairs or on the grassy floor in a garden room in Bloomingdale's, New York.*

In other rooms, it is the actual placing of items: a pair of cast-bronze feet on the carpet by a bed; a stone figure of a reclining woman stretched on an ordinary deck chair under a tree; a papier-mâché group of ill-assorted people sitting stolidly on a bench in a hall. In others still, it is the choice of objects themselves, for their incongruity perhaps, or for some macabre or fantastical quality: deliberate spoofs such as gilded lilies on a dining table, a piece of sculpture nestling in a coffin, a disembodied arm stuck through drawn curtains . . .

Sometimes the humor is decidedly childish, which is fine if it's just the odd joke or two and the house isn't crowded with a laugh a minute, which would be boring. Spectacles perched on the Roman nose of a dignified bust, or a green turflike carpet in a sitting room with a golf club and ball propped against the wall ready to drive up to the next tee, are mildly amusing. Then again, a room can be devoted to a single elaborate charade, like the powder room I visited which was a perfect reproduction of the Russian owner's great-grand-father's *cabinet de toilette* in his private, mahogany-lined nineteenth-century parlor car.

Bathrooms as such are notorious places not so much for lavatorial humor as for mild teasing. They are the perfect place for a wallful of printer's errors or misquotations, for collected absurdities, or for stern words of advice. One friend of mine, an expatriate American notorious for giving various distinguished decorators a ghastly time when trying to perfect her beautiful and historic house, could laugh enough at herself to frame a despairing letter from the last of her decorators (". . . Now that we have exhausted the possibilities of the whole United States, Great Britain, Italy, France, Switzerland, Scandinavia, India, Thailand, Hong Kong, etc., etc., and still not found anything to suit you, I feel that I can have little else to offer you in the way of ideas and therefore resign my commitment to you . . .") and hang it in the visitors' bathroom. It is all grist for the mill, and it serves to make a room more memorable than it would be without the leavening.

242

Above left: *Cards, scraps, badges, letters, mementos, and even clothes are pinned or hung up against free-form painted shapes in the converted Soho, New York, loft belonging to dress designers Jim O'Connor and Pamela Motown. With its vivid colors and carefree approach to storage, the space is exuberant.*

Above right: *A toy railroad made into wall sculpture in painter Gerta Conner's New York studio.*

Below: *Casual wall decoration made from chains.*

Right: *Although the Arne Naesses' New York apartment is grand on the surface, it is full of nicely turned touches of humor: in the choice of art as much as in the detailing, and with occasional joke furniture in serious and luxurious settings.*

Indoor Landscapes

I would not dream of accessorizing a room, any sort of room, without some sort of plant life. In America especially, it is the exception to find a thought-about interior space that is not planted—sometimes overplanted, in fact, so that one sits with palm fronds trailing in one's drink, the ends of a *Dracaena* prodding one's back, trying to part the leaves of a *Ficus benjamina* to catch a glimpse of a neighbor's face. All the same, tall plants and wide-spreading plants, clusters of small plants, flowering plants, and indoor trees add a new dimension, a liveliness and freshness that are gratifyingly cheap in relation to the pleasure that is given. And it is a real pleasure.

There is almost no gap in a room that a plant does not fill and improve, no piece of furniture that cannot be balanced and made to look better by a spread of leaves, no setting that is not softened by foliage. Obviously (well, perhaps not so obviously to some people, judging by the wilted, unhappy state of their greenery), the choice of plants is governed by the sort of light a room gets and its geographical location. If the setting is not right, no amount of cosseting in the way of fertilizing, spraying, and careful watering can stop the rot. In fact, some people maintain that they can tell in a week if the location is appropriate by the gloss on the leaves and a certain indefinable air of health—like the wetness of a dog's nose. On the other hand, if the place is right, most plants seem to thrive willy-nilly with remarkably little attention except for repotting as they grow and spread.

On the whole, the same varieties look best massed together —or anyway, grouped in twos or threes—rather than mixed up with a whole lot of differing species, although it looks good to put different sizes of the same species in a clump to make variations on a theme. Equally, a space will look interesting with perhaps three *Dracaenae* balancing each other in different parts of the room. Tall plants and indoor trees make subtle room dividers, and planters can be set on small castors or wheels for easy moving. I have seen them massed on shallow trolleys like captive jungles on wheels; have seen them used as a natural green balustrade against a dining platform in a living room; have seen a group of palms that gently divided a dining area from a seating arrangement.

Far left: *An old French baker's rack in a New York kitchen is filled with plants (and trays and plates), and a scarlet amaryllis lily in full bloom matches the scarlet of the two-toned table beneath.*

Center: *A vivid yellow sofa in front of a window in the Naesses' New York apartment is framed by burgeoning indoor trees in generous rush baskets.*

Above: *Flowering plants, nice pots, and a graceful indoor tree crowd on and around a table in front of a window in a heavily planted sitting room. It happens to be in California, where indoor planting, of course, has reached an apotheosis.*

Overleaf left: *A single perfect rose in a jar fits gently into a group of different objects.*

Overleaf right: *The feeling is one of tropical splendor in this profusely flowering, profusely green Californian conservatory. It is used for casual eating and sitting and opens right off the living room at one side, right into a garden at the other, so that indoor and outdoor greenery merge.*

A bushy indoor tree set in front of an uncurtained, unshuttered window can make it look completely dressed. A hanging plant strung in front of a small pane of glass is all that is needed for cover. Rows of plants on shelves strung across awkwardly shaped windows, or across a maverick window that does not fit in with the others in a room, solve the problem of unity in a minute. And drooping hanging plants (I mean plants that are meant to droop) liven up any series of shelves.

Put plants in baskets or stainless-steel planters, stone or terracotta pots, or wooden Versailles boxes—anything that suits the mood of the room. Put uplights behind them to throw shadows on walls and ceiling, or small spots to shine through them—though not so near as to burn the leaves. Put plants or a bowl of massed flowers directly under a downlight for a special brilliance. Make a group with plants and sculpture; ferns and pottery; a broad-leaved plant with a collection of any sort. Mass single flowers in specimen jars and old bottles. Indoor landscaping is just as exciting, and much less work, than the outdoor variety.

246

12.Furniture

What constitutes necessary furniture to any one person
is a question of life-style as well as of room function.
People often think that furnishings are so basic that
they should know what they want in toto and from the
beginning—or at the very least, that a decorator should
know for them. I find clients looking at me as if I were
totally incompetent when I suggest that they hang fire
on such and such a choice till the framework is further
advanced. For a time, I even used to feel guilty about it:
perhaps I *was* merely inept? Now I don't at all, for the
older I get and the more I see, the more I realize that
even those who are richest, most sure of their tastes,
and most determined find it difficult to get to exactly
what they want right away. And what is more, I know
that any truly individual room should evolve slowly,
not just come as an instant package.

Furniture

The first useful thing to do when planning the furniture is to make a list of any existing furniture, if only to decide what can or should be reupholstered, recovered, refinished, or repainted. Add to this list a note of all the other pieces that are wanted, what they are likely to cost (making a habit of pricing appealing pieces in shops, sales, and auctions keeps the eye in wonderfully), and what can actually be afforded—if not now, over the next five years. When working on these calculations, remember that prices have an unfortunate habit of creeping up each year, so make an allowance for inflation (say 10 percent), remembering also to add a contingency sum of about the same amount to the budget to allow for impulse buying, changes of mind, and the mistakes we all make with the best will in the world.

Finally, remember that taste as well as financial ability might change somewhat along the way. Neither of them is notoriously reliable, so keep an open mind and be flexible.

To Spend or Not to Spend

Think out what must be of good quality, and what can be improvised, made oneself, or rejuggled from junk furniture. Anchor pieces, that is to say any necessary large storage, beds (especially good mattresses), and conventional upholstered seating like sofas and large armchairs or lounge chairs, should be the most comfortable and best-looking that you can afford or find. It is pretty true to say that you pay for what you get in upholstery, and you have to take the quality on trust since you cannot see the frames, fillings, and springs, if any. They are invisible assets, and the better the assets the more you pay: it is as simple as that. And if long-term comfort is wanted, the anchor pieces must take priority over smaller pieces like coffee tables, side tables, lamp tables, worktables, occasional chairs, dressers, and low storage.

Most of these latter, in any case, can either be found very cheaply (and I do not mean at any sacrifice of aesthetic values) with a view to change later, or

250

A simple room looks luxurious because of the color.

they can be successfully improvised, as can dining tables. In a conventional dining room or dining area, I would far rather spend money on a good, handsome set of chairs, whose pair of armchairs—if they exist—could be used as occasional chairs in the living area, than on a grand table. So:

A plain round wooden table, to seat four, six, eight, or ten persons depending on space, might be found in a thrift shop or be constructed by a willing local carpenter. Even if it is covered with a different coordinating floor-length cloth for every day of the week, it will still end up costing something like a quarter as much as the real McCoy.

Cheap black tin trunks can act as coffee tables or side tables. So can Oriental (not Occidental) packing cases topped with an appropriately sized rectangle of wood or glass. See if a local Oriental import shop has any to spare.

Ready-cut slabs of thick glass can be perched on painted or lacquered plywood cubes. These cubes can equally well be used on their own and can be (apparently) painlessly homemade by following instructions in Clement Meadmore's *How to Make Furniture Without Tools* (not available in Europe). (Mr. Meadmore, mentioned in the first chapter, also explains how to make rectangular tables, desks, chairs, beds, and storage and seating units.) They can be carpeted with a layer of foam for extra comfort and used as seating,

with a couple of semiconcealed castors at the base for easy maneuverability.

Dressing tables and dressers-*cum*-bedroom desks can be made by painting or lacquering cheap unfinished wood chests, setting them a kneehole's width apart against a wall, and topping them with an inch-thick length of wood, Formica- or plastic-covered for practicality.

Good-looking desks can be made from old flush doors, stripped and varnished, or stripped and lacquered, and set on painted or natural wooden sawhorses or trestles, or 2 x 2 steel supports.

Bed bases can be dispensed with and space enhanced by topping a carpet-covered plywood platform with a well-covered mattress.

Shabby old Oriental rugs can be turned into coverings for large, plumpy floor pillows or cushions.

Forget about conventional sofas and chairs altogether. Build a plywood platform at one end of the room and cover it with carpet piled with floor cushions or pillows. For back support for a bed, hang covered rectangles of foam on the wall. Make a seating pit by boxing in a chosen area. Carpet both levels, and fill the center with floor cushions and a coffee table. Or build the surrounding platform higher and slightly further back and add a second carpeted level at a height to form seating units.

If storage space and seating are both at a premium in a small space, build in boxes with hinged lids for storage and add slabs of foam covered with a fabric to the top for seating. Again, suspend fabric-covered foam slabs along the wall for back support.

Scrounge around secondhand and thrift shops for bargains. As long as the shape is good, almost any piece can be revamped beyond recognition by stripping off old paint or varnish or dirt and painting or lacquering or just repolishing the cleaned surface. Old kitchen chairs look fine stripped and painted in a variety of primary colors, or lacquered black or white; try alternating colors around a table. Dreary reproduction chairs can be smartened up with paint, the seats covered in tweed or corduroy. Old dressers can be retrieved, sanded down, stripped, and waxed, or lacquered. Or paint each drawer a different color, for children (and not only for children, come to that).

Upholstered Furniture

Fully upholstered furniture must be well designed as well as comfortable, which is all too often easier said than accomplished. Proportions should be harmonious, coverings agreeable, and simple skirts should just touch the floor with no more fuss than a single pleat at the corner.

Pieces in this class consist of sofas; love seats or two-seater sofas and chesterfields; armchairs, wing chairs, and *chaises longues*, which are all more or less traditional or updated traditional, like a Corbusier *chaise*.

The modern equivalent of the first group are modular seating units and banquettes, which come in all sorts of permutations such as individual armless chairs, two- and three-seaters, corner units, and hassocks. Arms can be plugged in if wanted, or there are end units with arms, so that they can all be bought to make or fit into specific arrangements—U-shapes, L-shapes, zigzags, squares, and conversation pits —but are still easily maneuverable.

The modern equivalent of the large wing chair is the big sculptural chair like the Charles Eames club chair; either version is large enough in bulk to balance a sofa grouping. Smaller armchairs, on the other hand, are best used in pairs if there is enough space, or at least close together if there is not.

Open armchairs, or occasional chairs with upholstered seats and backs, are particularly useful because they do not take up too much room visually or in practice, are easy to move around, leaven the heavy look of too much upholstery, and, because they are smallish, can be used to add accent colors to a

Two antique chairs with twentieth-century furniture.

monochromatic scheme. These can be traditional or modern in style, ranging in materials from the woods and velvets of the eighteenth and nineteenth centuries to the steel and leather or canvas of the twentieth. Dining and desk chairs are sometimes semiupholstered, with fabric mostly on the seats.

Most good stores display a whole selection of upholstered pieces from traditional to modern in many shapes and sizes. What customers often do not realize is that sofas, for example, come in a variety of sizes and covers which cannot possibly all be shown. If something comes in an acceptable shape but the wrong size, do not just give up on it, but make inquiries. More often than not, it will come in at least six other lengths from 54 inches to 90 inches (137 centimeters to 229 centimeters). Arm and back heights can often be varied—after all, each one has to be built separately— and there is almost always a large choice of covers available within the price of each piece, and even more choice if the customer is prepared to pay any difference.

Hard Furniture

This group of furniture is generically known as "hard" and consists of anything that does not include upholstery: bookcases, armoires, secretary desks, and bureau bookcases in the larger range; consoles, sofa tables, desks, worktables, side tables, lamp tables, coffee tables, commodes, dressers,

chests, and dining and kitchen chairs in the smaller.

Most traditional living rooms seem comfortable with approximately a half-and-half mixture of upholstery and wood sparked, if possible, with a proportion of plexiglass, marble, glass, or mirror, edged or supported in the latter cases by brass or polished or brushed chrome. The deep polish of wood, the glitter of glass, the glow of brass and chrome, all offset the depth and softness of upholstery. More purely modern rooms often eschew wood altogether, or only use it marginally and in its paler versions, balancing the softness of upholstery with the hard, smooth finishes of marble and glass, mirror and plexiglass, and brass or chrome.

Arrangement

I talked of the importance of flexibility in chapter 1, "Planning," and flexibility holds as good in the choice and arrangement of furniture as in planning in general. Nevertheless, it is as well to have a reasonably clear idea of one's needs and preferences for any given space, and so to go about the arrangement of a room that it will always look complete in its way even when it has not yet reached the completion envisaged for it in the long term.

In the early stages of a master bedroom, use a chest or dresser which can be moved into a child's room when a better one can be afforded. Buy a pair of cheap canvas or cane occasional chairs for the living room which can end up on a terrace or porch, or perhaps in a bedroom. In short, keep the long-term needs of the whole home in mind and think of eventual as well as current distribution.

Except for living rooms, most rooms arrange themselves. The major points to remember are to offset the major elements—say, the bed—with another group or object of significance—an armchair and light or a dresser and a mirror —and to juxtapose hard and soft. Otherwise, there is not usually space for more than so many permutations, and if there is, chapter 2, "Space," might serve as a guide.

Living rooms, however, are a different matter. In the first place, they are public rooms in the sense that other people come into them more often than into other rooms, which means that traffic problems must be catered for in the arrangement. In the second place, they are multifunctional, and different functions require different arrangements. And in the third, since they are in some ways rooms on show, it is of particular importance to balance the relationship of one piece of furniture to another, as well as to its space.

Traffic, in the room sense, means the area that must be kept free to allow comfortable movement to and from the door and around pieces of furniture. Three feet (91.5 centimeters) is quite a good space to allow for a passageway. About 18 inches (46 centimeters) between coffee table and sofa or seating unit allows movement between and an easy reach for glasses, ashtrays, and so on; 30 to 36 inches (76.5 to 91.5 centimeters) should be allowed at the back of dining chairs around a table.

The talking, relaxing, reading, working, music-making, drinking, and eating functions carried on in most living rooms very often predetermine their own arrangement. Heavier pieces like upholstered seating, pianos, and tables act as anchors for the more flexible occasional chairs, stools, floor cushions, and side tables. When there are parties, these lighter pieces can be moved around at will either to the side of a room, out of it altogether, or to form parts of larger seating groups.

A good general rule when there is a sofa is to have a pair of occasional chairs, or another couch of some sort, at right angles, with opposite them another chair: a large, comfortable one if the room is big enough, or an open-arm chair if it is not. Every sitting place should have a table surface and light to read by within easy reach, so with this sort of grouping there should be a large coffee table and several small side tables appropriately distributed.

A desk or worktable of some sort is useful in any living room if there is space. It will balance the solidity of the upholstered group, act as a display table

252

Purple-painted junkshop chairs in a country room.

when it is not being used for writing, and perhaps serve as a dining surface if there is no other area or table for eating. Finally, think of the peripheral furniture to put around the walls of a room: the storage, the étagères, the secretaries or capacious armoires.

I dealt with the mechanics of planning furnishings to scale in chapter 1 (pp. 18-20) and talked of the importance of balance in chapter 11 (p. 231), so that it almost seems redundant to repeat that rooms do benefit vastly from a sense of balance and differences in height. Yet this point is so often neglected that maybe it needs to be repeated over and over again. Balance soft surfaces with hard, wood with the shine of metal or glass, horizontal lines with perpendicular, taut lines with the jagged edges of leaves.

Offset the major seating group with an architectural focal point of some kind —a handsome fireplace, a large expanse of window. If there is no such architectural largesse, try framing the existing ordinary window or windows with a lambrequin (a valance that goes over three sides of a window) made of painted or covered wood or stiffened fabric. Or frame a window from floor to ceiling with 1¼ x 6 stock lumber cut to order from a local lumber yard, and applied with the thin edge perpendicular to the wall to give added depth. This simple but impressive idea comes from American designer Emily Malino's *Super Living Rooms* (New York: Random House, 1976; $4.95), so far

available only in the United States. Such windows could also be edged by full-length folding screens or shutters, which might be louvered, painted, or lacquered, or covered with fabric or mirror. Any one of these alternatives will make a distinctive focal point out of the most ordinary opening.

Other focal points could be set against the perimeter of a room: a generous wall of books or storage; a dresser, commode, or console (old or modern) with a mirror, a grouping of prints or objects, or a large painting over it; a secretary-desk, a bureau bookcase, or an old armoire.

All these items will add height to a room as a foil to the low furniture. Back up whatever is chosen with a tall plant or an indoor tree or two, a tall floor lamp or a cluster of pendant lights, a piece of sculpture—free-standing if it is tall enough, on a simple pedestal if not. Height and depth, smoothness and roughness, solidity and delicacy are as important contrasts as light and shade.

A last point to remember is that the actual furniture that goes into a room is seldom as important as its background (the walls, floor, and window treatment) or its thoughtful arrangement. The grandest pieces will look depressingly undistinguished in a badly thought out arrangement set against insipid coloring. This fact was demonstrated to me quite startlingly when I revisited a family home that had been redecorated for the first time in thirty-odd years. Not only was it suddenly vibrant with color and light, but I was impressed—even envious—to see that the new generation seemed to have raked together enough money to replace the old furniture with a series of handsome new pieces. I was wrong: the furniture was unchanged. It had merely been revitalized out of recognition by the new background and rearrangement.

Mixing Styles

It is sad but true for the purist that rooms furnished all of a period rarely seem anything other than dull, however splendid the individual pieces. When all is said and done, however perfect the *mise en scène*, a *mise en scène* is all it turns out to be. The sense of balance that I am always going on about applies to *feeling* as well as proportion: the juxtaposition of curves with straight lines, flamboyance with simplicity, worthiness with flippancy.

At least one or two old things, even if they are only accessories (a painting, some prints, odds and ends), or an inherently architectural element like a turn-of-the-century fireplace or moldings, will make all the difference to a roomful of modern furniture and modern fabrics. In similar vein, modern lamps and lighting, a glass and steel console, neatly plumped sofas or banquettes, Louis XVI chairs covered in a twentieth-century fabric like tweed or corduroy, will all enhance a collection of eighteenth-century wood furniture. A collection of modern paintings and sculpture will look super in an otherwise antique room. A single piece of lacquer inlay will look especially rare in a roomful of monochromatic and spare modern pieces.

Normally, it is best to mix only a couple of periods. Seventeenth-century and earlier furniture from whatever country, Occidental or Oriental, looks particularly striking with modern furniture because of its austere solidity and its dull patina. The gentle curves of the early eighteenth century look well with steel and glass, plexiglass, and controlled but comfortable unit seating. Nineteenth-century furniture, especially japanned and turned bamboo, chesterfields or love seats, and bentwood rocking chairs, goes well with modern junk or ephemeral furniture, lacquered cubes, glass and chrome, and natural textures. Lucite or Perspex furniture can be juxtaposed with pre-Columbian sculpture; the careful simplicity of the Directoire, or the opulence of the Regency, with neutral twentieth century.

To experiment in mixing a great many styles demands experience, a sureness of taste, and certainly a unifying background. However eclectic the collection, if the general feeling of the pieces is right—and it is encouraging how often the common denominator of one person's taste is a natural harmo-

Old chest and screen against shiny modern walls.

nizer—they will almost all go with each other. But nothing must jar, and this is often difficult for the amateur. So look around, note the components of harmonious or exciting arrangements, and try to remember them: this is really the only way to learn.

In Conclusion

Although nearly all the points mentioned in the following room-by-room guide have been dealt with in other chapters of this book, I thought it might be helpful to end the book with a summary of this sort for easy reference.

Halls, Foyers, Corridors

Halls and foyers are the definite starting points for any living space, yet they all too easily end up at the bottom of a list of priorities. Whatever their size—and most often they are small—they should be cheerful, interesting, and welcoming. If space permits, there should be at least one comfortable chair and a big enough table to take the mail, a telephone, possibly telephone directories, and all the other small paraphernalia that collect, however ephemerally, in this part of the home. Add to these essentials a cupboard for coats and an umbrella stand.

If the space is too narrow for a table and chair, try putting in a bench or a shelf and stool. If there is no built-in

cupboard for coats, provide a coat and hat stand, or pegs in a row on a wall that is not too much in the mainstream of traffic; a row of disheveled outdoor wear is not the best-looking sight.

If a staircase or corridor leads out of the hall, it should be decorated and carpeted or floored in the same or at least coordinating colors. Walls should be covered in a hard-wearing fabric or vinyl if it can be afforded, or in dark, rich paint if it cannot, since all the traffic through, the (occasional) moving in and out of furniture, parcels, bicycles, prams, strollers or push-chairs, and other accessories to family life, take their toll on wallpapers and pale paints.

Flooring should be tough, hard-wearing and practical. It is hopeless to expect carpeting by the front door to remain clean in either town, suburb, or country unless there is a large mat to take off excess shoe dirt, preferably fitted into a mat well for neatness. This is less of a problem in apartments, since most of the dirt will probably have rubbed off en route through the public areas of the building.

If carpet is laid, it should be the best and heaviest quality affordable, and of a color and design that blend in with the floor coverings of rooms opening off the hall. When space is at a premium, or even if it is not, the same floor covering throughout enlarges and exaggerates that space.

In the country, I think it is best to avoid carpet and have easily cleaned tiles. Stairs do not have to be carpeted. Wooden stairs look good stripped or stained a pleasing color, but remember that if carpet is used it is more practical to cover the entire tread of a stair, because the paint at either side will not get scuffed and there will be less dusting and cleaning.

Lighting should be clear, bright, and central (see pp. 68, 74). Take careful note of the position and size of windows in halls and on staircases in making the decision whether to curtain them, shade or blind them, or leave them alone. Windows in halls or halfway up stairs and on landings look neater and let in more daylight if they are covered with blinds and shutters or some sort of

Cane furniture and plants in a small garden room.

grille or trellis work. If long curtains are used, they should be tied back. Very small windows are better left uncurtained, with perhaps a plant or small flower vase or some object on the windowsill.

Halls and corridors are good places for displaying prints, paintings, drawings, objects, and curiosities. If there is enough light and if there is space on a landing or in the turn of a stair, a small table, a chair, and a large tub of plants or flowers or a plant on its own will all add interest and give the illusion of more space and air than there is. Odd alcoves and awkward angles can be filled with cupboards and bookshelves, since halls and landings are practical areas for any overflow of books. And with ingenuity, it is sometimes possible to make quite adequate studies or workplaces from those alcoves or recesses halfway up or at the top of stairs in some nineteenth- and early-twentieth-century town houses and in many country and suburban houses of whatever period. If there is a large window in one of these spaces, they can also make small but glamorous conservatories strung and hung with plants.

Kitchens

Almost everybody has quite definite ideas on kitchens. On the whole they can be divided into three groups:

Those who think a kitchen should be designed purely as a workroom with

254

all family activities going on in other rooms.

Those who think of a kitchen as a room for cooking where some or all family meals are taken.

Those who think of the kitchen as the real center of the home: a family room where cooking is done, where meals are taken, and where people spend most of their leisure moments.

A good solution for a young family (given sufficient space to begin with) is to have the available area divided up into working and playing space, with a demarcation line of working top and cupboards and suspended wall units. This could have a gap in the middle for convenient nextdoor viewing and perhaps a breakfast counter on the other side for the casual meal.

This is only one suggestion, but before planning think around the pros and cons. Are the present numbers likely to remain static or might there be more children and more guests to feed in the future? What kind of meals are likely to be cooked, for how many, and how often? The kind of cooking done is relevant to any planning, for a succession of simple meals needs far less preparation and storage space than a succession of more ambitious menus. But here again, people's tastes change, as do their cooking abilities.

Other basic questions to ask are:

Does the cook work? If so, is it all day, and is he or she likely to go on working all day? This will make a difference in deciding whether or not to invest in a big freezer. Is the home far from shops, so that more bulk-food storage space will be needed?

Is it likely that extra space will be needed in the future for a dishwasher, a washing machine, a bigger refrigerator, or a freezer that is not needed or cannot be afforded now?

Will there be more than one person working or cooking at any given time, and what is the likely maximum? Kitchens that work well for one very seldom work as easily for two or more.

A useful breakfast area in a white-tiled kitchen.

Is there a separate utility or washing room, or space for one? If so, all that sort of equipment can be separate from the kitchen proper, which will be much more convenient.

When the sort of kitchen has been decided upon, the space can be planned. Usually, kitchens are best arranged according to a work diagram based on the sequence of operations. Sort out what is done and what is likely to be done, so that everything has a specified place. A U-shape—which presupposes a squarish kitchen—is usually considered the ideal, but this is of course impossible to achieve in long narrow kitchens (or short narrow kitchens, come to that), where a ship's-galley arrangement works best since every last bit of space is utilized for maximum efficiency. In this sort of space, try hanging baskets from ceilings for storing small things; hanging an extra shelf from a high ceiling for pots and casseroles; or hanging a circular iron saucepan and utensil rack like those old French ones (or reproductions of them) to be found in good kitchen-accessory shops. If there is room, fit in extra shelves at a suitable height above the stove. Extra work surfaces can be made by attaching hinged, folding flaps to the ends of existing surfaces.

If the kitchen is big enough to eat in, or is part of a large family room, many people like to have an island unit containing hot plates and rings, perhaps a sink and dishwasher, and possibly a small refrigerator, which does keep all the bulkier appliances in one place. In any case, it is aesthetically desirable to have all appliances on a level, with the exception of the refrigerator and freezer, which pretty well have to be big to be good, and a split-level stove.

Kitchen floors get a good deal of wear and tear, so they should be tough, waterproof, grease-alkali-and-acid-rejecting, easy on the feet, not so hard that dropped china and glass will automatically break, able to withstand great heat (in the case of low-level ovens when dishes might be stood on the floor for a second), and good-looking. See page 125, for suitable, comfortable flooring materials.

Kitchen decoration depends on taste as much as it does on whether it is a straightforward workroom, a kitchen-dining room, or a proper family room. I personally think the best background for food preparation is a room that is as cheerful and unclinical as possible, with the emphasis on natural finishes and a good clear color, or on white with a contrasting color like mustard, deep blue, orange, or red. But this is only personal. I also like wood tables that are scrubbable, rush-seated chairs or good plain pine, and roller blinds at the windows, or shades that are not slatted and so do not collect much grease. (Curtains can get in the way, unless they are the café variety.)

If it is impossible to change a rather dreary kitchen in any major way because of expense or the fact that it is a furnished rental, it can still be given a whole new look with color, fabric, and accessories. If even a coat of paint or a change of window treatment is difficult, a few baskets, pots and casseroles, bowls of fruit and vegetables, strings of herbs and onions, and maybe a salami or two will make a difference quite disproportionate to the cash involved, which is cheering. For although a kitchen generally needs more intricate and accurate planning than any other room, it can equally well be brightened up more easily and more cheaply than most other spaces. In any event, a kitchen that is well used, well cared for, and well cooked in acquires a comfortable patina that no amount of efficient planning and expensive equipment can supply.

Bathrooms

Preliminary questions for bathroom planners could be:

How much space is there?

What is wanted: a luxurious bathroom with the emphasis more on the room than the bath; or a practical, hygienic, but comfortable splashing place?

How much money is there to spend?

My personal feeling is that the bathroom should be comfortable, relaxing, and decorative, and that to achieve this, it is not at all necessary to spend vast sums on the actual equipment. In fact, people often spend small fortunes on equipment only to end up with an ostentatious but uninteresting display.

If the room is to be started from scratch, it is useful to bear in mind the occasions when more than one person will be using it at a time. Clearly, it is quite impractical in most spaces to have more than one of most items, but if at all possible, it is useful to have two washbasins embedded in a vanity unit, or a unit with storage cupboards underneath and a large mirror over the top.

If the room is large enough, a free-standing bath looks good; it can be in the middle of the floor, perhaps on a plywood platform. If space is adequate, there is no real reason why the bath should always be huddled up in a corner—except convenience to the plumber. If a bath is at least centered on a wall, it can be framed by useful cupboards or shelves taking up the rest of the space, and the alcove so formed can be tiled all over and even curtained. An ordinary standard bath will look vaguely sunken and more glamorous if it is boxed in and tiled with a wide ledge of tiles all around. Carpet—preferably nylon, because it dries more quickly— can be run up the sides of a boxed-in bath, still with a rim of tiles.

If there is no question of starting from scratch or of embarking on any new equipment, do not despair. Cracked and discolored baths can be renovated and resurfaced, and baths and basins can be moved around for a more practical arrangement of space if there is any sort of leeway. Even if nothing can be changed, it is quite possible to transform the smallest, meanest, dreariest bathroom by purely cosmetic processes.

Washable wallpaper or a vinyl paper covering walls, ceilings and even flush doors (edged and held in place with narrow beading) works an immediate change. Felt is cheap and can look luxurious as long as there is sufficient tiling or some other sort of splashback protection above the bath and basin. A dark paint covered with pictures or a collection of some sort can disguise a mass of pipes. Walls can often be covered with tongue-and-groove boarding or prefabricated wood panels, both available from lumber merchants.

Horrible tiles that cannot be stripped off (this is always an expensive business) can be whitened with an abrasive cleaner and painted any color, shiny or matte. For a shiny surface, use one coat of eggshell yacht or deck paint, followed by one coat of eggshell or satin gloss; for a matte surface, use a good flat paint for the second coat.

Plants, too, are a great transformer, and many of them flourish in the moist heat of a bathroom. A set of open shelves filled with neatly folded, carefully chosen colored towels is always decorative—as are shelves filled with anything interesting, for that matter. A carpet will always add a more comforting touch to a hard floor.

Condensation—that bathroom bugbear—can usually be avoided by steady warmth and good ventilation. If a heated towel rail or radiator is not enough to keep up a good level of warmth in winter, install a wall-mounted fan or infra-red heater and insert a fan in the window for extra ventilation.

Powder rooms are generally small and can therefore be as fanciful as one likes and can afford. It is sometimes best to tile unisex powder rooms all over and let specially good towels provide any decorative softness that is needed. If tiling all over is too expensive, just tile the floor and paint the walls, or cover them with a washable wallpaper or vinyl. They can always be hung with prints, posters, and oddments to provide diversion, and a couple of shelves can hold plants and objects. Alternatively, powder rooms can be turned into velvet-lined boxes, carpeted and mirrored and hung with rich wall fabric that might never be afforded in a larger space.

As far as equipment is concerned, much the same rules apply to powder rooms as to bathrooms, but on a smaller scale. Basically, they need a toilet and a washbasin, an outlet for an electric razor, a good well-lit mirror with a shelf or cupboard for a clothes brush and a clean spare brush and comb. If there is any spare space, consider putting in a shower, especially in a family house where children are growing up and extra bathing space never comes amiss.

Living Rooms

Living rooms are certainly the most taxing on the imagination and the rooms for which most people feel the most responsibility. They do not arrange themselves as well as bedrooms do, they are normally on show all the time, and they have to encompass so many activities and needs for general living.

Questions that might help clarify thought processes on the subject are:

Do you prefer a formal room or a casual one?

How often do you entertain and in what way?

Do you ever eat in the living room? If so, is it regularly, just sometimes, or only for parties?

What exactly will the room be used for as well as for relaxing and entertaining? Working and daytime office, perhaps? Listening to music? Watching television? Playing bridge, backgammon, or other games? Interests such as needlepoint or sketching? The children's homework?

256

Armchairs and reading lights by a blazing fire. Chairs and a hammock in Calvin Klein's room (right).

Clearly the design of the room will hinge very much on whether it is for single, a couple's, or family use. Often a couple have no real idea of what their partners want from a room. If they are asked separately, the answers can be a revelation, so honest communication on this subject is important. A family room, of course, will need a different approach. On the whole, I think it is best always to bear children in mind when choosing a living room's ingredients. A single or childless state does not mean that children will never enter a room, and if all surfaces are pretty practical anyway, they will stand up alike to the ravages of toddlers, teen-agers crouched over homework on the floor, the amiable wanderings of dogs, and the carelessness of convivial guests—often the worst of the lot.

Decoration—as in most rooms—is a matter of taste and of what can be afforded, but colors should be restful without being boring, stimulating without being frenetic. If money is short, my advice would be to pay particular attention to the wall, floors, and windows and probably the plants. An interesting background will always make a room's other components look good, although good components will not do the same for a shabby background. Suggestions for walls, floors, windows, and lighting are all dealt with in separate chapters; but a living-room floor will bring the disparate elements in a room together as nothing else can, so choose it carefully.

I have proposed some furniture arrangements and talked about balancing the various components in the furniture guidelines section of this chapter, but remember that whatever combination of hard furniture and upholstery is chosen, it should be as good, or at least as adaptable, for a quiet evening as for an evening's entertainment. Try to seat at least six comfortably—this should be possible in even the smallest room. A sofa and two easy chairs with a couple of occasional chairs or a banquette or a bench is the average format, with as much air as possible all around. In cramped space, shy away from conventional upholstered pieces and use comfortable chairs around a low round table to make a seating island, or use all banquette seating, or just use floor cushions and low tables.

If a room is big enough and is to be entertained in frequently, have some extra mobile seating on hand (not necessarily permanently in the room): really *occasional* occasional seating that can be brought in from the hall or a bedroom but will still fit into the room's style, such as upholstered cubes, ottomans, stools, and light cane or canvas chairs.

I rather like a big table in the living room, if the size allows, so that eating space, whether for every day or parties, is not a problem. (After all, ideally, one should be able to eat anywhere in the home, since the formal dining room is now a comparative luxury.) Anyway, when the table is not in use for dining, it can be used for books, periodicals, or working, or homework, or games, or just for the display of objects—although it is much more of a bore to have to keep moving these latter than to dump books somewhere else.

Living-room storage needs to be especially well thought out because it will probably need to encompass so many things. A wall of storage units with a desk flap to let down is one solution, or a permanent table set at right angles to the shelves and cupboards for work, games, and any particular interest. Such systems can hold books, tapes, records, stereo equipment, television, and a liquor cabinet as well

An old urn and a chair make good use of a corner.

U-shaped kitchen working surface with a dining table.

A round antique table in a tiny kitchen-dining room.

as space for other impedimenta. One big beautiful armoire or a secretary-desk will hold a comfortable amount of family paraphernalia, and many people use the cupboard over a secretary-desk for drinks or records. A simple serving cart drawn up to the side of a sofa is always practical for storing and serving drinks, and a good many essential things can be stashed away quite neatly in nice-looking baskets, or in Lucite or Perspex cubes turned upside down.

The essentials for any particular interest or hobby often add character to a room if left on neat display instead of being bundled away. Painting and sculpture materials are out for a start, if only on grounds of neatness, but the skeins of wool and silk used for embroidery and tapestry work can look brilliant arranged in some order on shelves; and plans and drawings can be stored in neat rolls in large baskets or drums, or laid flat in thin drawers set into a wall for storage, which can look interesting in themselves, with their severe horizontal lines.

A room that has to act as office by day and a living room by night can still perform both functions admirably. Papers can be kept in drawers in a storage wall or area or in an old pedestal or rolltop desk. If a modern desk seems too officelike, place a thick glass top on two neat white or colored filing cabinets. Or a glass and chrome side table can be used, with a slide-out typing table underneath if necessary.

258

Dining Spaces

In most homes the luxury of a single-purpose room like a dining room is a thing of the past, and unless a great deal of entertaining is done, there is seldom need for a formal dining room anyway. If the kitchen is big enough, eating there is ideal for most occasions; but if it is not, a dining area in the living room is a good alternative.

If there is some sort of alcove where chairs and a table can be put, so much the better; if preferred, it can be treated like a separate small room: lined with mirror, for instance, or with the curtain or shade fabric, or painted or papered in a color out of the room but different from the main walls. If it is treated like the main room, the tablecloth could be the same fabric as the window curtains or the upholstery. If the alcove is rather narrow, use a bench with suspended cushions for backrests on the inside, and chairs around the outside of the table.

When there is no separate alcove, a distinct dining area can be made by raising a table on a plywood platform at whatever height is preferred. Again, it can be separated a little from the main-stream area with a low wall of cup-boards, which can also act as a serving top with storage for glasses, china, cutlery, and drinks. Or it can simply be screened off slightly with tall plants or indoor trees.

It does not actually matter if a dining table is not much divorced from a main

living area, because once people are sitting around a table with candles or lowish lighting, the table becomes an island on its own anyway. The real problem is hiding the ghastly debris from sight afterwards, which usually means whisking it away on a serving cart or organizing some other efficient routine for quick clearing.

One nice solution for dining, if the room will take it, is a long old refectory table, which can be used for stacking books or objects and for working and eating surface all at once. It is very relaxing to eat like that. And a good-sized round table that can also be used for books or work or whatever is equally handsome and useful. Both these can be effective balances for a seating area. If space is short, find a table with flaps that can be kept by the wall as a side table when not in use for eating.

It may be financially impossible to find a table good-looking enough to leave standing on its own most of the time. If so, have one made up under my improvisation scheme (see p. 250), keep it covered with a floor-length cloth, and put a fresh short cloth over the top for meals. Dining chairs can be kept scattered around the room as occasional chairs, or a neat pyramid of stacking chairs can be tucked away somewhere or even hung from a small cleat.

A table, of course, presupposes rather formal eating. Informal eating can take place on cushions by a low coffee table, or on whatever seating

A long table at one end of a sitting room in Provence.

Covered mattresses make sofas by day, beds at night.

Centrally placed bed in a tiled Italian bedroom.

there is in the living room with individual small tables. All the same, unless there are either just two persons or a large party, eating like this never has quite the shared and comfortable conviviality of sitting around a dining room proper.

If a hall is wide enough, a dining area can be fitted in quite neatly there, keeping to the same table precepts as in the living room. And again, a study might double effectively as a dining room, for the table would be a library table in its dual role, and the walls might be lined with books, which is always very handsome.

A dining room proper is an interesting room to decorate, because, like a bathroom, it is generally used for comparatively short periods at a time and then mostly at night. As long as its main purpose is borne in mind—that of providing a relaxed, enjoyable, and comfortable area for eating—it can be as stimulating, as curious, and as experimental as one likes, though I do think it should still be a good background for food. I remember one completely black room that resembled nothing so much as a jeweler's black velvet gem box; the relief was in the tablecloth and napkins, which varied from spanking white to black-and-white to red and canary yellow. The lighting was subtle, and the room always looked beautiful except on a gloomy winter's day. It was definitely a night room.

The choice of table depends very

much on the shape of the room. Round tables are usually more sociable in that they make it easier to hold general conversations, hold more people in less space (or less square space anyway), and take odd numbers better. In a narrow area, try placing a long table against a window or a wall, with a bench running along that side and chairs along the other; this gives a little more circulation space than a similar table in the middle of the room.

Circulation always takes up more space than one thinks. Each place setting with an armless chair should be about 2 feet 2 inches (66 centimeters) with 2 inches (5.1 centimeters) more allowed for arms. A long table should be at least 2 feet 6 inches (76.2 centimeters) wide if both sides are to be used. Each person will need at least 2 feet 6 inches (76.2 centimeters) per chair to allow for easy getting in and out. And of course there must be an ample passageway around the table; 3 feet (91.5 centimeters) would be ideal.

Dining-room lighting and flooring have been treated in the appropriate chapters on those subjects, but I repeat that lighting should be soft and subtle and flooring practical. It is almost impossible to prevent people dropping food on the floor at some time or another; and a hard floor is easier to keep clean. If having a carpet is unavoidable—as in the living room—try standing the table on a rug that can be cleaned more easily.

Bedrooms

Bedrooms are essentially personal and should be more than just places to sleep, store clothing, and get dressed. They make good workrooms and studies as well as extra sitting rooms and should be carefully planned if the basics of bed, storage space, roomy bedside tables, writing space, and a couple of chairs are to be fitted in with any regard for looks and comfort.

Decide upon the following points from the beginning:

Is the bedroom to be a room specially for the bed, or more of a room in its own right?

Is it to be cool or highly personal?

Can it be designed from scratch, or must it all be done cosmetically?

The bulk of a bed is difficult to minimize, although the base can always be dispensed with and the covered mattress set on the floor if a hard-based bed is acceptable. A bed can also be built in with storage units so that it becomes a logical extension of the built-in furniture. If a room can be planned from scratch, remember that plywood platforms make a lot of sense when a comparatively small area needs to be expanded. Whether the bed is raised up on such a platform or sunk into it, it adds interest and makes use of all that space between ceiling and floor, as well as providing seating and bedside table space. If the platform is high enough, it can incorporate an extra storage area underneath, or be used for a separate desk and working area.

People do not necessarily want to minimize beds, of course; they may even want to emphasize them. There are various models on the market now which are to all intents and purposes relaxing oases rather than just beds, with built-in hi-fi, television, ashtrays, tape recorders, and a good many other gadgets. There are beautiful suede and leather beds, beds with a soft foamy lip all around them, and beds like upholstered Russian sleighs. Also, as I pointed out in the chapter on fabric (pp. 160–64), an astonishing number of variations can be achieved with fabric around the bed.

A sitting-room atmosphere can be injected into a bedroom by covering the walls with felt or a woolen fabric or paint or a plain wallpaper in good, rich colors with perhaps a border, and having either a matching carpet and bedcover, or a bedcover in an untraditional bedcover material like tweed or Supersuede or corduroy. If the bed is single, tailor the cover to make it look more like a sofa and pile it with cushions. A bedroom-workroom could have the bed surrounded by a wall of shelves and cupboards, or have the wall opposite to the bed used for a wall system instead. Small bedrooms can be made to seem more spacious by covering walls, ceiling, windows, and bed with the same pattern. Extra space can be gained by building wardrobes around a window with a linking shelf under the window to act as a dressing table. Alternatively, a bed can be fitted into the space between full-length cupboards so that it seems to be tucked into an alcove.

An ideal bedroom has sitting space as well. Two armchairs, or an armchair with its own reading light and a *chaise longue* or couch or comfortable chair with its own footstool, are ideal. There should be an upright chair or stool for the dressing table and a chair for the desk, if there is one. Bedside lighting should be good for reading in bed, but not disturbing; lighting over the desk or the dressing table should be good for

260

Occasional table in a bedroom seating corner. Mattress on a sheepskin for one-room living (right).

working or for putting on makeup. And in addition, there should be adequate general light.

In a small family house or apartment, the guest bedroom used for that purpose alone is getting to be as rare as the dining room. But even if the room is used for a study or a playroom or a dining room in its alter-ego form, with a convertible or studio couch rather than a bed proper, or if it happens to be one of the children's rooms with a willing child moved someplace else, much the same precepts apply as to a guest room proper. That is to say, the room, when used as such, should seem particularly welcoming and be stocked with ashtrays, carafes of water, (or bottles of mineral water), boxes of tissues, absorbent cotton, needles and thread, writing paper, plenty of coathangers, books, possibly a jar of cookies, and enough drawer space to make a guest feel wanted and welcomed.

I think it is a mistake to make guest rooms look like hotel rooms. If they can't be personal, they can at least be idiosyncratic and full of odds and ends that can be examined at leisure and, one hopes, with pleasure. If I had space, I would certainly add a desk or writing table to every guest room, or at least the sort of dressing table that can be written at; a comfortable chair with its own foot-

stool and a reading light; and perhaps a combination of a blackout-lined shade and curtains, so that those who hate the faintest chink of morning light can be kept comfortable, and those who like to be awakened by the sun can use curtains on their own.

Children's Rooms

Children's rooms, whether they are combined sleeping-playrooms, playrooms proper, or fenced-off areas of the kitchen, have to be capable of growing as their occupants do. Modifications have to be made over the years so that cribs give way to cots and cots to beds, playpens to trains and cars and paints, and toy cupboards and chests to wardrobes and storage for adolescent paraphernalia with the minimum of fuss and untoward expense.

Ensure safety by seeing that electrical outlets are flush with walls and preferably not down near the baseboards or skirtings and in crawling reach; that cords are short and nontrailing; that windows, if they are above the ground floor, are well barred or guarded in the most efficient manner compatible with not looking like a prison (and never use horizontal bars, which only make good ladders).

As for decoration, choose fabrics that are tough, colorful, and washable and wall finishes that can be scrubbed, washed, or retouched with impunity. Try to make as big a play space as possible, with plenty of seating and storage as well as floor space for games. A strip of pegboard is useful, as children get older, for pinning up drawings, schoolwork, trophies, and their own bits and pieces.

Appropriate furniture for postbabyhood is not so much difficult to find as difficult to choose. Unless there is money to burn, avoid all small-scale children's furniture in favor of pieces that will last through most of their upbringing. Try to find beds that slide under each other during the day and pull out at right angles or to form separate beds when needed. Even in a single child's room, this sort of arrangement can supply a useful spare bed. If

bunks are chosen, look for ones with sturdy, safe sides for small children, and for the kind that can be transformed into single beds later. A good-sized dresser is obviously something that is going to last, and there is no reason at all to install a less than a full-sized hanging cupboard. The rod can always be lowered and then raised as the child grows.

Storage is important if any sort of order is to be kept. Wall units will absorb an immense number of games, books, mechanical toys, and models; a wide shelf on brackets running the length or width of the room will make a practical play bench for drawing, modeling, painting, construction, and puzzles and, later on, for homework. Narrower shelves could be continued up the wall for books and small toys that are best taken care of and therefore kept out of very small children's reach. Another idea is to build in a series of boxes with lids for storage along the wall, perhaps under a window. Put slabs of fabric-covered foam and pillows on top of these boxes, and they will make good seating as well.

Lighting should be clear and bright. Table lamps, which can be knocked over, should be avoided in the early stages. Night light of some sort is important, because so many children are frightened of the dark. In a family of several children, it helps if a baby can be fed at night without an extra light being turned on and waking a child in the same room. Install a special low-powered night light, or use a dimmer switch in conjunction with an ordinary light. If this is difficult—as in a rental—leave a low-wattage bulb alight in the corridor outside.

Adolescents, I feel, should be allowed to choose their own room schemes. If this seems too mind-boggling, at least offer them a number of choices, so that the final decision is theirs. Necessities will be a bed; a worktable–dressing table; at least one chair; shelves; storage space; and a full-length mirror. If there is room, two beds could be placed at right angles and used as a corner seating area, as well as for putting up friends. Large cushions and stacking chairs, sack chairs, and bean-

262

bag chairs are good for extra seating, and there should be at least two lamps, for working and for reading in bed. If the adolescent children can keep to the budget allowed, and the necessary items do not happen to be in stock at home, they could go along on the buying trip and choose the various items of furniture for themselves.

A grouping of sculpture and plants on a tiled floor. A sheepskin rug set into the floor (right).

Offices and Studies

It is rare to find a home office or study that serves as a one-function room. Usually it is allied to the bedroom, guest room, or dining room; often it is simply a corner of the living room or the kitchen. But the principles are the same whatever the location. However small the area, it should be bookish, comfortable, well lit, and inviting. (Even the desk in the kitchen can be surrounded by cookbooks and account files; it is a particularly good place for a working corner.) There should be plenty of shelves, if there is enough space; these could be either built-in or part of a wall system. And cupboard space of some sort is always useful.

Desks come in many shapes, sizes, and materials. Some people prefer the flat surface of a writing table; others, a bureau so that they can shut the flap on their disorder and have some privacy

for their papers; others still, a kneehole desk with as much drawer space as possible. Some wall systems have built-in desks, and convenient desk tops can be built in across corners to use every last bit of space.

Study areas wedged into landings and alcoves halfway up the stairs, or under them, or in hallways, need to be no more than close-fitting shelves surrounding a desk, or a series of shelves with a deeper shelf underneath at desk level to act as a working surface, and a couple of filing cabinets.

I do not think it is mere convention that the walls of studies are generally dark and often covered with a fabric of some sort. Books definitely look better against a dark, rich background, and wall fabrics help deaden the sound of a typewriter. If there are many bookshelves, they can be lit by wallwashers, or by strip lighting concealed under a pelmet at the top of the shelves. The desk light should be glare-free. Filing cabinets come on castors for easy moving and in quite domesticated colors and shapes. Old dressers can be turned into adequate filing cabinets, painted up either conservatively or in zany colors and designs. Run a wood counter over the top of a couple of them, with kneehole space in between, and there is a ready-made desk and filing system all in one.

Terraces and Patios

These are the indoor-outdoor spaces of a home that are so often unexploited, or anyway not used to their full advantage. Whether they are an extension of the home into the outside or of the outside into the home, they have enormous decorative possibilities, and not only with greenery. The imaginative interplay of indoor and outdoor spaces and clever planting can alter the feel of the most cramped urban spaces. Any potential, however unpromising at first, should always be explored.

If it is at all practical, and the indoor space could do with exaggeration, it is a good idea to try to continue the color or feeling from the room behind out onto the deck, terrace, or patio. If the room

colors are coordinated with the outside colors, there will be particularly harmonious integration between the interior and the exterior. There are choices of brick, wood, slate, tile and concrete floors, all of which can be laid in many different ways. And if the room is carpeted and the deck or terrace tiled, the tiling could be extended a little way into the room to give a sense of continuity. Sliding glass doors or French windows, or a mixture of fixed glass panels and a glass door, will all add to the sense of light, space, and freshness. If the same sorts of planters are used indoors and out, the merging of the glossy green of house plants with that of the outdoor foliage will heighten the impression.

A terrace or deck, however pleasantly seductive, can get unbearably hot in midsummer unless it has some sort of cover or shelter. Fiberglass roofs can protect the space without darkening it, although they are not particularly beautiful. Folding canvas awnings are more festive. A wooden pergola strung with a tangle of climbing plants that form a cool roof of dense green, or a pergola thatched with reeds or rush, is more romantic. If there is room, a roof and screens can make the area doubly useful, because the space can be used on fine days in winter, with some booster heating, and possibly planted like an old-fashioned conservatory with all sorts of exotica if the temperature is kept at the right level. In any event, try to plan for shelter and shade that can be used if necessary.

Permanent outdoor furniture should be tough and waterproof. Other furniture should be easily portable and storable, capable of being used indoors or out. And if the space runs off a living room, it could complement in some way the furniture inside, whether by color, texture, shape, or material. Use the same fabric on seat cushions as at the windows, for example, or at least a coordinating color. Match tablecloth and napkin colors, and possibly any sunshades over tables.

Do not forget to install electric outlets for lighting, and perhaps for cooking, and to provide barbecue facilities.

Index

Page references in italic type refer to illustrations.

268

Vocabulary

Because this book was written for my
American publisher but is nevertheless
quite as applicable to Europe, there are
certain American words and terms that
might need translating, quite apart from
measurements. These are as follows:

apartment = flat
baseboard = skirting
burlap = hessian
chest of drawers = dresser
curtain rods = tracks
latex paint = emulsion paint
matchstick blind = Pinoleum blind
padding = underlay
pillow = cushion
plexiglass or Lucite = Perspex
    or acrylic
rental = rented flat or house
satin gloss paint = eggshell paint
serving cart = trolley
shades = blinds
wicker = cane

Photo Credits

Grateful acknowledgment is made to the following for permission
to use the photographs listed below:

Gil Amiaga for photographs on pages 17, 194-5, and 202 (top
    and bottom)
Manfredi Bellati for photographs on pages 88 (left), 161 (right),
    220, 221, 235, 251, and 259 (right)
Ralph Bisdale for photographs on pages 60, 66-7, 68, 69, and 190-1
Richard Knapple of Bloomingdale's for photographs on pages
    140, 172, 182, 189, 196, 208-9, 214, and 240-1
Michael Boys for photographs on pages 116-7, 144 (bottom), and 170
Concord Lighting for photographs on pages 58 (top, bottom left,
    bottom right), 59, 66 (left), 72 (right), 73, 75 (top), 78-9, 79
    (right top), and 258 (center)
Condé Nast Publications for photographs on pages 102, 162
    (bottom right), and 188 (bottom right), taken by James Morti-
    mer of rooms designed by Hilary Green for *Brides and Setting
    Up Home*, published by Condé Nast.
Hyde Park Hotel, London, for photographs on pages 157 (right),
    162 (top), and 163 (bottom left)
André Lamoth for the photograph on the title page
Lightolier, Inc., for photographs on page 61 of LyteTrim units to
    be installed under shelves or in cabinets
Wendell Lovett for the photograph on page 40 (bottom)
Maison Française for photographs on pages 70 and 71 (right top
    and right bottom)
Brian Morris for photographs on pages 33 (top far left and top
    second from left), 42 (top), 50 (top left), 93 (far right), 115
    (right bottom), 122 (left bottom), 138-9, 143 (right), 163 (bot-
    tom right), 191 (center), 219, 231 (bottom), 237 (bottom right),
    and 246 (left)
Louis Muller and William Murphy for the photograph on page 261
Otto Maier Verlag and Van Nostrand Reinhold Company for the
    photograph on page 87 from *The Elements of Color* by Johannes
    Itten. © 1970 by Otto Maier Verlag. Published in 1970 by Van
    Nostrand Reinhold Co., A Division of Litton Educational
    Publishing, Inc.
Robert Perron for the photographs on pages 12-13, 22, 25, 40
    (top), 43, and 211
Stan Peskett and William Waldron for the photograph by Robin
    Clifford on page 137 (right top)
George Powers for the photographs on pages 76-7, 110, 132, 183,
    188 (top left), and 199 (right), taken by Michael Boys and
    Spike Powell
William Waldron for the photograph on page 238 by Arthur Gordon
WestPoint Pepperell for the photographs on pages 152-3 and
    163 (top), courtesy of Martex, WestPoint Pepperell
Elizabeth Whiting for the photographs on pages 28 (left), 39
    (left), 77 (right), 92, 107, 124, 129, 134-5, 135 (top right, middle
    right, and bottom right), 136-7, 137 (left top and right bottom),
    168 (left), 170, 184 (top, bottom left and bottom right), 186
    (left), 186-7, 191 (right), 194, 197, 200-1, and 230 by Michael
    Boys, Steve Colby, Geoffrey Frosch, Clive Helm, Tim Street
    Porter, Spike Powell, and Gerald Tubby.

About the Author

Mary Gilliatt runs a successful interior design practice of her own and writes about decoration in books, newspapers, and magazines on both sides of the Atlantic. She is Design and Furnishing Coordinator to Liberty's of London, one of the leading British stores. Her books include *English Style in Interior Decoration, Kitchens and Dining Room, Bathrooms, Doing Up a House, A House in the Country,* and *Setting Up Home.*

Graphic Credits

The text of this book was set in a film version of Century Old Style. The display type is various versions of Lubalin Graph, designed by Herb Lubalin. This typeface is based on the original Avant Garde Gothic series. The type was photocomposed by Superior Printing, Champaign, Illinois. The color separations and halftone reproductions were executed and printed by Mondadori in Verona, Italy. Production and manufacturing coordination was directed by Constance Mellon. Graphics were directed by R. D. Scudellari. Book design concept and graphics are by Janet Odgis.